Heightened Mayhem

Heightened Mayhem

Dakota Destruction Book 5

Millie Copper

Written by Millie Copper

Edited by Ameryn Tucker

Proofread by MDC Proofreading

Cover design by Dauntless Cover Design

Also by Millie Copper

The Havoc in Wyoming Series

When a series of coordinated attacks devastate the United States, the people of Bakerville, Wyoming, must come together to survive. Unfortunately, not everyone has the town's best interest at heart. Some are striving for personal gain during the apocalypse.

The Montana Mayhem Series

A group from Bakerville, Wyoming strikes out on their own while searching for the desires of their heart. Unfortunately, the road will not be easy, and sometimes the heart is hardened and deceitful.

The Dakota Destruction Series

After a series of coordinated attacks devastate the United States, Katie and Leo sacrifice everything to help their country. But some things aren't as they seem. Is it time to go home and start fresh, or can something good come out of this terrible situation?

Wyoming Fall Series (In The October Fall World)

In the blink of an eye, an EMP changed everything for Lauren and her family. Now they are in a fight for survival, trying to keep their loved ones alive as society collapses around them.

Nonfiction Books

Millie has penned seven nonfiction, traditional food focused books, sharing how, with a little creativity, anyone can transition to a real foods diet without overwhelming their food budget. Many of her books also include preparedness and food storage tips.

Find these titles at:
MillieCopper.com

Join My Reader's Club!

Receive a complimentary copy of *Looming Mayhem: A Dakota Destruction Prequel*. As part of my reader's club, you'll be the first to know about new releases and specials. I also share info on books I'm reading, preparedness tips, and more. Please sign up at:

MillieCopper.com/Join

Chapter 1

Katie

The pickup truck plows through the snow-covered streets of Rapid City, the cold seeping through every crack and crevice. I huddle close to Leo, my breath visible in the icy air.

"So . . . how's the family?" Josiah Talbot asks, a chuckle in his voice as he scans the area.

The city, now draped in a white blanket of snow, looks both serene and ghostly. The crunching of the tires echoes through the silence, broken only by the distant howling of the wind.

"We haven't made any firm decisions yet," I say, following Josiah's lead of scanning the area.

"But that Mindy woman asked you to take her baby, right?" Josiah persists. "And Kemeera told the boy—what's his name? Nico?"

"Right. Nico." Leo nods as he slows for a right-hand turn.

When this trip was first planned, new medic Austin Chambers was supposed to be our driver. I'm not sure why the plans changed, but they did, and now Leo is driving with Josiah riding shotgun.

I glance over my shoulder at the passengers in the covered bed of the truck. Private Elliot Tillman, his dad, and Jesse Talbot, along to help with security and as a medic, visibly brace themselves for the turn. I slide the window open between the pickup cab and camper shell. "Everything good back there?"

Elliot's dad, Duncan Tillman, gives me a wide smile. "Good enough. Mite chilly, but the cover at least cuts down on the wind. Sure am glad they let you use a vehicle instead of making us walk."

"I'm not much up for walking right now," his son says with a laugh. "Give me a few weeks at the rehab hospital and maybe it'll work out then."

"You'll be fine, son. You'll be fine." His dad rests a hand on his arm.

Private Tillman was one of many injured in the Christmas Day explosion at Camp Rapid. Many more members of the South Dakota

National Guard were killed. Tillman was among those given little hope of survival and wasn't even treated in the beginning. We simply attempted to keep him comfortable.

When he was examined nearly six hours later, we discovered he might have a chance. In the almost six weeks since then, he's stabilized and is improving. Captain Williams arranged for him to have inpatient therapy at the Monument District Hospital, formerly known as Monument Health Rapid City Hospital before the EMP changed our world twenty months ago.

"How about you, Jesse?" I ask. "Warm enough?"

He scoffs as he turns away from the camper shell window. He, too, is scanning and searching to ensure our safety, rifle in hand. "Not sure I'll be truly warm until summer."

"Stop your complaining, big brother," Josiah says. "When it warms up, you'll be spoutin' off about it being too hot."

Leo and the Tillmans laugh, while Jesse says, "You're probably right about that. I'll take the cold over the hot any day. But does it have to be this cold?"

I let out a sigh. It is cold, but not the bitter cold we had a few weeks ago. Those windy days with temps below zero were almost deadly. I should know.

Taking my dog Gerry outside before bed nearly killed us both when what appeared to be a case of mistaken identity led to our assault. If Leo hadn't found us when he did, neither one of us would've survived the night.

I reach my hand toward my ear. The scab left from the frostbite itches. My pinky finger, still bandaged, is also stinging. Even though I'm fortunate to have made a nearly full recovery from my ordeal, as did Gerry, there's still some concern I may lose the tip of my pinky. Captain Williams and Dr. Wolff have been keeping a close eye on it.

I glance at Leo as he drives with one arm. His left arm is tight against his body in a sling, and he still has the external fixation device holding the bones together. The purpose of our trip to the main hospital today is two-fold. Not only are we delivering Elliot for his inpatient therapy, but Leo is to be examined by the orthopedist responsible for putting his arm back together.

If Dr. Bollinger is happy with what he sees, he'll remove the external fixation device, and Leo can begin to strengthen and use the arm. Then once they deem his arm healed, we're supposed to take our place as members of the South Dakota National Guard.

At least, that was the plan.

Now, the possibility of instantly becoming parents to the orphaned infant Caleb, young Nico, and Kemeera's abandoned newborn Zach has disrupted our plans. I'm not entirely sure I'm upset by that.

"I suppose they could always go to the orphanage if you can't keep them," Josiah suggests softly.

"Nope, no way," I say, while Leo shakes his head. Each Rapid City district has an orphanage, and they certainly do the best they can to care for the children, but it's not an option as far as Leo and I are concerned. If we decide we can't keep the boys, we'll find suitable homes for them.

I've never visited the Guard District orphanage, but Leo has. Our doctors do rounds there once a month, and he's gone with Captain Williams before. He admitted there were simply too many children for the workers to give the attention they needed.

As we approach a narrow alley between dilapidated buildings, Leo narrows his eyes. "Something isn't right," he mutters.

A sudden barrage of snowballs pelts the windshield, startling everyone in the truck. Leo slams on the brakes, and the bandits emerge from the shadows, their faces obscured by scarves and gaiters.

"Out of the truck! Now!" the apparent leader shouts, his voice cutting through the cold air like a knife, as the sun glints off the steel of his rifle.

Leo's gaze meets mine, a silent understanding passing between us. We can't afford to lose our only means of transportation in this frozen town. His fingers tighten on the wheel, his breath visible in the frigid air.

"Where'd they come from?" Josiah shouts over the engine's growl, his hand instinctively reaching for the rifle at his side as his other hand cranks down the passenger window. In the truck's bed, Jesse orders Duncan to lie next to his son as Jesse slides open the window of the camper.

Leo slams the truck into reverse and spins the tires on the icy ground. Other assailants emerge from the shadows, caught off guard by our unexpected maneuver as they open fire with bullets instead of snowballs.

The street transforms into a chaotic battleground. Projectiles pierce the air as Josiah and Jesse unleash a barrage to fend off the approaching threat. The assailants, only momentarily disoriented, retaliate with a hail of gunfire. Stuck in the middle seat of the pickup, I'm unable to help defend against the attackers and drop my head into my lap. I cling to the edge of the seat, adrenaline surging through my veins.

Josiah's rifle barks with controlled precision. With limited ammunition, he knows to make each shot count. Jesse fires steadily, too. The bandits' shots ring out with menacing intensity.

"Hold on!" Leo orders as he expertly drives in reverse. The backend slides, and I send a silent prayer heavenward. "Please, Lord, please get us out of here."

A metallic ding, followed by a yelp from Josiah, catches my attention. "Are you hit?" Another hail of gunfire and the cracking of the windshield drown out my question.

"Keep moving, Leo!" Josiah shouts over the gunfire. "Get us out of this mess!"

Leo's jaw clenches with determination as he navigates the truck through the maze of alleyways. Our attackers, relentless in their pursuit, continue to fire at us. A window in the camper shell shatters, and shards of glass scatter across the bed of the truck. Duncan offers several choice words about the situation.

"We're almost clear!" Leo yells.

The truck slides around a corner, leaving the bandits behind in the snow-covered maze. The gunfire fades, replaced by the howling wind and the engine's strained growl. Josiah, his face etched with pain, leans against the door as the battered vehicle carries us away from the ambush and chaos.

I cautiously lift my head as Leo asks Josiah, "How bad is it?"

"I'll be fine," Josiah insists, though his face shows the pain. "Jesse? You okay back there?"

"Been better," Jesse responds. "We've got glass everywhere."

Jesse's tone of voice clearly shows that he is unaware of his brother being shot.

Leo, now driving forward at a speed much faster than the road conditions warrant, says, "Let me get a little more distance between us and them, then we're going to make sure Josiah is okay and check everyone over."

"Josiah?" Jesse calls out, pure fear now lacing his words.

"I–I'm okay. Just caught a stray one." His eyes meets mine as he gives a small shake of his head.

I've already repositioned myself so I can apply pressure to Josiah's wound. The bullet hit him in the meaty part of his thigh, but I'm unable to assess the damage because of his heavy winter garments. I survey the amount of blood, not only on his pant leg but on the seat of the truck, and my heart clenches. "Jesse, grab the compression wraps out of the kit."

"I'm already on it. We're far enough, Leo."

Leo takes a quick look in the rearview mirror before pulling the truck to the curb. We're not even at a full stop when I hear the back window of the camper shell squeak open. "Duncan, see if you can clean up some of the glass," Jesse directs. "We're only stopping long enough to bandage my brother, so don't get out."

Seconds later, Jesse is at the passenger door. "It's jammed," he says through the open window.

Josiah, now pale and weak, gives a nod. "Not surprised."

"Give me the bandages." I reach for the supplies. "I'll wrap it around and we'll go. How far is it to the hospital?"

"A mile, maybe two," Leo responds. "With the roads slick and the snow unbroken in places, it's going to take some time."

I push a large square of cloth onto the wound. As near as I can tell, there isn't an exit wound.

We've had snow in the past twenty-four hours. Not a lot, but a couple of inches. Add that to what we already had on the ground and the lack of snowplows . . . the distance to the hospital is concerning. Josiah needs proper treatment now. "You have a syringe in your kit?" I ask Jesse as I continue doing what I can to stop the bleeding. "No needle, it's for fluids."

"I'll get it."

I pause for a moment, contemplating whether the bandage is the best option or if a tourniquet is required.

Sensing my question, Leo asks, "Is it spurting blood or seeping?"

"Seeping."

"Use the bandage then. Wrap it up and we'll get moving."

"Okay. Yes." Less than a minute later, the homemade compression bandage is in place. The bandage should not only control the bleeding but also protect the wound. The latching system, similar to a ratchet on a tourniquet, allows for the bandage to be pressed tightly onto the wound.

Josiah groans as I crank it down. "Sorry," I whisper.

"Here's the syringe. I've already filled it," Jesse says. "Brought the jug of water, too, in case you use it all."

Nodding, I say, "I've got the bandage in place. Let's get going." Jesse disappears from view. Reaching across Josiah, I crank the handle to raise the window.

When nothing happens, Leo says, "It was probably hit and shattered inside the door. Might be part of the reason the door won't open."

The motion of the pickup indicates Jesse's in the back. "Let's go." With the window between the bed and the cab still open, his voice booms.

"Everyone, hold on," Leo instructs as he shifts the truck into gear, spinning the tires as he takes off.

As soon as the truck smooths out, I check Josiah's pulse. Fast and weak. His breathing is rapid and shallow. "Jesse, send me a blanket through the window." As I talk, I crank up the heater in the old pickup truck.

With the heater blasting and the blanket tucked around Josiah to help ward off shock, I squirt a little water into his mouth using the syringe. He needs intravenous fluids to replace the blood he's lost, but that will have to wait until we reach the hospital. For now, I'll orally rehydrate him with small amounts of water, hoping to modulate his plasma volume. Emergency medicine in the apocalypse often results in trial and error.

"Please, Lord, please help our friend," I whisper.

Leo chimes in with, "Amen."

Chapter 2

Katie

God's response to our brief prayer is the appearance of tire tracks in the road. The broken snow allows Leo to increase our speed. Josiah's head is now lolling to the side, his breathing erratic.

Jesse, still in the covered bed of the truck, positions himself close to the cab so he can keep an eye on his brother while also watching our backs. "Is he . . ."

"He's still breathing," I quickly assure him. Not adding the rest of what I'm thinking: *for now.*

The old truck presses forward, its wheels crunching through the snow. With each passing moment, the urgency to reach the hospital intensifies, as do my prayers.

"There it is." Leo motions with his chin toward the extensive building looming in the distance. My eyes scan the area.

The Talbot brothers were with us the last time we were here, too. After Leo visited with the doctor, the four of us had gone to a nearby church festival. The festival took a tragic turn when the preacher and his followers set off explosives and shot at those attempting to escape.

As we approach the hospital, Leo sounds the horn. "Wish we would've brought a truck with a CB, then we could've had help waiting for us."

I nod, recalling our earlier discussion about which truck to take. We had chosen this one because its camper shell would offer Elliot and Duncan some protection from the wind. Unfortunately, that shelter vanished when the attackers shattered the windows.

The blare of Leo's horn alerts the hospital guards, who quickly make themselves seen; their rifles ready to respond in case we're a threat. "Lean across me and roll down my window," Leo says.

The awkwardness of him driving and his arm in a sling, allows me to have the window down only a few inches before we reach the roadblock.

"We're from the Guard District!" Leo hollers. "We're expected. Someone attacked us on the way, and we have an injured man!"

"Critically injured!" I add, as the guard waves us through.

Dear Lord, let him live. Please let him live. Use Your healing touch to stop the bleeding and give him health.

As I complete my silent plea, Josiah lets out a long sigh. "It's okay," he whispers, a soft smile on his face. "I'm okay. I'll dance for Jesus."

A sensation floods through me—one that reminds me of the last days of my mom's life. She had uttered similar words and wore the same serene expression before slipping away.

In the past few months, Josiah had started attending the men's Bible study Leo goes to. Leo returned home one evening with a grin splitting his face as he shared Josiah's newfound love for Christ.

That night, Lieutenant David Paul shared his own story of coming to Christ. Josiah had never fully grasped the depth of the Gospel until that moment. He hadn't comprehended that Jesus died for his sins, for Josiah's own sins. It was that night when Josiah came to realize his need for Jesus as his personal Lord and Savior.

"I know where I'm going . . . Thank you, God. Thank you . . . Jesus . . ." Josiah lets out a long breath as Leo skids the truck to a halt. Three armed guards meet us at the parking area in front of the hospital door.

"Everyone stay where you are," a guard orders. "Where's the injured man?"

I put my hand on Josiah's neck. His breathing is shallow, and the pulse in his neck is barely there. "Here! He's here," I call through the window. "He needs help now."

Jesse lets out a growl from behind me and mutters something unintelligible before yelling, "Hurry and get him inside!"

"His door's jammed," Leo declares. "We need to take him out from my side."

A new person calls out, "Let's go. Let's go. Get him out and on the gurney."

"You." A guard points at Leo. "Get out. Let me see your hands the entire time."

Leo reaches across to open his door with his uninjured arm. "I've got my left arm in a sling. That's the reason we're here. I have an appointment with Dr. Bollinger." His words come out in a rush as he exits the truck.

I'm right behind him, urging him forward. "Hurry! We've got to get Josiah out and treated!" Assuming the woman in scrubs standing nearby is part of the medical staff, I give a quick report. She nods and asks a couple of clarifying questions.

With Leo and I held at gunpoint by one guard, the other two quickly, yet with surprising gentleness, take Josiah out behind us. From the bed of the truck, Jesse orders them to be careful with his brother.

They put Josiah on the gurney and whisk him away with hardly a pause. My knees are shaking, and tears well in my eyes.

The guard turns to us. "Now tell me again why you're here, other than because of your friend being shot."

With his voice surprisingly strong and calm, Leo says, "We are expected by Dr. Bollinger, who will check my arm, and by the head of the physical therapy department for Elliot Tillman." He motions to the shell of the truck. "Josiah and Jesse were acting as guards for our trip. Jesse is a medic at Guard District Medical Center. Katie and I are in the med school program and also work in the hospital. She's a nurse. I'm a medic on medical leave."

Leo motions to his arm before pointing at the shell of the pickup truck again. "Elliot's dad, Duncan, is also with us to spend time with his son before his inpatient treatment begins."

"And you ran into trouble along the way? Where was this?"

Leo gives the approximate area, which is right on the line between Main Street District and Monument District. The guard motions to his associate, who takes a few steps away to use his radio. It's important to send the deputies or Citizen Patrol for the district to find the attackers. If they're attacking people as they pass, they need to be stopped.

"Can we hurry this up?" Jesse requests. "I'd like to be inside with my brother."

The guard narrows his eyes. "If you really work at Guard Hospital, I'm sure you know we're under tight security."

"Absolutely." Jesse's voice booms. "My brother is one of the main guards at our hospital, so I'm well aware of the procedures to vet people. We've given you our credentials. You can see our vehicle has the proper markings to identify it as one of the district's ambulances—

along with a variety of bullet holes, thanks to the shooters. I'm just asking you to hurry it up."

Unmoved by Jesse's impassioned plea, the guard asks for our ID cards. Not only do Leo, Jesse, and I have the district identification cards we show when using our ration chips, but we also have our hospital IDs. Elliot produces his National Guard ID, and we also give the orders we have from Captain Williams, the lead doctor of our hospital.

Elliot's dad only has his district card. In the past few weeks, after recovering from his injuries caused by the ration center explosion back in November, Duncan started working in the laundry that supplies the hospital and care centers for our district. Although he works with the hospital, the hospital doesn't officially employ him as part of their crew, so he doesn't have a hospital ID.

After scrutinizing all the identification cards, the authorities give Jesse and Duncan permission to step out of the truck. Both Jesse and Duncan have cuts on their faces or hands, evidence of the broken glass from the shootout. Thankfully, none are more than scratches.

I point at one of the cuts and ask, "Elliot?"

"Nope. Duncan shielded him," Jesse replies. "He's fine."

Duncan moves his hand to the back of his neck. Pulling it away, he looks at it before showing it to us. "Guess I got nailed." There's blood on his fingers.

"May I?" I ask of the nearest guard, still waving his weapon in our general direction.

After a nod from the main guard, he lowers the rifle. "Go ahead."

While I check the cut at the nape of Duncan's neck, Leo informs the guards that Elliot will need a gurney or wheelchair to transport him inside. The main guard instructs one of his associates to retrieve not only a wheelchair, but also a medic to help with transferring.

"See if they have news of my brother," Jesse calls after the guard.

Without stopping, the man lifts a hand to acknowledge he heard the request.

"Probably not much more than a scratch," Duncan informs me as I ask him to squat slightly so I can take a look.

After a quick eval, I agree with Duncan's assessment. "It isn't bad, but we still need to have all your scratches cleaned. The last thing you or Jesse need is an infection."

It's almost ten minutes later before we're deemed not a threat and are able to move inside the building. The guards escort Jesse and Duncan to the emergency room where Josiah is being treated. Jesse has permission to see his brother, and the doctors will tend to their scratches. They move Elliot to a gurney and take the three of us to the waiting room. Before he strides away, the main guard informs us he has notified Dr. Bollinger and the PT department of our arrival.

Within a few minutes, someone from physical therapy shows up to take Elliot for his evaluation. We ask about sending Elliot's dad to them once he's been treated, and they give directions on how to find the rehab area.

Half an hour later, Duncan reappears. He's now sporting a few small bandages on his neck, face, and hands. "I'm going to go find my son. Jesse is asking for you to go back with him."

"Did you see Josiah?" I ask.

"I did. It's not good. He lost a lot of blood."

I scrunch my forehead as I recall the amount of blood on the seat and the floorboards. Replaying the attack and his injury in my mind, I try to determine whether I could have done anything differently.

As Leo and I get to our feet, memories of the past couple of years flood over me. It wasn't until our world changed that I knew much of anything about medicine. Before the attacks on our country, I was an artist and attending college at K-State in Manhattan, Kansas, while waiting tables to make ends meet. In the days after five planes were deliberately crashed and explosions were set off at the airports targeting first responders, a series of related terrorist attacks changed everything.

When bridges around the country were targeted, people began fleeing the cities. Interstates became impassable due to the sheer number of travelers. Many people fleeing Kansas City ended up stranded in Manhattan. The college town soon became dangerous. Leo and I, not yet married but in a serious relationship, left to join my family at their home in rural Wyoming.

It was there, after my sister was attacked and nearly killed on a supply run, that I became part of the medical team. I never would've thought that less than two years later, I'd be in an apocalyptic med school, training to be a doctor as a sergeant in the newly formed United Volunteers.

Leo and I wanted to do our part to help rebuild the country. Originally, Leo wanted to rejoin the Marines, but regular service was difficult then, and still is. The alternative offered was to join the United Volunteers. The Volunteers are the apocalyptic answer to the Armed Forces. There's very little screening and no background checks, thanks to the destruction of most computers. Even though the United Volunteers are doing a lot of good while helping to rebuild the country, there have also been some difficulties.

Among those was an altercation in a ration line that ended in the death of several civilians in Rapid City. This event resulted in the governor of South Dakota removing all federal forces from any sort of policing duties and forbidding the Volunteers from operating in the state. Leo and I had already been in the area for several weeks, stationed at the Guard District Medical Center under the direction of lead physician Captain Chris Williams of the South Dakota National Guard.

When the Volunteers were ordered to leave, several of us petitioned the Guard to allow us to enlist with them. The request was granted, though not unanimously. We would've already been in service, but before the approval was given, Leo broke both arms when he fell from a horse. While his right arm, broken at the humerus, healed perfectly, his left wrist didn't. When he was attacked by a couple of burglars, the arm was rebroken and minor surgery was needed to install the external fixation device.

While I hate that Leo's had such a difficult time with his injuries, the delay in joining the Guard has given me time to consider if it's what I really want. I love being a nurse, and even though I've only officially been a med student for a few days, I can envision becoming a doctor. I'm just not sure I want to be in the military.

I don't have a passion for it, not like Leo does. Especially now that the children have come into our lives. Caring for them over the last few days has brought me true joy. Right now, we consider it a temporary situation. We don't know where Kemeera is and if she may return for her newborn, Caleb. If she does, there's a good chance she'll be arrested and face charges for her part in the atrocities committed by the preacher and his followers.

Originally, she insisted she was innocent and had no knowledge of the explosions and murders they had carried out. Her actions and the hints she dropped before she fled seem to contradict those statements.

If Leo and I become the guardians of her baby Caleb, deceased Mindy's baby Zach, and Nico—orphaned sometime last summer—I don't believe the Guard will be the right choice for me, or that they'll even accept me as a mother of three. I do hope I can continue with med school, but even that may not be possible.

Currently, Alice Williams, wife of Captain Williams, is helping care for the children. She'd always wanted to have a family of her own and wasn't able to carry a baby to term. Now past childbearing age, she takes her role as grandma seriously. In many ways, Alice reminds me of my own mom and how she was with her grandchildren.

Leo informs a nurse of our destination, and with a wave, she guides us through with concise directions. After holding the door open for me, Leo leads the way into the emergency section of the hospital. We've been here before when assisting with treating the injured from the festival explosion. As we make our way to the curtain at the end, I see a familiar face.

Dr. Callahan was one of the physicians we met then. Seeing us, she walks in our direction. "Good to see you again. Wish it was under different circumstances. Your friend . . ." Her voice trails off as she shakes her head. "His brother is with him now. It's just a matter of time."

Tears fill my eyes as I absorb her words. Even before he was brought into the hospital, I believed it would be only a matter of keeping him comfortable. In our apocalyptic world, we don't have the resources to repair the damage he sustained. Josiah knew it, too. He told me he was okay, that he'd dance for Jesus.

Just last night, at our neighborhood church service, we sang the once-famous song containing that line. Soon, Josiah wouldn't just imagine what it'd be like to be in God's presence.

His glory will surround Josiah.

Chapter 3

Merissa

"So, Merissa, how long have you lived in Rapid City?" He tilts his head as he questions me.

I purse my lips at the new medic. "A few months. Now, during quieter times without an immediate need for assistance, it's an opportune moment for cleaning."

I'm on a 0600 to 1800 medic shift with new medic Austin Chambers shadowing me. Leo, Katie, and Jesse are all at the main hospital, and Kerry Hendricks is on leave, prompting Captain Williams to suspend med school classes. As a result, he has been in his office for most of the morning, catching up on paperwork, while our newest physician, Dr. Murphy, is on shift.

I'm still not sure what to think about Murphy. He seems to be an excellent doctor based on the few times I've seen him in action. Not exactly a friendly sort, but I'm okay with that. I don't feel the need for much chitchat while I'm working.

Nurse Jacquie Haley, though, says she doesn't trust him at all. He's much too uptight. She asked him about his family and where he came from, and he straight out told her he wasn't interested in discussing it. That certainly sent the nosy nurse into a tizzy. Since then, she's made a point of avoiding the new doctor and badmouthing him to anyone who will listen. Jacquie may be a decent nurse, but she isn't happy unless her tongue is wagging.

"I heard you're dating Ritchie Kasubowski," Chambers says while staring at my expanding waistline.

I straighten my shoulders and turn away from him. Whoever I'm dating is none of his, or anyone else's, business. Besides, I wouldn't exactly call the friendship I share with Bowski dating. It's more of a . . . I shake my head as I spray the disinfectant on the exam room counter.

Whatever's between Bowski and me, I've zero desire to discuss it. Especially considering I've heard rumors of my own regarding

Chambers and Bowski's former wife. It's no wonder the two men don't get along.

As I give a swipe of the counter, the radio on my hip springs to life.

"Guard District Hospital, come in, over."

The voice on the other end is vaguely familiar. "This is Weaver. Go ahead," I respond, as I try to place the caller.

"Uh, yeah, Weaver. Good. This is, um . . . We've spoken before." There's a long pause, and I almost think I've lost him. "Yes, Weaver, this is Dr. Wainwright from Deadwood. Over."

I'm already moving, heading toward the main base at the nurse's station. The doctor's name isn't familiar, but it's not unusual to receive calls from other hospitals. A direct call from Deadwood is unusual, though, especially coming over the walkie-talkie.

How's he even reaching us? Usually, we converse with them via the CB and have other operators between here and there relaying the messages. Maybe they were able to set up a new system for direct contact? I would've thought we'd heard about that, but it's certainly possible Williams or the National Guard were told and the information had yet to trickle down to hospital staff. But still . . . via the walkie-talkie?

"Go ahead, Doctor," I respond.

Chambers is right behind me as he whispers, "What's he want?"

I lift my shoulders in response and motion in the direction of the captain's office. "Please let the captain know Dr. Wainwright from Deadwood is on the radio."

A loud squeal sounds over the handheld radio. "We've received reports of a mysterious illness spreading in your area," Wainwright explains, his voice low. "People are exhibiting strange symptoms, and there are concerns it might be an unknown threat or biohazard."

My eyebrows shoot up. A biohazard? We've dealt with our fair share of challenges in post–apocalyptic Rapid City, including a severe flu strain around the new year that left many dead and many others weak and still recovering. But why would he call the flu a biohazard?

Is it possible that the new synthetic drug Ploy is connected to it? Former Sheriff Melvin Cabal was one of the main ringleaders in the distribution of the drug, but who actually makes it remains a mystery. Cabal refused to divulge any information. Geoff Landers, his nephew, had promised to tell all he knew, but he's been unable to speak since his supposed girlfriend poisoned him.

"Please hold for a moment, Doctor. I need to locate our head physician." I crane my neck toward the captain's office. Chambers has already knocked on the office door and is holding it open as he relays the need for Williams to join us at the radio.

"You're the one who can help with this, Weaver," Wainwright insists. "I'd like to meet with you . . ." His voice fades away as the static increases.

I wrinkle my forehead. Meet with me? That doesn't even make sense. Is he confused about my position here at the hospital? There's most certainly something familiar about Wainwright's voice. His name is unfamiliar, but I'm certain I've spoken with him before.

Williams is on his way toward me. I can hear the combination of his walking boot and cane tapping against the cold tile floor.

"Captain, there's someone on the walkie-talkie. Dr. Wainwright from Deadwood. He says there's a mysterious illness spreading in our area."

"Another round of the flu?" Captain Williams responds. "Let me speak with him. You said his name is Wainwright? If he's in Deadwood, how's he using the walkie?"

"Unknown, sir. He called the situation a biohazard." I hold off telling the captain that Wainwright requested to meet with me.

"Biohazard? That doesn't sound good." He puts the radio to his mouth. "Wainwright? This is Captain Williams. Please repeat the information you provided to my medic, over."

After a prolonged silence, he repeats his transmission. When there's still no response, he asks, "Did we lose him?"

As the captain finishes his question, I realize why the voice sounded so familiar. "It's a prank call," I blurt out. "Like before, remember? It even sounds like the same guy."

"Why that— " Williams stops short of finishing his statement as he shakes his head. "Probably just some kids with too much time on their hands."

"Prank call?" Chambers asks, confusion painting his face.

I tilt my head in Williams's direction. At his nod, I share with Chambers what happened. "A few weeks ago, we received a similar call from someone claiming to be Deputy Garcia from the Main Street

District. In that radio call, he said they had reports of a group of raiders heading toward our hospital."

"Raiders?" Chambers raises his eyebrows.

"Yes. When I asked him to hold while I brought Captain Williams to the radio, he hung up. Just like this time."

"Why make prank calls over the radio? Where'd they even find a radio?"

"That is the question, isn't it?" Williams says. "Last time, they used Garcia's name, an actual deputy with the Main Street District."

"I even met him a short time later," I add, while refraining from mentioning that the last time the prank call came in, we contacted local law enforcement. Trooper Schroeder responded, only to confirm he hadn't heard about any raiders. In that instance, he contacted Garcia directly, only to find out Garcia hadn't made the call either.

Since then, it came to light that Schroeder was part of Cabal's drug distribution ring. He met his end after he, Cabal, and Geoff Landers took several of us hostage at the hospital. I must admit, it was quite a blow. He was the last person I would've suspected of being involved in something so abhorrent. He certainly never struck me as a drug dealer.

Having had a few pleasant interactions with Schroeder, I found him to be naive and almost innocent, with a boyish charm. His wife, who happens to be Melvin Cabal's sister, is expecting a baby a few months after mine is due. Currently, she, along with Cabal's wife and Geoff Landers's parents, are all in custody as the authorities work to uncover the extent of their involvement in Cabal's illicit activities.

Captain Williams shakes his head. "The entire thing is rather suspicious. Let's get Deputy Shaw or whoever is in charge tonight on the horn. Maybe . . . maybe it isn't a prank and we just lost transmission? You said he was calling from Deadwood? How's that even possible?"

"He said he was calling from Deadwood. I agree, sir, it shouldn't be possible. These are FRS—or Family Radio Service—walkie-talkies. We know how limited they are."

"Correct, Weaver. That's one reason we all live near the hospital, so we're within range."

Nodding, I recall times when I was on call and had a radio at home, but the reception wasn't always great. Even though I'm within the proper range, the house I share with my mother-in-law, Pearl, tests the limits of that range. Chambers, who's still in training, lives outside the area and will move to a house nearby, where the radio will work, as soon as he's approved for full duty.

Moving to the CB base, I use it to call dispatch and ask them to have Deputy Shaw, or whoever is on duty tonight, reach out to us. Shaw is in command of our district's law enforcement.

Within seconds of my summons for the deputy in charge, a response comes through the walkie-talkie. "This is Shaw, go ahead."

Captain Williams takes the lead, giving Shaw the basics on the call we just received, including how it came through the walkie-talkie.

"Biohazard?" The surprise in Shaw's voice is evident. "I haven't heard anything. Do you know this Dr. Wainwright?"

"I do not," Williams responds. "But Deadwood is far enough away that I'm not necessarily in the loop about who they may have brought in recently."

"You think it's like before?" Shaw asks. "With the fake Garcia?"

"Could be. Or . . ." Williams shrugs. "It could be legitimate. None of us really knows what's happening at Sanford."

"Sanford?" Chambers asks while shaking his head. "You think whatever they're doing at Sanford Underground Research Facility could cause a biohazard?"

Williams returns to the radio. "I'd call Deadwood and ask for the doctor, but we need to go through the radio relays, and— "

"Right. Gotcha. Best to keep this quiet. I have someone I can trust. He and I have developed a code, so he knows what frequency to switch to. Give me some time. I'll see what I can find out. I'm leaning toward it being a crank, especially considering he used a walkie-talkie. In the meantime, you may want to think about setting up your procedures in case this isn't a false alarm."

"Agreed. We'll do what we must. Get back to me when you can. Williams, out."

He eases into a chair. "This is interesting. What are your thoughts, Ms. Weaver?"

I take a moment to think through the information. Sanford Underground Research Facility, or Sanford Lab, is in Lead, South Dakota, close to Deadwood. It used to be a gold mine. After the mine closed, it became a dark matter and neutrino physics research facility.

Because of the depth of the facility, it's said to have been unaffected by the EMP. They are now working on something—no one knows what exactly—that will help put our country back on its feet. Could they be doing something there that would put us in danger?

I shake my head. "I don't know, sir. Not for certain."

"Well, that makes two of us. I'm leaning toward it being a prank—to what end, I'm not sure. But perhaps this Wainwright fella stumbled upon a situation he wasn't prepared for and is making exaggerated calls."

"Could be, sir."

Chambers clears his throat. "Doesn't make much sense to me. Why call the hospital pretending to be someone you're not and make false reports?"

"Unknown," Williams responds. "We never figured out who did it last time. We changed our frequency channels after that, for all the good it's done. Guess we'll need to make changes again."

"Did it happen to any other hospitals?"

"Not that I've heard of."

"And just the one time?"

"That's correct."

Chambers furrows his brows. "Weaver was the medic on duty then, too?"

I narrow my eyes. "What are you implying?"

He lifts his hands, showing me his palms. "I'm not implying anything. Just asking questions. I'm as curious about this as you are."

"It is a good point."

"Sir— " I start.

Williams lifts a hand. "Let's consider this for a minute. The previous call came in when you were on an overnight shift. I was on duty then, too. Who was the nurse on duty that night?"

I close my eyes as I try to recall the circumstances of that event. It was around the same time Katie was attacked and left for dead. We were treating her for her injuries and hypothermia. I was acting as a medic but following Katie's treatment, along with the treatment of Elaine Ebright, an older woman who developed sepsis following a skin infection. The nurse who was on that night isn't on duty today. And even though Captain Williams is here today, he isn't the doctor on duty. That's Murphy.

I inform him the nurse isn't here today, and he replies, "That's how I remember it, too."

I hesitate a moment, considering if I should tell the captain about a conversation I had with Bowski a few days ago over lunch. Bowski mentioned he'd heard about the prank call via one of his sources and thought it wasn't really a prank but somehow related to the Ploy drug trade. He said he was going to talk to Deputy Shaw about the rumors he heard.

I glance toward Chambers, who's closely following our conversation. I choose not to mention what Bowski told me. When I can get Williams alone, I'll bring it up then.

"Please let me know when you hear from Shaw," the captain says as he shuffles toward his office.

The screech of the desktop radio brings him to a stop. "Guard District Hospital, please come in, over."

I shake my head. I'm not sure who it is, but it isn't Deputy Shaw or the mysterious caller from earlier.

"That's Leo Burnett," Williams says as he scurries toward the base. "This is Williams, go ahead."

"Captain? It's Burnett. We're, uh . . . we're going to be delayed in returning. We were attacked. It isn't good."

Chapter 4

Katie

Leo walks toward me, his steps slow and measured. His gaze, filled with a mix of sorrow and understanding, never leaves mine as he makes his way to the chairs in the waiting room. I wipe my eyes, to no avail. We made it to the exam room only minutes before Josiah quietly passed, with Leo holding one hand and Jesse holding the other.

The weight of loss hangs heavy in the air, clinging to the memories of the moments leading up to Josiah's death. It was peaceful, with Josiah simply not regaining consciousness from his last words in the pickup's cab.

I have little doubt he truly is dancing with Jesus.

While I'm rejoicing for him, my heart aches at our loss. Josiah was a wonderful friend to us, especially Leo. Our pain is nothing compared to that of his brother. I know Jesse feels an emptiness that words cannot describe. Losing someone you love changes you.

Leo takes the chair next to me and reaches for my hand. The warmth of his grip is a comforting anchor in the sea of grief that threatens to overwhelm me. He squeezes my hand gently, a wordless promise to be there through the healing process.

"I reached Captain Williams," he says. "We switched frequencies several times and pretty much spoke in code. He suggested that if Jesse can't travel in time to reach home before dark, we spend the night here. He and Mrs. Williams can handle the children and Gerry. He'll shift the hospital schedule to give Jesse a few days off."

I wordlessly bob my head as my tears continue to stream. "We're already shorthanded at the hospital with Kerry not working. Another death . . ." My voice comes out in a squeak. "At least Jesse was with Josiah and knows that he passed. Poor Kerry. I'm wondering if we'll ever find out what happened to her husband."

A few days ago, during the time Melvin Cabal was holding us hostage at gunpoint, Rand Hendricks disappeared. At first, we didn't realize he was missing. The day was so chaotic. Then, as things calmed,

Kerry started asking about him, wondering if anyone had seen him. We performed a cursory search that night, checking all the obvious places.

The next day, an organized party started a more in-depth search, combing the area and checking near the hospital for any trace of him. The grid widened the following day. As of now, his whereabouts are completely unknown. Some believe he ran off, deciding to start a new life. Others, including Kerry, firmly believe that he's dead.

Leaning back in his chair, Leo lets out a sigh. "Dr. Bollinger will be ready to check me in a few minutes."

"Do you think they'll remove the fixators?" I motioned toward the hardware nestled under his sling. He's had the external fixator in place since before Thanksgiving, much longer than originally expected. The delay resulted from a myriad of issues, including the explosion at the National Guard Camp and a nasty flu sweeping through the region.

There is some concern the removal won't be a simple process because it's been on for so long, and we may have to look at other options. No one has mentioned what those other options may be. I've grown used to Leo's somewhat bionic-looking arm, but it'll be wonderful to have him in a less cumbersome splint or cast. We're both praying the healing is complete this time.

After a few minutes, Jesse joins us in the waiting room. His grief is clear in the way he clenches his jaw and avoids meeting our eyes. "Have you seen the doc yet?"

"Soon," Leo says.

"I plan to take Jo—my brother's, um . . . I want to take him back with us."

"Of course." Leo updates Jesse on his talk with Captain Williams and the arrangements.

"I'll be ready to go as soon as the doc says you are," Jesse insists. "Whether that's today or, if need be, tomorrow. Our mom . . ." He shakes his head. "I'm not delivering this news over the radio."

"Understood. Williams and I used a system of codes. I don't think it'll get out, and he knows to keep it quiet. He said he won't even tell Shaw yet. Not until we get back."

"Good. Thanks." Jesse's shoulders drop, and he heads back toward the emergency room and his brother's remains.

I close my eyes and let out a breath. The events of the past couple of hours replay in my mind, each one filled with our collective sorrow. My thoughts drift to Kerry and the anguish she must be feeling over Rand's disappearance. The uncertainty of his fate weighs on my conscience, reminding me of life's fragility. I make a mental note to check on her when we return home and offer whatever comfort I can.

Leo's sigh pulls me back to the present, and I send him a reassuring smile as Dr. Bollinger approaches, his expression grave yet determined. "Sergeants," he says with a lift of his chin. "I heard about the trouble you had. I'm sorry for your loss."

"Thank you, sir," Leo responds while I give a nod. While Bollinger is undoubtedly a good doctor, I'm not a fan of him personally. He seemed to have something going on with two of the doctors from our hospital when they worked here at Monument Hospital, though I don't think at the same time. When he worked at our hospital as a rotating doctor, it was awkward enough to cause a rift between Nettie Wolff and Chastity Morrow.

Now Chastity is dead, and Nettie is . . . I don't know exactly what, but something's off with Dr. Wolff. The friendship I believed we shared is now strained, and she seems curt with almost everyone.

"Let's head back to the surgery center. I'll give you a quick exam, and then we'll see about removing your pins. Sound good?"

"Sounds great, sir."

As we make our way to the exam room, Bollinger says, "I guess it's good you brought the truck. Had you been with the team and wagon, you may have lost more lives."

I pull my lips tight as I consider a response to his insensitive comment.

Leo's hand brushes against my arm as he replies, "Indeed, sir."

"How are you all doing on fuel? Have they cut your rations on biodiesel?"

"I-I'm not sure," Leo replies, glancing in my direction.

I lift my shoulders. Biodiesel and the supply of it, or even how it's rationed, aren't something we hear much about. Other than rare occasions when we travel more than a few blocks from our home and our hospital, we walk. Bringing the truck today was a necessity due to the distance and weather.

Even if biodiesel rations were being cut, it wouldn't be as big of a deal as the cuts to our food rations that we've noticed in the past several weeks. Even though it isn't a lot, it's definitely being talked about.

"I heard we're getting pretty low in our district," Bollinger continues. "In fact, we're not even supposed to use our ambulances. Back to the handcarts and wagons until this year's crops of seed oils come in. They need oil to make the biodiesel, you know. Here we are." Bollinger opens the door, holding it wide until Leo and I are inside. "I'll be right back. Just need to find my assistant."

Leo and I sit on the chairs in the small exam room. We're quiet as we wait just a few minutes for the doctor and his nurse to arrive. The doctor opens the door and strides in, followed by a slight woman with downcast eyes and a hesitant demeanor.

After instructing Leo to move to the table, Bollinger examines Leo's arm, his movements deliberate as he assesses the condition of the fixators.

My heart races as we await the verdict. I steal a glance at Leo; his eyes are fixed on Dr. Bollinger with a mixture of anticipation and apprehension.

After what feels like an eternity, Dr. Bollinger finally speaks, his voice steady despite the gravity of his words. "The healing process appears to be progressing well, but we'll need to proceed with caution following the removal of the fixators. There's a risk of complications due to the extended duration they've been in place, but I'm confident we can manage it with proper care."

Relief floods through me at his words, and a wave of gratitude washes away some of my apprehension toward Bollinger as a person.

Leo releases a noisy breath. "Do you think I'll have full use of my arm?"

"Well . . . for that, we'll need to wait and see. You're still going to be in a splint for six weeks or so. It'll be three to six months before we know your exact capabilities."

"Will you give me exercises for strengthening?"

"Some, yes. I'll have you meet with our PT department before you leave. As late as it is, you'll probably want to stay the night. Will that— "

"That'll be fine," Leo interrupts. "We've made arrangements with our hospital. Will we be able to get a room in the third-floor dormitory? We stayed there the last time we were here."

"Shouldn't be a problem. Give me a few minutes while we prepare a procedure room. We'll use a local, so you should only feel a little pressure. Your wife can be in with you if you wish."

As Dr. Bollinger and the nurse step out to prepare, I turn to Leo, feeling a surge of mixed emotions. Relief mingles with lingering worry, and I find myself searching for words to ease his concerns. "This is good. I think this is good." I offer a too-wide smile. "You've made it through so much already, and I have no doubt you'll come out of this even stronger."

"He doesn't sound too sure about how much I'll be able to do. I don't think the National Guard will take me unless I'm a hundred percent."

"You will be." We both know I'm overly optimistic.

"We'll see." He shrugs. "It'll be fine. Besides, I've still got one good arm to hug you."

I laugh. "Isn't that from a movie?"

"Pretty sure it is." He gives his own laugh before turning somber. "But it's true, Katie. I know the last few months haven't been easy. *I* haven't been easy. And it may sound corny, but hugging you is one of my favorite things to do. I couldn't do this without you by my side."

Warmth spreads through me at his words, a reminder of the strength of our bond, even in the face of uncertainty. "We'll take it one step at a time. And no matter what, we'll find our way through together."

Leo's gaze softens, gratitude and love flickering in his eyes. "Thanks, Katie." He leans toward me. I meet him partway, and his lips brush against mine. "Thanks for sticking with me, even when I'm a jerk." He waggles his eyebrows.

I snicker as the nurse enters the room, looking much more relaxed than a few minutes ago. "We're ready for you, Mr. Burnett. Do you want a wheelchair, or are you okay walking to the procedure room?"

"I'm happy to walk." Leo slides off the exam table, his expression focused and determined.

Ten minutes later, Leo has changed into a hospital gown with a cap covering his hair. I've scrubbed and am dressed as if for surgery.

As Dr. Bollinger prepares to begin the procedure, I offer a silent prayer for a successful outcome, for a glimmer of hope amid the darkness that threatens to engulf us. In this shattered world, even the smallest victories are worth celebrating, and I cling to the promise of brighter days ahead, no matter how distant they may seem.

Chapter 5

Katie

After a night of restless sleep in the dorm-style rooms of the hospital, Leo and I make our way to the physical therapy area. Leo's arm is still tender from the procedure, and he moves with caution so as not to jar or bump the splinted and slinged arm.

The exercises given by the therapist are simple, designed for him to increase the strength and mobility of his long-injured arm. The woman cautions Leo to take it slow and easy. "You first broke your arm in what? September?"

"September 16," I offer while Leo nods.

"Right. So today is . . ." She looks upward briefly to recall the date. "February 9?"

"That's right," I answer. "The ninth."

"So nearly five months ago. I'm sure you can see the size difference in the two arms." She gestures toward both of them. With the splint removed, the injured arm is noticeably scrawny, wrinkled, and pale.

Yesterday, after the surgery, I was able to gently clean Leo's arm to remove the buildup of dead skin. We'd done a decent job of keeping it clean with the fixation device in place, but there were some areas where the pins and screws made it difficult to reach. There's little doubt that the muscles in Leo's left arm—his previously dominant side—have shriveled.

"I'll take it easy," Leo assures her. "Believe me, it's been a long road so far, and I'm ready for it to end. This has definitely put a damper on our plans." He glances at me, a slight smile on his face. "Well, for the most part, anyway."

The therapist observes the bandage on my ear and the scab on my nose. She had already taken note of my wrapped fingers. "It's not easy when there's an injury in the house. I presume your wounds are more recent?"

"Frostbite. It isn't terrible." I choose not to mention there's a probability I may lose the top of my ear and the tip of my pinky finger, considering how much worse it could've been when I was stuck outside on a night in double digits below zero and beaten within an inch of my life. Not to mention the attackers kicked my little dog, leaving us both for dead. Gerry, dragging his bruised and battered body near mine, likely kept us alive.

She raises her eyebrows before turning back to Leo. "Do you have children?"

Leo and I both laugh.

"What? Is that an odd question?"

"It's more like one we don't know how to answer," my husband says. "At the moment, we're taking care of three children—two infants and a five-year-old—with the help of another couple. It's . . ."

"Complicated," I finish for him.

"All right. Let's just say, for the sake of caring for your arm, you have children." She continues talking about how she wants and doesn't want Leo to pick up the babies or play with Nico.

Although we've only had the three boys in our lives for a few days, we've already grown attached to them. I keep telling myself we don't need to decide our long-term plans right now, but it's getting more and more difficult. Being away from them last night felt completely wrong. All I really wanted was to cuddle the babies and play with Nico. Being with the three boys and Gerry might make Josiah's death hurt just a little bit less.

Before the physical therapist finishes, Dr. Bollinger enters the room. "You get the sergeant here all squared away?"

She gives the doctor a quick glance before muttering, "He's good to go." She slides the rolling stool and quickly stands, passing off the chart to the doctor. "Leo, Katie, it was nice to meet you. Do the exercises and take it easy. Have fun with your children."

As she walks away, Dr. Bollinger takes the chair she vacated and glances over her notes. "Children? I didn't realize you had kids."

We give the briefest of explanations to the doctor. When we mention that Captain Williams and his wife are also helping care for the children, he hoots out a laugh. "That makes sense. They always wanted kids. Tried for years. Even looked into adoption. Surrogacy, too. Finally decided they were fine having each other. Leave it to the apocalypse to give them something they always wanted."

His face takes on a serious look as he lowers his voice. "I've been hearing some scuttlebutt about the good doctor having some trouble. Something about that rotten Melvin Cabal blackmailing him?"

Leo shrugs while I avert my eyes and look around the room. We'd agreed before leaving our own hospital that we had no desire to add to any gossip concerning the situation with the Williamses. In the far corner of the room, Elliot Tillman is on his back on a floor mat, a therapist gently helping him stretch out his legs. His dad sits on a chair nearby. Duncan Tillman catches my eye and gives me a hearty wave.

"The way I hear it, Cabal thought he had a smoking gun. Accusing poor Alice of euthanasia. If the rumors I hear are true, what she did was truly compassionate. No one should fault her. I mean . . ."

Bollinger glances around before scooting his wheeled chair closer to us. In a low voice, he says, "It's no different from what's happened here, time and time again. I'm sure at your hospital, too. How many times have you had to make the hard choices during triage? How many times have you decided whom you have the resources to save and who you can simply try to keep comfortable? It's a blessing—a blessing I tell you—that Alice had the gumption to help those people die with dignity."

While people may consider the actions of Mrs. Williams during the early days of the apocalypse as euthanasia or a mercy killing, maybe even assisted suicide, I'm not entirely sure I share his thoughts on it. I believe she did what the long-married couple requested of her, but I still struggle with whether that was her choice to make.

It doesn't change how I feel about her, though. She's a friend. I think of the captain as a friend, too. Different than his wife, considering he's our boss at the hospital and is a ranking officer. And I hate the way former sheriff Melvin Cabal bullied the captain into accepting his nephew into the medical school.

The medical school, a brainchild of the captain's to train people with limited medical knowledge but who show promise to become doctors within two to three years, is an experimental project. We laughingly refer to the school as Doctors of the Apocalypse Training Academy. It doesn't have any sort of official name, but the title seems to fit. In the few months since the school's been in operation, there have already been several changes.

One of the students came down with the flu and couldn't keep up. She's decided she'd rather be a nurse and will soon start nurses' training—an offshoot of the med school.

Stella Swenson, an experienced herbalist and wildcrafter, decided she didn't need the stress of being a doctor. Instead, she'll continue working with her herbs and will act as our pharmacist and assist in other ways as appropriate.

Kerry Hendricks is currently weighing whether she wishes to continue training in the wake of her husband's disappearance. She's asked for a temporary leave of absence from both the school and her janitor job at the hospital.

After an issue at the hospital revealed Geoff Landers had a drug problem, the captain kicked him out. Landers is the nephew of Melvin Cabal. He was the first to leave. Come to find out, it was much more than just an issue of using drugs.

The doctor's gaze lingers on Leo for a moment, giving him the opportunity to add his thoughts before he speaks again. "Have you worked with Dr. Murphy yet?"

Leo furrows his brow, confusion flickering in his eyes. "Not exactly. I'm not on full duty yet. Unless you'd like to change that?" Leo gives a sheepish grin.

"Soon, Sergeant. Soon. Let's get a little strength back in that arm first. I'll be taking rotations again in early March. I'll evaluate you then, and we'll see if we can't get you back to work. Are you still assisting Chris with his med school?"

"Assisting and learning. The captain has added both Katie and me to the school roster."

Bollinger leans back on his stool. "Is that so? The both of you, huh?" He glances toward me. "Are you still nursing, too?"

"I'm still a nurse," I agree.

Bollinger shakes his head. "Don't know how you're going to do it all. Kids, nursing shifts, and doctor training. Aren't you supposed to be joining up with the National Guard, too? How's that going to work?"

I swallow and paste a smile on my face as I give a shrug. "At the moment, I'm not entirely sure. We're praying about it and are waiting to see how God leads us."

"Humph. That's— "

"Am I good to go, Doc?" Leo interrupts. "We'd like to get on the road. We want to make sure we're back before news of our friend's death leaks and his mom finds out."

Bollinger's jaw tightens as he gets to his feet. "Do your exercises, and I'll see you in a few weeks." He takes a step away before turning back to us, his voice clipped. "About Dr. Murphy . . . tell Chris to keep in touch with the new doctor's progress. Be sure to fill out his eval reports regularly."

"Um . . . yes, sir. I'll remind him of that."

Dr. Bollinger gives a curt nod and strides away, his movements sharp and suggesting irritation.

"What was that about?" I whisper.

"You mean with Dr. Murphy? I have no idea."

"Not just Murphy. The way Bollinger was acting."

Leo shakes his head. "Let's go tell Elliot goodbye and gather his father."

With everything in order, we load the pickup. We decide that Duncan will drive with me riding shotgun in the cab. Leo and Jesse, along with Josiah's remains, are in the bed. The shootout yesterday took out most of the windows on the camper shell, leaving it an even chillier ride than it had been. We discussed blocking the windows with cardboard but decided that would limit the views from the truck bed.

For our return trip, we took the time to map out a different route. The hospital received a radio call last night informing us the sheriff and patrollers in the district had gone in search of the group who attacked us. While they easily located the area of the shootout, they didn't find the assailants. It was at their suggestion we searched out alternate routes, choosing to take streets they said they'd make sure and patrol today.

Duncan keeps his hands on the wheel, at ten and two. His knuckles are white from his grip. We don't speak, both of us keeping our eyes trained on our surroundings. Thankfully, the journey home is completely uneventful. We don't even see anyone except a couple of kids walking through a park. When they see us, they quickly run behind an outbuilding.

As we finally reach the familiar streets of our home district, relief washes over me. The tension that had coiled tightly in my chest since the ambush begins to loosen its grip, to be replaced by a profound sense of gratitude for our safe return.

After being cleared by the guard at the front entrance, Duncan pulls the pickup to a stop at the hospital. Dr. Nettie Wolff and Captain Williams, along with several other staff members, meet us outside under the covered awning, their expressions a mixture of sympathy and solemnity. Merissa stands tall and somber, her eyes shimmering with tears.

Our new medic Austin Chambers assists Jesse in unloading Josiah's remains and placing him on a gurney. "I'm sorry for your loss," Austin mutters.

Captain Williams quietly says, "I've called Hugo. He should be here shortly."

"Thank you, sir. I'd like to go and tell my mom. Give her a chance to see him . . . if she wants."

"Understood. Take the pickup. We'll put Josiah in exam three."

"I'll take him in. Would you— " His voice cracks as he turns in my direction. "Katie, do you mind staying with him?"

"I will," I whisper, my own voice sounding off.

As Jesse takes hold of the head of the gurney, guiding his brother's remains feet first toward the door of the hospital, I watch him with a heavy heart. My thoughts drift to his mother, to the pain she'll soon face and the agonizing choice of seeing her son one last time. I can only imagine the turmoil she'll soon go through, and I silently offer a prayer for her strength and courage in the days ahead.

Chapter 6

Merissa

The dimly lit hospital corridor is completely quiet, the air heavy with the scent of antiseptic, a homemade version that's brought in by horse-drawn dray carts from Deadwood. A former moonshine distillery, wildly popular with tourists, now uses its knowledge and still-working equipment to produce various alcohol-based sanitizers.

Josiah's mom and brother are still in exam room three, saying their goodbyes. Captain Williams and Dr. Wolff are in Williams's office, along with the Burnetts and Duncan Tillman.

Austin Chambers is shadowing me again today. If all goes well, he'll be put on the permanent roster and will need to move to his new home just down the street from where I live. While I have a small house that I share with my mother-in-law, Pearl, Chambers will stay in a shared house where another medic and several orderlies from the care centers live.

The radio on my hip clicks, with the front guard's voice coming through. "Hospital, over."

I fumble trying to get it off my belt and up to my mouth. "This is Weaver. Go ahead."

"The transport truck is here. Can I let him through?"

I release a sigh and glance toward the exam room. This is always a tough part—when the coroner arrives to take away a loved one. They'll be expecting it, Jesse knew Hugo had already been called, but they still won't be ready. To make things worse, there won't be a burial. Not anytime soon, anyway.

Until spring, the bodies lost over the winter remain unburied due to the frozen ground. With the deaths from the preacher's attacks, the attack on Camp Rapid—which the preacher insisted he wasn't a part of—combined with the terrible flu, the number of dead is staggering. Storing the dead is a challenge for sure.

Hugo, the coroner, mortician, and coffin maker for the Guard District often arrives to pick up remains. I can't help but hope it's not

Hugo picking up today, but rather Bowski. It's been a few days since I last saw him, and I really want to talk to him. I'd also like to tell him about the radio call that came in yesterday.

He knew about the first prank, having heard about it from a separate source before asking me about it. He planned to have a conversation with Deputy Shaw about some rumors he had heard that were potentially related to that prank call. The captain may be right. It may just be some kids playing on the radio. Then again . . . I shake my head.

While I like to think of myself as someone who's level-headed and handles issues as they arise, sometimes my imagination takes off on its own and the worry begins. Mother Pearl and my baby are always among the top of my concerns. Is my mother-in-law getting enough to eat? Am I eating enough to allow my baby to grow as she or he should? Will the birth go well? Even though we have knowledge that people from the past didn't have, our infant mortality rate is terrible, rivaling that of the Middle Ages.

All of us working in the hospital have experienced the death of an infant—either at birth or under a year of age—or the death of a mom in labor. Sometimes we lose both. If I think about that too much, I could send myself into a tailspin. Having a child in today's world is a risk, but so is driving across town, as proven by the loss of Josiah.

Katie told me Josiah's last words, *"I'm okay. I'll dance for Jesus."* Hearing what he said makes me realize that is what I'd want, too. I've been attending church services both at Opal's ranch, where Opal's son Shawn acts as the pastor, and at a nearby service that is offered daily.

It's been interesting. More than interesting, even. Before the EMP, when Braedon and I were married, I rarely went to church with him, which was one of the reasons we separated. Another reason was his desire for children, while I didn't want any.

My hand moves to my stomach as my babe within gives a solid kick. I stifle a laugh at the appropriateness of the timing. After Josiah is tended to, I plan to talk to Katie about how I can also dance for Jesus. Although I've been attending church for over a year, I still don't have the personal relationship with Jesus that I've heard others speak of, and with each day that goes by, I realize that's something I want.

Something I need.

As I pass the nurse's station, the front bell sounds, and the door swings open. A shaft of sunlight streams in from the doorway, momentarily blinding me. Shielding my eyes, I squint against the glare, trying to discern the figure that stands silhouetted in the light.

And then he steps forward, his impossibly tall frame cutting an imposing figure against the brightness behind him. Bowski's broad shoulders fill the doorway, and his presence commands the room. His rugged features show determination, with his jaw set in a firm line. My heart rate kicks up several notches.

At the nurse's station, Chambers lets out a groan. "Great, Prince Charming," he mutters.

Ignoring him, I step toward the doorway. When we finally reach, Bowski's lips lift in a half-smile, revealing a glimpse of white teeth beneath a bushy mustache. "Merissa," he greets me, his voice a deep rumble that sends shivers down my spine.

"Hey." My voice cracks. I clear my throat and try again. "Did you hear? Did you hear who the fatality is?"

His forehead wrinkles. "Hugo didn't say."

"I'm not sure if Captain Williams announced it over the radio. He used the base, but I wasn't there." I take a few steps toward him. It's no longer a secret now that the family knows, but I feel it's respectful to keep my voice low. "It's Josiah. Josiah Talbot."

Bowski's eyes go wide before he closes them and shakes his head. "How?" His voice is unsteady.

I share the minimal details I know. Katie wasn't really in any shape to go into depth about what happened, but I do know it was an ambush.

Nodding, Bowski says, "I heard about it. I didn't know it was our people involved. Just heard about the trouble in the Main Street District. They were looking for the perpetrators. I had no idea . . ." His voice fades away as he looks over my shoulder, his features contorting into a hard mask of disdain.

I shift slightly, feeling the tension in the air thicken. Chambers is there, his arms crossed and a smirk covering his face. Placing my hand on Bowski's arm, I try to defuse the situation before it escalates.

Chambers's jaw clenches, a flicker of annoyance crossing his features.

"Well, Bowski," he bites out. "Should've known they'd send you."

"So, Chambers, how's the new job? Holding up the wall as usual, I see."

"Better than dealing with arrogant know-it-alls like you."

"We both know— " Bowski starts, but I interrupt.

"Please." I increase the pressure of my hand on Bowski's arm, feeling the tension radiating from him. "Can you two just try to get along? You're both adults, right? And professionals."

Chambers snorts, his derisive laughter filling the air like poison. Bowski looks in my direction, as the muscles in his arms relax slightly under my touch.

"Looks like someone's got you wrapped around their finger," he taunts.

I turn toward him. "That's enough, Chambers." The new medic smirks as I turn back toward Bowski.

Bowski's eyes narrow, but he stays quiet, his eyes fixed on mine, the tension in his shoulders revealing his inner turmoil. Without glancing at Chambers, Bowski asks, "Where's Josiah?"

"Exam room three."

He gives a slight dip of his chin. "I'll go pay my respects. I'm sure Jesse will help me move him."

"I'm sure."

Chambers steps to the side, his eyes following Bowski as he walks away. As Bowski stops to knock on the exam room door, he glances back in my direction. I send him a slight smile and a nod before he disappears into the room. With only Chambers and me in the corridor, I can't shake the frustration washing over me. With a heavy sigh, I turn to face him.

"That was uncalled for. You should know better than to engage in petty conflicts, especially while you're working. Especially today."

Chambers's jaw clenches, his gaze shifting uncomfortably under my scrutiny. "I know, I know," he admits grudgingly, his tone softer now, devoid of the earlier hostility. "But Bowski just knows how to push my buttons."

"That's no excuse for unprofessional behavior. We have a responsibility to our patients and to each other to maintain a level of professionalism at all times, regardless of personal grievances."

His expression is contrite. "I understand. I'll do better."

"I trust you will. The trouble between the two of you needs to stay outside of this building. He's here in a professional capacity, just as you are. We need to support each other, not tear each other down."

He tilts his head, and the smirk reappears. "What do you see in him?"

"Pardon?" I heard his question perfectly clear but am shocked he has the gall to ask such a thing.

"I mean, really. You're an attractive woman, even with the— " He motions toward my stomach. "You don't have to settle for a neanderthal like Ritchie Kasubowski."

As Chambers's statement lingers, a cold, calculating gleam enters his eyes, revealing the motive behind his inquiry. He's not seeking understanding; he's probing for weaknesses to manipulate. My stomach churns with a blend of anger and apprehension as I grasp his true intentions. He aims to capitalize on my vulnerabilities.

"None of your business. And as for Bowski, he's a far cry from the likes of you, Austin Chambers. At least he respects boundaries."

"Respects boundaries? Sure he does. You might think you know what went on in the past, but you don't. My guess . . . you're just another notch on the old rifle butt." He winks before he walks away.

A surge of anger rises within me. "You don't know anything about me, or what I know."

He stops moving and turns to look at me, a smirk on his face. Taking in my determined glare, his smirk falters, his confidence seeming to wane.

"And if you ever dare to speak to me in this manner again, you'll regret it. I promise you that."

The tension between us crackles like electricity in the air. Chambers's smirk fades entirely, replaced by a flicker of uncertainty as he gives me a nod.

Satisfied he received my message, I walk away, leaving him standing alone in the corridor. As I resume my duties, I feel a sense of satisfaction knowing I stood my ground against his manipulative tactics. I'm also concerned it won't be the last time I'll need to put Austin Chambers in his place.

Chapter 7

Merissa

Wisely, Chambers makes himself scarce and slinks away to the storage room. Part of me wants to report him to Captain Williams, but I can't come up with a complaint that doesn't sound like something belonging on a kindergarten playground.

I'll admit, I have doubts about whether Chambers is suited for this kind of work and the hierarchy of the hospital, but I'm willing to give him another chance. I figure if he's not cut out for it, I won't be the only one who has issues with him. His true colors will show soon enough.

Besides, today is not a day for petty differences. It's a day of mourning. I wish I could've had a few minutes with Katie to make sure she's doing okay. I know she's no stranger to death. None of us are, but to have a friend die at your side . . . it isn't easy.

A creaking door draws my attention down the dimly lit hallway. Bowski emerges from the room where Josiah is, moving with a cautious grace as he quietly closes the door behind him. His gaze briefly meets mine, and he offers a subtle nod, a silent acknowledgment that speaks volumes. In turn, my heart does the crazy little flip thing that so often happens when he's around.

As Bowski approaches, his boots clicking on the tile of the corridor, I can't help but notice the tension in his demeanor. Tension and sadness. He knew Josiah Talbot, too.

"How are they?" I inquire softly, my voice barely above a whisper. As soon as the words leave my mouth, I know it's a stupid question.

Bowski hesitates for a moment, looking toward the closed door behind him. "Did you know their mom used to be the public librarian?"

I shake my head.

"When the boys were really young, she'd take them in there sometimes. Not usually while she was working, but if she had a quick reason to stop by. I spent a lot of time at the library during the summer months. Jesse's, what . . . ten years younger than me? He must have been four or five. Josiah, he was just a baby. He was probably the first baby I was ever around. I didn't have any siblings or relatives living nearby. It was just my mom and me. My dad died when I was a toddler.

"Anyway, Mrs. Talbot asked me if I wanted to hold him. I didn't. He was so small, and I was afraid I'd drop him or something. I got a job the next summer and didn't have time for the library. Didn't see much of Mrs. Talbot or the boys for years. I'd heard about Jesse joining the Army. Hoped he'd be okay, of course. Then, when the EMP hit, we all just sort of came together again. How could we not? Josiah turned out to be a good man. His death . . . it's just wrong." His eyes drop to the floor.

The image of a young Jesse and infant Josiah, surrounded by the hushed tranquility of the library, takes root in my mind, a snapshot frozen in time amid the ebb and flow of years gone by. "It's remarkable how life has a way of circling back upon itself. The ties that bind us, they endure even in the face of adversity."

A glimmer of melancholy dances in the depths of Bowski's eyes. "Josiah," he murmurs, his voice tinged with a mixture of reverence and regret, "he was more than just a friend. Since the EMP, he'd become family."

As his words hang in the air, laden with the weight of shared memories and unspoken truths, I find myself nodding in silent agreement as my eyes fill with tears.

A fleeting smile graces Bowski's lips. "He went out of his way to help people. Both he and Jesse did all they could. In the early days after the EMP, they went from house to house, making sure people had clean water and food. That first winter, before the crews were fully functioning, they'd split wood, snare squirrels and rabbits . . . whatever was needed to help people survive. Things have become more organized now. And he had his job with the Citizen Patrol. I suppose you saw a lot of him since he was often stationed as a guard here at the hospital."

"Yes. He was usually assigned to walk us home. Not only would he provide a secure escort, but he'd also take it upon himself to tell us any funny story he could come up with. He liked to laugh and make others laugh. But he also knew when it was time to be serious."

We spend a few more minutes sharing memories of Josiah before I ask if he knows if they'll have a memorial service or wait until the spring burial.

"They didn't say. Sometimes, people other than family arrange the memorial. It wouldn't surprise me if the Citizen Patrol or deputies organized something to honor him now instead of waiting until the weather warms."

"True. That could happen."

There's a weighty and slightly awkward pause before I say, "Oh, I was going to tell you, we had another prank come over the radio yesterday. You know, like the one before."

He furrows his eyebrows. "You did? What'd they say?"

I repeat the basics of the conversation, informing him the man stated he was a doctor from Deadwood—a name Captain Williams didn't recognize—and they'd received reports of a mysterious illness spreading, with people exhibiting strange symptoms, and they thought it was some kind of biohazard.

"Biohazard? What does that mean? Another round of the flu?"

"I didn't take it that way, but I don't know what he intended to imply. When he first called, I thought I recognized his voice. And then when we lost him, after bringing Captain Williams on, it all clicked."

"Hmm. Let me ask around. I brought up the drug trade rumors to Shaw the other day."

As his eyes meet mine, warmth spreads over my cheeks as I remember how we discussed the first prank call over lunch. That lunch at my house was essentially the beginning of something serious between us. A date, of sorts. "What'd he say?" My voice comes out hoarse.

"That he would ask around and see what he could find out. Did Williams tell him about this call?"

"I'm not sure. It was only a few minutes later when Leo called about Josiah. Things got a little crazy from there."

"I'll take care of notifying him. In fact, I'm surprised Shaw isn't here. I would've expected him to show up for Josiah."

I purse my lips. "I don't know if the captain told him Josiah's remains had arrived. We were trying to keep things quiet so Josiah's mom could hear it from Jesse."

"That makes sense. Does Shaw know about his death?"

"Yes. Captain asked him to come to the hospital last night. He told him in person."

"Good thinking."

I touch his arm. "There's something else. The radio caller said something weird this time. He said I was the one he wanted, that he wanted to meet with me."

"You were the one he wanted?"

"He used my name . . . but, uh, maybe that isn't really that odd. I told him my name was Weaver when I answered the call. But he did say he wanted to meet with me."

Bowski looks like he wants to say something, but the exam room door screeches as it opens.

Jesse takes a breath before saying, "We're ready."

"Let me get the captain," I whisper.

Bowski walks toward Jesse, and both of them disappear into the room.

Before they return, Deputy Shaw and several from the Citizen Patrol arrive. The captain shakes the deputy's hand and says they're just getting ready to take Josiah.

"I'm glad we made it, then. We'll have a chance to honor him."

We line the corridor as Bowski and Jesse move the gurney toward the front door. Mrs. Talbot walks behind them, her head held high.

As they proceed through the corridor, a hushed reverence fills the air, punctuated only by the soft shuffle of footsteps and the occasional sniffle. The hospital staff, standing in silent tribute, offer a solemn acknowledgment of the profound loss we collectively bear.

Amid the somber procession, I catch sight of Katie wiping away a tear, her eyes reflecting the gravity of the moment. Leo is next to her, one hand pressed behind his back as he stands at attention. As Mrs. Talbot passes, several of us fall in behind her.

Two men from the Citizen Patrol hold the doors open, revealing the bright daylight beyond. Deputy Shaw, a couple of patrollers, and Leo—using only his good arm—gently load Josiah's remains into the back of a truck used by Hugo and the mortuary team.

With Josiah in place, Bowski helps Mrs. Talbot into the front seat while Jesse climbs into the bed with Josiah's remains. The gathered group continues to stand in reverence as Bowski starts the motor. Mrs. Talbot holds her back straight and her head high, staring ahead as they drive away. None of us move until they pass the guard station and turn toward the mortuary, finally disappearing from view.

Chambers is the first to go back inside, followed by the nurse and a new janitor replacing Rand Hendricks. There's a second temporary janitor covering for Rand's wife while she's off, helping to search for her husband.

I turn to Katie and drop my hand on her arm. "How're you holding up?"

She closes her eyes and shakes her head. "It never gets any easier. Losing someone. It just . . . it's terrible. And to see Mrs. Talbot like that, it reminds me of my friend Doris from back home. She lost her daughter when we were attacked. She'd said losing a child was the worst possible thing." Katie's eyes meet mine. "Losing a husband . . . that's terrible, too."

My hand instinctively moves to my stomach. "It is terrible, but I think your friend is right. I can't imagine losing my child."

I'm about to ask her if she has a few minutes to talk, to discuss what Josiah said about dancing for Jesus, when Deputy Shaw approaches.

"Katie? Leo mentioned they didn't interview you while you were at the hospital. I'd like to get your statements. Duncan's, too, so they're on the record. I'll make sure both the Monument and Main Street Districts get a copy."

Katie glances toward me. "Did you want to talk about something? I can do this and then find you."

"Sure," I respond. "I'll be here until 1800 hours."

She wraps me in a hug. "You're a good friend, Merissa."

Chapter 8

Katie

"Thanks for sticking around and giving me your statements." Shaw closes his notebook with a snap. He wrote with a pencil, but he'll take the handwritten notes to the Guard District Station, where they have an old manual typewriter.

Currently, they still have a supply of typewriter ribbons. They were found with an old typewriter. The ribbon, which someone had to explain to me since I've never used a typewriter, functions as the inkwell for the keys. While I think the whole thing is fascinating, I still haven't had the opportunity to use one of the old typewriters.

In the hospital, we use ink pens, wanting to preserve the notes as best we can, but do nothing beyond that. There's also a woman who was working as a reporter and was setting up a mass printing press to release a newspaper. She'd tried to make it a weekly newspaper and had succeeded in that effort during the warmer months, but with winter here, it's dropped to monthly. I've heard she plans to get it back to weekly when the weather breaks.

Duncan Tillman leans forward in his chair. "Do you think they'll find them?"

"We're going to try. They looked for them yesterday without success. Right before I made my way over here, someone notified me of another attack. No fatalities this time, but a couple of injuries. It's bad enough they killed one of our own, but if they're keeping at it . . ." Shaw raises his hands as he shakes his head.

Leo rubs his good hand against the sling, holding his left arm close to his body. "What's the plan?"

"A good old-fashioned posse. Several districts are joining. Deputies, Citizen Patrol, and just regular old volunteers."

Shifting slightly, Leo catches my eye. I respond with a shake of my head. "You're not released for duty yet."

His lips pull into a tight line as he gives a singular nod. "I'm sure I could be of some use."

"Let's hold off on that," Shaw says. "There are plenty of people willing to join the fray."

It's clear that Leo has more to add, but Duncan cuts him off. "Leo, you need to focus on your recovery." His voice is firm but not unkind, almost fatherly-like. "We can't risk you aggravating your injuries by jumping into action prematurely. I'll admit, I'd like to offer myself as a volunteer, but I know I'm not up to it. I still haven't fully recovered from the explosion, and that's been what? Over three months now? Don't know if I'll ever be a hundred percent. It's frustrating."

Leo sighs, his own frustration clear in the furrow of his brow.

Shaw leans back in his chair and rubs his temples. "Believe me, Leo, Duncan, I understand. And I know you'd both be helping us if you could. We'll handle it for now, but your time will come."

Leo nods reluctantly, conceding to their reasoning. He looks at me, silently asking for support. I give him a reassuring smile, trying to ease his tension.

"All right, then," Shaw says as he stands and gathers his belongings. "I need to get back to coordinate my part in this."

Duncan glances from me to Leo before also standing. "I'm going to head on home. I'm back to work tomorrow, so will undoubtedly stop by here."

"Would you like us to walk with you?" I ask.

He gives a shake of his head. "Unnecessary."

Once we're alone, I turn to Leo, keeping my voice as soft as possible. "Listen, Leo, I get it. You want to help, and you will. But you have to be patient. You got your hardware removed yesterday. You heard— "

"I know," he says with a sigh. "I just . . . I feel responsible for Josiah's death and want to do whatever I can to find them and make them pay."

I don't know what to say, especially since I feel the same way. Not that Leo's responsible, but that I should've done more. I should've been able to stop the bleeding. My mind knows it was a fatal wound almost instantly, but my heart argues that I should've been able to save him. I'm not a doctor yet, but I will be soon, and doctors save lives.

Staying silent, I move in front of Leo and wrap my arms around him. He pulls me close with his good arm, and we stay that way for many minutes.

As we hold on to each other, a mixture of emotions swirl within me: grief for Josiah's loss, worry for Leo's well-being, and a fierce determination to see justice served. But amid it all, there's also a sense of gratitude for the strength we find in each other during these trying times.

After several minutes, Leo loosens his grip, his breathing steadying. He presses a gentle kiss to the top of my head before pulling away. "Thanks, Katie. I don't know what I'd do without you."

I gently smooth the wrinkle between his eyes with my fingertip. "You don't have to figure this out alone. We'll handle it together, Leo. Just like always."

"With God's help." He takes a deep breath and rises from the chair, wincing slightly as he adjusts to the movement. "I'm exhausted. You ready to head home? We have a long day ahead of us tomorrow."

"Is school starting up again?"

"Captain Williams says we need to get back at it. Kerry's going to take a few more days off, but the rest of us will meet here at 0600 hours."

I close my eyes for a moment. I'm still recovering from my injuries of a few weeks back and, like Leo, am on a light-duty schedule. Tomorrow, I'm scheduled for a four-hour nursing shift from 1600 to 2000 hours.

We've found that we tend to be busier in the late afternoon, so it's helpful to have two nurses on then. People who are finishing up their own work schedules often get off between 1500 hours and 1800 hours—or as I still think of it in my head, 3:00 p.m. and 6:00 p.m. Sometimes I wonder if the twenty-four-hour clock will ever become second nature to me like it seems to be for Leo.

"Let me go tell Merissa goodbye. I think she wanted to talk to me. Maybe we can steal a few minutes tomorrow."

"Go ahead and see what she needs. I need to check in with the captain, anyway."

"Okay," I agree. "I won't be long, though. I'm ready to get home, too. Before we go to bed, I want to spend some time with the children and Gerry."

"Same. I have to admit, Katie, I'm surprised."

"Surprised?"

"At how much I miss them. I keep thinking . . ." He lifts his hands. "Never mind. Let's get a move on so we can get home . . . I mean, back to the Williamses' house."

Right now, Captain Williams and his wife Alice's home is our home. We've been staying with them since the night of my attack. Hiding out is probably a better phrase. At first, we weren't sure if my attackers would return and try to finish what they started. Even though we believe it was a case of mistaken identity, and our neighbor Oscar Harrington was the actual intended target, we don't want to risk it.

Now, using information provided by Melvin Cabal and his nephew Geoff Landers, we know that the leader of that attack, Julius MacAllister, is dead. At least, we think he's dead. Landers said Cabal made sure the man wouldn't hurt me again.

While we don't have confirmation of his death—and Cabal refuses to say anything about anything—we'd like to think I'm safe. Not only me, but also Oscar. For now, though, we're staying put with the Williamses, and Oscar and his family are staying with Deputy Shaw. Better to be safe. When Cabal talks, or Geoff Landers recovers enough for questioning, then maybe we can have some actual answers.

In the hospital corridor, Leo finds Captain Williams at the nurse's station, engrossed in something with Dr. Wolff. Hearing a rustling noise from one of the storerooms, I knock on the door before pushing it slightly open in hopes of finding Merissa. Instead, it's Austin Chambers, squatting down while working on a lower shelf. "Oh, hey," I say. "Sorry. I was looking for Merissa."

He leans back on his heels. "She's cleaning up exam three. Said she'd prefer I not help her." He screws up his face, his irritation evident. "Guess she's happy doing it on her own."

I consider my response. Even though Merissa and I have become friends, she's not the easiest person to get to know. She's on the quiet side. Good quiet, in my opinion, but still quiet. That is, until she has something on her mind.

Recently, she made it clear to me that I needed to decide what I wanted from my life, especially regarding joining the South Dakota National Guard. She basically told me to either do it or don't do it but stop whining over it.

I'll admit, I was considerably upset at her at first and thought she was way out of bounds. But the truth is, what she said was what I needed to hear. Joining the military was never something I was interested in.

The United Volunteers was a way for me to run away from the grief I was feeling over the loss of my mom. With only a one-year commitment, I figured, why not? But the Guard requires eight years, and if we're still in a state of emergency, they could choose to keep me even longer. Eight years sounds like a lifetime. I didn't like it, but Merissa said things I needed to hear, and I'm grateful to her for it; she's a genuine friend.

On the surface, Austin is Merissa's complete opposite. He talks a lot, laughs loudly, and can be a little much. He doesn't seem like a bad guy and is actually fun to be around, but his energy can be excessive.

I haven't worked with him directly, but it's clear he might be too much for Merissa. She likes things quiet, and he is anything but. He probably tries to talk her ears off. Plus, I've heard rumors about some trouble between Austin and Bowski.

I glance around the room. "The sorting and organizing seems to never end."

"Seems so." He gives me a nod. "I'm sorry about your friend."

"Thank you." My voice comes out in a squeak. Taking a deep breath, I fight back the tears, but they come anyway. I step out of the room. With the door shut, I blink rapidly, trying to regain my composure. I'm exhausted and want nothing more than to go home. I need a long sleep. A hot bath would also be wonderful, but that's unlikely to happen. The need to haul and heat water leaves the luxury of a bath a rarity.

I can't shake the feeling of unease settling over me. Things are such a mess right now. Minor, and even major, attacks are escalating, and despite the efforts of our law enforcement, the perpetrators remain at large. We're living on the edge of chaos, and I fear what may happen if we don't bring an end to it soon.

Chapter 9

Katie

The clinking of utensils against plates fills the cozy dining room as we sit around the table, sharing the simple meal that Alice has prepared. The aroma of savory stew and freshly baked bread wafts through the air, mingling with Nico's laughter and the warm glow of candlelight. He's really come out of his shell in the days since he's been living with us.

I remember the first time I met him. He barely spoke above a whisper, and his slight frame appeared almost lost in the room. He kept his head down and his hands fidgeting nervously in his lap, as if trying to disappear into himself. When we wanted to engage him in conversation, he offered only fleeting glances and hesitant responses, as if unsure of how to interact with us.

But now, as he sits at the table, animatedly recounting his latest adventures in the backyard, his eyes shine with newfound confidence, his voice ringing clear and strong. He gestures enthusiastically, fully immersed in the moment's joy. It's a remarkable transformation. While I wanted nothing more than a bath and a nap, I now know Nico's bright laughter is the best thing for me. For Leo, too.

Just as we're finishing up, there's a sharp rap on the door. We exchange puzzled glances, wondering who would visit at this hour. Captain Williams rises from his seat, his expression a mixture of curiosity and apprehension.

"Sir?" Leo also rises, his hand on the butt of his pistol.

The captain responds with a nod as Alice and I each grab a baby. "C'mon, Nico," I urge him off the chair and offer him my hand. My voice trembles slightly. "Let's move to the back of the house while the captain and Leo check the door."

The simple act of opening the door shouldn't cause my heart to pound in fear, but I can't ignore the dread gnawing at me as I worry about our safety . . . about the children's safety. Nico seems to understand the necessity of it. Even at his young age, he knows we need to be safe.

We move to the hallway near the door to the garage. If things go bad, we'll have an easy escape route. I glance at Alice. Her face is white, and her lips are pulled tight. Like me, she has a pistol on her hip.

I also have a smaller pistol on my ankle and know she, too, carries a backup, but I'm not sure where it's stashed today. She has a few options. It could be in a brassiere holster, an armpit holster, built into her undergarments, or, like me, strapped to her ankle. We take our personal protection seriously in the apocalypse. "Ready?" I ask.

She dips her chin. "Tell them to go ahead."

In a low voice, I let Leo and the captain know we're in position. Although I'm out of the line of sight, I can envision what's happening. The captain will go to the door while Leo stands back and out of the way, using a large masonry yard statue—brought into the house specifically for this purpose—as cover.

The captain clears his throat and calls out, "Yes?"

From my location, the reply is inaudible, but I can hear the captain commanding Leo to stay alert.

I take a sharp breath as Alice whispers, "What's wrong?"

I shake my head in response.

"Major Stone?" the captain says loud enough for us to hear. "I wasn't expecting you."

"Hello, Williams," a smooth voice says. "The lieutenant and I need to speak with you. May we come in?"

"Of course. Please, come in." He raises his voice slightly. "We're okay, Alice. Come out."

"Sorry." I immediately register the voice as belonging to Leo's good friend, National Guard Lieutenant David Paul. "We should've realized we'd catch you off guard by coming this late."

"No, no. It's fine," the captain responds, a slight quiver in his voice.

Alice and I, each cradling an infant, walk alongside Nico toward the living room. My guess is that as soon as Leo and I give our greetings, we'll take the children to our bedroom, believing this to be an official visit.

"Sergeant Burnett," Lieutenant Paul says. "Mrs. Williams. Good to see you both. How are the children doing?"

"Very well," Alice answers. "The babies are growing so fast, and Nico is such a help." She drops an affectionate hand on Nico's shoulder. "Aren't you?"

He responds with a wide smile and a vigorous nod.

Alice glances toward the man standing next to David Paul. "Major."

"Mrs. Williams." He looks at me and then Leo, who's standing at near attention. I briefly wonder if I'm supposed to be in the same stance.

"I don't believe we've met," he says, "but I've heard about the Seargent Burnetts of the United Volunteers." There's a hint of contempt in his words, his upper lip curling slightly.

Lieutenant Paul clears his throat, the tension in his shoulders confirming my suspicion: this isn't a social visit. I turn to Alice. "Let me take Zach. We'll go to our room."

She slowly hands Zach to me, giving me time to reposition in order to hold both infants safely. Leo glances from the major to the captain with a slight lift of his eyebrows.

"Major?" the captain says. "Would you and the lieutenant like to go to my study? Did you wish for Alice to join us?"

He shrugs. "No reason we can't say what we've come to say in front of the Burnetts. They'll know soon enough, anyway." He moves toward the couch and plops down. "Have a seat, everyone," he commands as though he owns the place, ignoring the fact that it actually belongs to the captain and Alice.

With my arms full of babies and Nico by my side, I give Leo a subtle shake of my head, signaling my desire to take the children to our room. I suspect I already know the gist of this conversation, and Nico doesn't need to be involved.

"Perhaps Katie should take the children to the bedroom?" Alice suggests, her demeanor timid.

The major's expression shifts to one of irritation. "Everyone. Sit. Now."

A flash of annoyance crosses Alice's features before she pastes on a neutral expression and opens her arms to take Zach back. "Here, dear. You and Leo sit on the loveseat. Nico, you can squish in between them."

The major taps the toe of his boot against the hardwood floor, a rapid rhythm punctuating his impatience. Alice moves in almost slow motion as she hands me Zach. She gives me a wink before taking a seat in the easy chair.

"Finally," the major mutters.

From his spot on the far end of the couch, Lieutenant Paul leans in Captain Williams's direction. "I'm sure you know why we're here. We've come with news regarding the recent events concerning you and Mrs. Williams."

The captain gives a single nod but remains silent, waiting for the lieutenant to continue.

The major clears his throat and shoots David a look. "I'll handle this, Lieutenant. We reviewed the situation and consulted with higher authorities. It was decided there will be no charges brought against you, Captain. You should know that not everyone agrees with this decision. I, for one, believe at the minimum you should be tried. And believe me, if things were normal, that is exactly what would happen. We know how that trial would end, too, don't we? You'd be found guilty, imprisoned, and dismissed."

If he was expecting an argument from the captain, he didn't get one. Instead, the captain remained composed, matching the major's gaze.

Major Stone narrows his eyes. "No comment, Chris?"

"I appreciate you bringing me this information."

"I'm here to make sure you understand that, even though you may have been given a free pass this time, you will be subject to intense scrutiny. These actions bring other concerns to light. The fact you not only hid your wife's illegal acts but also allowed yourself to be blackmailed to keep them hidden . . ." He pulls his lips into a tight line as he shakes his head. "Beginning tomorrow, I'll be on site at the hospital, acting as the commanding officer."

Captain Williams inhales sharply, eliciting a smile from the major. Leo's attention is fixed on David Paul. David, in turn, is staring intently at the major.

"I guess that got your attention, didn't it?" The major smirks.

"Thank you, sir," the captain responds. "I'll appreciate your assistance at the hospital. Am I to assume you'll also oversee the medical school? And the nursing school, which will start in just a few days?"

"We'll be discussing the future of your so-called schools in depth. As far as the hospital is concerned, you'll continue to handle the medical end of things, but all personnel issues will go through me. Do I make myself clear?"

"Absolutely, sir."

Lieutenant Paul chimes in, his voice tinged with a sense of solemnity. "The governor has also clarified that there will be no further pursuit from a legal standpoint. You and Mrs. Williams are to be left alone to continue your lives in peace."

The major shoots the lieutenant a look before his gaze locks onto Captain Williams, cold and unyielding, asserting his authority with an unmistakable air of superiority. "You should consider yourselves fortunate, Captain," he remarks sharply, his tone leaving no room for argument.

Captain Williams maintains his composure, though a flicker of annoyance flashes across his face. "Understood, sir. I appreciate the consideration and look forward to complying with your directives."

The major's smirk widens, a silent declaration of his perceived victory as he bounds to his feet. "Good. I expect nothing less."

He strides toward the door with an air of self-importance, Lieutenant Paul trailing behind like a reluctant shadow, his expression tinged with sympathy for our predicament. Captain Williams beats them to the threshold, holding it open as the pair exit. I catch a small shake of the lieutenant's head as he departs.

The room descends into an uneasy silence as the gravity of their words settles among us. In Alice's embrace, the baby stirs, oblivious to the tension. Her hands tremble slightly as she cradles baby Zach.

I'm truly happy there won't be criminal charges against Mrs. Williams. I didn't really expect there to be with the way our world is, but I also wasn't sure if the military might enact laws even now. From the sounds of things, the major would've certainly liked to escalate the situation.

Leo's jaw is tight, his expression steely as he looks at me. He quirks an eyebrow and barely moves his head in a shaking motion. I lift my chin in response, understanding we'll discuss this later, in the privacy of our bedroom.

Returning to the sitting area, Captain Williams clears his throat, his voice cutting through the tension. "Well, I suppose we have our work cut out for us."

Alice nods in agreement, her voice steady despite the underlying tremor. "Will he go out of his way to complicate things for you?"

"I'm certain he will."

She snorts. "I've never had any fondness for that man. Since his arrival here, he's made it his mission to be a constant annoyance to you—to just about everyone. But we'll handle it, Chris. We always have."

A sense of solidarity passes between the long-married couple as he reaches out to squeeze her hand. "Yes, we have."

Sitting in the dimly lit room, I'm struck by the resilience of Captain Williams and Alice. They face challenges head-on, a trait I've always admired.

The flickering candlelight dances across the walls, casting fleeting shadows that seem to mirror the uncertainties of our future. Yet, amid it all, determination grows within me. With Leo by my side, I know we'll navigate whatever obstacles come our way. We're ready to tackle whatever life throws at us, united in purpose and resolve.

Chapter 10

Merissa

Tension fills the medical school conference room, anticipation thick in the air as we await Major Stone's arrival. His impending presence casts a shadow over the proceedings, sowing uncertainty among our once-unified team.

Poppy Gardner, the soon-to-be nursing school leader, sits beside me, her expression a mixture of defiance and apprehension. I can see the fire in her eyes, a reflection of the simmering anger that pulses through each of us as we brace ourselves for what lies ahead. I glance toward Katie as she sits quietly with her chin dropped toward her chest.

Shortly after Captain Williams said we'd all be joining him for a meeting before we started our med school classes, she pulled me aside to tell me about the major stopping by their house last night. The good news is that Captain and Mrs. Wiliams will not have any charges brought against them for the assisted suicide of their neighbors.

Well, Mrs. Williams won't have charges for that, and the captain won't have charges for the coverup that followed. His punishment, however, is he'll no longer be in charge of the hospital. They're bringing in Major Stone to run it.

I'm surprised by this for several reasons. First, he isn't a doctor. Second, other than the captain and, loosely, Katie and Leo, the rest of the hospital employees are civilians. My guess is, this is nothing but a show of power to make it clear to Captain Williams that he is under scrutiny.

The door swings open with a resounding thud, echoing through the room as Major Stone strides in, his steps heavy with self-importance. As he takes his place at the head of the table, his gaze sweeps across the assembled staff, each glance exuding an unmistakable aura of superiority, leaving no doubt who holds the power in the room. Or at least he believes he holds the power. Personally, I'm not impressed.

"Good morning," he begins, his voice much too loud for the size of the room. "I trust you're all aware of the changes that have taken place. As of today, I have assumed command of this hospital, the medical school, the nursing school, and the long-term care centers."

There's a murmur of discontent that ripples through the room, but the major pays it no mind, his expression stern and unyielding. "Under my leadership, there will be no room for the laxity and incompetence that plagued this institution under Captain Williams's command. I will not tolerate any deviation from protocol or any attempts to undermine my authority."

Poppy Gardner bristles beside me, her fists clenched tightly in her lap as she shoots him a defiant glare. "With all due respect, the hospital and care centers have been running smoothly under Captain Williams's leadership. We've saved countless lives and provided exceptional care to our patients. I fail to see how your presence will improve upon that. Not to mention, you're not a doctor, and other than Captain Williams, we are not under your command or part of the National Guard."

I hide my smile, impressed that Poppy came out of the gate swinging. I'm also impressed that she covered my two biggest concerns.

The major's lips curl into a sneer, and his eyes narrow with disdain. "Your failure to understand this necessity is not my concern. I am here to ensure that this hospital operates with the utmost efficiency and discipline. And make no mistake, I will be watching each and every one of you closely."

"Again, I'm not in your military, and these buildings are not military buildings."

"That's where you're wrong," he interjects swiftly. "As of 0600 hours this morning, the governor gave control of all the Rapid City district hospitals, clinics, and care centers to the South Dakota National Guard. In fact, all hospitals and medical buildings across the state are now under the Guard."

Katie and Leo exchange a look before she glances in my direction and gives a slight shake of her head. Even Captain Williams gasps at this announcement as the major leans back in his chair, a satisfied look on his face. "Aren't executive orders wonderful?"

My heart sinks at his words, and a sense of foreboding settles over me like a heavy weight. I can't help but worry about what the future holds under the major's tyrannical rule.

"As of today," the major says, "you will follow very specific guidelines. I understand some of you have been receiving special treatment and shortened shifts. That changes today. You will work your regular shifts. Should we continue with the medical school and begin the nursing school, you will work your regular shifts plus keep up with your schooling."

Did he just suggest eliminating the medical school?

The captain clears his throat. "Major, perhaps we should discuss the— "

"No discussion needed," Stone says, raising his hand. "I am familiar with the expectations of medical students before the EMP. You may think you're doing them a favor by coddling them, having them attend school part time and work part time. You're not. If they can't handle the workload, then they have no business in classes."

He pauses for a moment and glances at a paper on the table in front of him. "Also, based on the numbers I have, this meeting is lacking several people. Did I not make myself clear that all employees and students were to be in this meeting?"

Williams crinkles his brow. "You did, sir."

"Then where is everyone?"

"Two of my staff are on bereavement, and I left one nurse to oversee the hospital."

"And I have one nurse at each of my care centers," Poppy interjects.

The major's face contorts with anger, his features twisting in disbelief. "My orders were to be followed to the letter. All the employees means all the employees."

While the captain's lips go into a tight line, Poppy laughs. "You do understand, *Major* Stone, that we can't leave the patients completely unattended? I realize you're not a doctor, and you apparently have zero medical training, but I would think you'd at least have a little common sense to understand— "

"Enough, Poppy," the captain says, his voice low and controlled.

She gives another light laugh and waves her hand. "It's really not enough, Chris. It's one thing for the governor to decide the military is in control of everything medical. But it's entirely something else to put someone like this . . . this . . ."

Nurse Jacquie Haley, who's sitting on my left, whispers, "Nincompoop."

Poppy finishes with, ". . . this *man* in charge."

I assume the major didn't hear Jacquie since he didn't comment or look at her. It's already obvious he isn't the type to let something like that slide. He certainly heard everything Poppy said and implied.

"You would do well to watch your tongue— " he glances at the paper in front of him " —Ms. Gardner. That's who you are, right?"

"*Mrs.* Gardner. Poppy Gardner."

"Well, *Mrs.* Gardner, let me make myself clear," he says through gritted teeth, his voice a low growl that sends a shiver down my spine. "I will not tolerate insolence under my command."

Poppy lifts her chin defiantly as she refuses to back down. "With all due respect, Major, I'm simply stating the facts. You may have the authority, but that doesn't make you infallible."

Major Stone's nostrils flare with barely contained rage, his hands pressed firmly against the table as he struggles to maintain his composure. "You seem to forget your place, Mrs. Gardner. I will not hesitate to remind you."

As the standoff continues, I exchange a worried glance with Katie, her expression mirroring my own apprehension. It's clear that Major Stone is not to be trifled with, and his wrath knows no bounds.

With a shrug, Poppy slides out of her chair. "No need to remind me. I know my place exactly, and that is treating and caring for patients. Also to teach the nursing school how to treat and care for patients. At least it was. I am not in the military, nor do I have any desire to be in the military. I refuse to be spoken to as if I'm a second-class citizen or a slave.

"My home is one of the care centers, and I will allow it to continue to be used as such for exactly one week from today. At that time, the patients will need to be moved." She seems to glide toward the door, her former training as a supermodel clear.

"Not so fast, Mrs. Gardner," Stone says. "I informed the governor not everyone would understand this need for a leadership change. As a result, we are putting all crew assignments or reassignment requests on hold for the next sixty days."

Poppy's eyes go wide as a rumble travels through the room.

"You've got to be kidding me," Jacquie mutters.

The major hears her this time. "I'm completely serious. Not only in this district, but in all Rapid City districts and the rest of the state. This will allow time for everyone to adjust to these changes."

"The governor can't do that." Poppy shakes her head.

I have a terrible sinking feeling in my stomach. Even though South Dakota isn't officially under martial law, my guess is the governor can do whatever the governor desires. As the major said earlier, the wave of a pen and an executive order was enacted. As things are, we don't even have an upcoming election to oust the current governor. All elections throughout the entire country have been given a moratorium by order of the president of the United States.

"The governor can and did," Major Stone says with a smirk.

Seemingly undeterred by this information, Poppy continues her stride toward the door. Her graceful exit only serves to magnify the tension in the room.

Major Stone's face contorts with fury, his fingers turning white from the pressure against the table. His eyes bore into Poppy's back, a silent warning of the consequences of her defiance.

The room buzzes with murmurs of disbelief and indignation as the implications of the governor's decree sink in. Sixty days of uncertainty loom before us, a daunting prospect in the face of the major's oppressive leadership.

Jacquie's muttered words echo the sentiments of many, a testament to the growing discontent among the hospital staff. If we can't switch crews, we're stuck working for this tyrant. The only other option is to leave town. Not just leave the town of Rapid City, but the state of South Dakota.

Meanwhile, Captain Williams sits stoically, his jaw clenched in frustration. It's clear that he's powerless to challenge the major's authority in the current political climate.

As I glance around the room, I can see the fear and frustration etched into the faces of my colleagues, a silent acknowledgment of the challenges that lie ahead.

The major glances around the room. "I see these new orders come as a bit of a shock. You will soon enough accept the way things are.

I'm sure you'll eventually understand that my management style will result in much smoother operations. You are all dismissed.

"If you are on duty today, you will show up for your shift on time. There will be no medical school classes today. In fact, I'm suspending all classes until I've interviewed each student and can determine if they are appropriate for this school. I understand the nursing school was to begin operations within a few days. How many of you are supposed to be students in that school?"

Several people raise their hands.

"I wouldn't count on the nursing school moving forward at this time."

"Major?" Captain Williams says, his voice more timid than I've ever heard it.

The major raises an eyebrow in his direction.

"The medical school and nursing school were both created with the governor's knowledge and blessing."

"Of course they were." The major's tone is less than convincing. "But after Mrs. Gardner's recent performance, I highly doubt that *blessing* will continue. If you don't have another instructor lined up, I will suggest shelving the program."

He turns back to the rest of the room. "That will be all. I'll allow you to wallow in your self-pity for today. Tomorrow, we will interview everyone—and I mean everyone this time. I will determine if there is a place for each person on the hospital roster or as part of either of the ill-fated schools. I expect everyone to be here at 0800."

The major wastes no time in leaving the conference room. The rest of us remain in our seats, staring in stunned silence. My hand moves to my stomach as my baby delivers a sharp kick.

Amid the turmoil, a spark of determination ignites within me, a resolve to resist the encroaching darkness and fight for what's right. I may be just a medic and med student, powerless against the National Guard and the governor, but I refuse to be silenced in the face of injustice.

I've proudly served my country, and I certainly understand how following orders is important. Necessary, even. But something feels wrong about this. Wrong and completely off.

I know little about the governor of South Dakota, especially considering I lived in Montana until only a few months ago. Prior to the EMP, when the twenty-four-hour news stations were still running, the South Dakota governor was a popular and controversial figure, loved by many and hated by others. During the time since the EMP, the governor has done much to help with the rebuilding efforts. To be honest, this feels completely out of character.

I rise to my feet and take a deep breath before speaking to the room. "Captain, please forgive me if I'm speaking out of turn." His nod prompts me to continue. "This is a shock to all of us. I know I'm certainly questioning my place here, in this hospital, but from the sounds of it, we're left without a choice in the matter . . . to a point. We can stand together, united against— "

I pause while I shake my head. "Against whatever may come. Our primary job is to care for and protect our patients. They depend on us completely, and we're the ones who can make a real difference in their lives. They need us now more than ever."

The room falls silent as my words sink in. I exchange a determined glance with Katie, and I can see the same resolve reflected in her eyes. We will face whatever comes our way with commitment to our patients and each other, resolute in overcoming the challenges ahead.

Chapter 11

Katie

Merissa's words hang in the air like a solemn vow, deepening the silence. Jacquie Haley breaks it, her voice cutting through the tension like a knife.

"You're right, Merissa." Her tone is resolute, and a determined expression marks her face. "Our duty is to our patients. We can't let this . . . this neanderthal prevent us from doing what's right. But at the same time, I feel trapped. Trapped in what may become a nightmare of tyranny, with no way out."

I must agree with Jacquie. We're bound by the orders of Major Stone, unable to escape the clutches of what's sizing up to become an oppressive regime. No matter how bad it gets, we're stuck.

A voice speaks up from the back of the room, breaking the spell of despair settling over us. "We leave. We leave South Dakota. That would be our only option."

I turn to see Austin Chambers, his jaw clenched and his eyes blazing with defiance. Several others mutter their agreement, their expressions a mix of fear and determination.

"They can't stop us from leaving," he continues. "We aren't required to stay in this state and work under these conditions. I, for one, refuse to be a pawn in the major's game."

His words resonate with me, stirring a sense of courage deep within my soul. I could go home. Be with my family. Although I am committed to serving with the United Volunteers, I prefer not to stand idly by and watch our freedoms get stripped away before our very eyes.

"Who has the handheld radio?" Captain Williams asks.

Austin raises his hand as he steps forward. "I do, sir."

"Who will you call?" Jacquie asks.

"This all seems a little too— " he hesitates as he seems to search for the word " —*convenient.* For there to be such a switch of plans almost overnight. I'm just not sure what to think. I still have a few contacts and ways to reach them."

Captain Williams takes the walkie-talkie, his hands shaking slightly as he reaches for the radio. He presses the call button, his voice steady as he pages a friend who he uses for relays via ham radio to reach the governor's office. The captain has his contact switch to a new frequency before passing on the message.

The voice on the other end says he'll be right back. After several moments, he returns. "There's no response. You want me to try again later and call you when I get through?"

"Please do so. Tell him it's urgent."

"Roger. I'll get back to you when I can. Out."

"What about the general?" Leo asks.

"I plan to pay a visit to General Truss," Captain Williams says. "However, I need to be delicate in voicing my concerns. I don't want it to seem like I'm being insubordinate. In the meantime, let's not make any rash decisions. While Mr. Chambers is correct that leaving South Dakota is an option, I would think you'd want to wait until all other options are exhausted. Let me check with my contact at the governor's office, plus see if I can carefully feel out the general."

"Do you think that will do any good?" Austin asks. "No disrespect intended, but if they've taken the hospital away from you, it would seem to me you're on the outside now."

Captain Williams gives a sad nod. "You may be right. But let's still wait and see what we can find out. I have a few other resources, too, that may know more about what's happening. Let's get through today. The major expects you all back here tomorrow at 0800. I'm not exactly sure how we'll handle the hospital and care centers being unstaffed, but we'll figure it out. Maybe I can convince the major of the importance of it and rotate through people."

One of the nurses from the care centers raises her hand. "What about Poppy?"

The captain releases a breath through his nose. "I'll talk with her. I understand she's upset, especially considering she came to me offering her private home as the first care center. She's put a lot into making sure the long-term facilities operate as they should."

As the captain addresses the group, unease gnaws at the edges of my consciousness. His words offer a glimmer of hope, but the gravity of our situation lingers in my mind. We're trapped in a precarious position, with no clear path forward and no easy solutions.

Poppy's defiant stance was remarkable, and Merissa's unexpected contribution was both impressive and surprising. She's usually quiet and reserved and only speaks up when something truly matters to her.

Austin's correct about people having the option to leave. Well, most people. Leo and I might not be able to go without being considered AWOL. Merissa likely couldn't either, especially with her pregnancy being so advanced. The travel would be too strenuous for her. Besides, she and Pearl came here specifically to be with Opal Maher, who's Pearl's sister. Merissa had made a point of staying with her mother-in-law after the deaths of her husband and brother-in-law.

Undoubtedly, they wouldn't release the captain from his commission with the Guard. If the others did go, that'd certainly leave us in a pickle. Would the threat of them leaving be enough to cause the major and the governor to back off? Unlikely.

The major seems the type to dig his heels in and make things even more difficult for the rest of us if part of the staff went.

"Everyone, return to your shift if you're on duty today. Students, we'll get our rounds done. Even though the major said there's no med school today, he didn't say you couldn't do rounds as planned." The captain offers us a strained smile.

As the group breaks up, I tell Leo I'm going to walk over with Merissa and I'll see him soon.

"You okay?" he asks.

I shake my head. "I know the captain and Mrs. Williams said they didn't trust the major, but I don't think they thought it'd go this far, do you?"

"The captain seemed as blindsided as we were. Especially the part about no crew changes. I hate to say it, but Austin might be right about people leaving. Only— "

"Only probably not us."

"Right. Probably not us. Not until our year is up. That's not until the end of June."

I tilt my head and furrow my brow. "But if we join the Guard?"

He shakes his head. "I don't know. We'd most certainly be under the major's direct supervision. I'm not sure it's something I'd want to do. I'm certain you wouldn't. Besides, I've been thinking, with the babies and Nico . . ." Leaning in, he whispers, "I kind of like the idea of being a mom and dad. I know we could still be soldiers with the children, but should we?"

My breath catches as my eyes fill with tears. "I don't know," I whisper back. "I'll—Let's chat later, okay?" I'd like nothing more than to discuss this now, but it's certainly not the time or the place.

"We will," he promises. "Go talk with Merissa. I'm going to catch up with the captain. See you in a minute."

As I walk over to Merissa, her expression is a mix of determination and concern. I can tell she's still processing everything that happened in the meeting, just like the rest of us.

"Hey, Merissa," I say, falling into step beside her. "That was something back there. Crazy."

Her brows are furrowed with worry. "I'd like to say I'm surprised, but I've known men like the major before. Give them a little bit of power and they run with it. The terrible thing is, he's not a doctor. Probably doesn't know the first thing about medicine beyond how to put a bandage on a paper cut."

I snort out a laugh while I shake my head. "No doubt. I met him last night when he and David Paul came to the house to let the captain know there wouldn't be charges. We found out then he'd be taking over the hospital and schools, but I had no idea it'd be like this. I'm sure the captain didn't either." I slow my pace to allow the others to get ahead of us. "Leo and I can't leave South Dakota. Not without permission."

"Right. I know. I can't go either." She rests her hand on her belly. "But the others, they could. Will they?"

"The captain is right about not making any rash decisions."

"Everything you said is true. Our patients need us, but it's going to be difficult. Especially if we really are stuck here with Major Stone controlling us. If the governor is allowing this, what can we really do?"

"I don't know. And to be honest, I'm kicking myself for saying anything. I wish I could take it back."

"Why? You were amazing."

She tsks. "Hardly. It's like you just said. I'm stuck. You're stuck. The captain is stuck. The others may be able to leave, but will they? And how does that help? The major will just make it more difficult for the rest of us."

"But we can't let the major take away what we've done. The hospital, the care centers, and the schools . . . they'll make a difference. They already make a difference. We can't let him destroy them."

"It's tough," Merissa says sympathetically. "I want to agree that we'll figure something out. We must. I'm just not sure what."

"Maybe the captain can get some answers from his contact at the governor's office. Or from the general or . . . who else do you think he plans to ask?"

She shakes her head but stops mid-move. "Bowski," she whispers, her cheeks taking on a pink hue.

"Bowski." I nod in agreement. "He seems to know everything that goes on in the Black Hills."

Merissa tilts her head. "If he doesn't know about it, he knows how to find out. I didn't get to talk with you much yesterday, you know, with Josiah— "

"I still can't believe he's dead."

"It's terrible. The captain understood the cryptic message when Leo called on the radio. I had a hard time following the conversation, but the captain and Leo seem to have a language all their own."

"It surprises me, too, how they can talk in half sentences and understand each other. Leo didn't want it to get out before Jesse could tell his mom."

"That was smart. Anyway, that wasn't the only cryptic call from the day. I had another one of those prank calls come in, like I had last month."

"What? Really? Someone pretending to be someone else?"

"Yep. This time he said he was a doctor and there was a biohazard threat of some sort."

"Biohazard? Another virus?"

"I don't think so. We really do think it's a prank, but Shaw's going to check it out. I told Bowski about it, and he also intends to investigate it quietly. The caller said he was a doctor from Deadwood. Williams didn't know him but admitted he didn't know all the doctors there, since they're a fair distance from us and with the communication issues. Shaw said he had a few contacts. They want to keep it off the radio. Which was something else odd. The man said he was calling from Deadwood but came over the walkie-talkie."

"How'd that work? It doesn't have the range."

"Exactly. Another mystery. The captain suggested this biohazard, if it even exists, might be related to whatever they're doing at Sanford Underground Research Facility. Maybe one of those experiments could cause a biohazard."

"What are they doing at Sanford?" I ask. "Does anyone know?"

"I'd guess the governor does, wouldn't you?"

I stop walking and grab her arm. "You got that strange call the day before yesterday? Then, last night, the captain was relieved of his command over the hospital. And today we find out the governor is behind it."

"You think it's all related?"

I lift my hands and shake my head. "That seems like a weird coincidence that these things that involve the governor are all coming up at the same time, doesn't it?"

"I don't know. Maybe." She lifts her chin in the hospital's direction. "We'd better get going."

As we walk, I say, "You're right that it's probably nothing. A coincidence or something. But let me know what Bowski finds out. Tell him about this whole thing, too. Even though we think the captain will go to him, you kind of have an inside track, right?"

She rolls her eyes at me. "I wouldn't call it that."

"Mm-hmm," I murmur. "I think you two make a good couple."

She sighs. "It's too soon. My husband— "

"Died fighting so you could live."

She gives a nod but doesn't look at me.

"Things aren't the same now as they used to be. My sister had the same thing happen, you know. Well, similar anyway. Her husband went missing. We assumed he was dead but didn't know, not right away. She met another man and had all sorts of guilt over it, but she knew her husband would want her to keep living. To be happy."

Merissa's expression softens, a hint of sadness lingering in her eyes. "I appreciate your perspective, Katie. And I'm sorry about your sister's loss. It's just . . . it's hard to move on, you know? Especially when the wounds are still fresh."

"I get it, Merissa. But life goes on, even when it feels like it shouldn't. We owe it to ourselves to find happiness wherever we can, even amidst all this chaos. And Bowski is a good guy."

She offers me a slight smile, gratitude shining through the pain. "Thanks, Katie. I needed to hear that."

As we approach the hospital entrance, a sense of determination settles over me. Despite the uncertainty of our future, I refuse to let fear dictate my actions. Together, Merissa and I push open the doors, ready to face whatever challenges lie ahead.

Chapter 12

Katie

As Merissa and I enter the hospital, our group is making their way toward the nurse's desk. We've shed our coats but are still in our boots since we'll need to visit each of the care centers after we finish with the hospital patients.

Captain Williams waits for us to approach before saying, "Dr. Murphy will lead you on rounds today." He turns to the newest doctor to join our team. "Doctor?"

Doctor Reginald Murphy glides his hand through his close-cropped hair. "I understand we all are plenty concerned about this morning's meeting. But let's remember, as Weaver mentioned, we're here for our patients. They still need us at our best—no matter what else may be on our minds. Narrow your focus and concentrate on what's important. Understood?"

There's a chorus of "Yes, Doctor."

"I'll leave you to it, then, Doctor." Captain Williams delivers a strained smile. "Dr. Wolff? Please join me in my office." Nettie Wolff gives a nod before trailing behind him.

Dr. Murphy starts the rounds by describing Lisa Fadden, the first patient we'll see. She sustained injuries in the November bombing of the ration center.

I shake my head. I remember Lisa. She's been in and out of the hospital since the bombing. The original injury was a massive cut to her leg caused by flying debris. The cut doesn't want to heal right and keeps getting infected. She was here only a few weeks ago, at the same time I was a patient, thanks to the beating and frostbite my dog Gerry and I sustained. According to Dr. Murphy, Lisa's fever has returned.

"Stella Swensen was here last night, bringing both topical and oral herbal remedies. These are remedies she responded well to last time. The question is, are we dealing with the same strain of bacteria as before? Weaver? Treatment suggestions?"

Merissa takes a breath before saying, "We need to take a sample and see what grows."

Dr. Murphy crinkles his nose. "Simplistic, but correct."

I hide my smile behind my hand. Leave it to Merissa to get her point across in as few words as possible.

As we discuss potential treatment options for Lisa Fadden's recurring infection, I notice Merissa's brow is furrowed in thought. When Dr. Murphy opens the door to the patient room, I whisper, "What's wrong?"

Merissa shakes her head. "Probably nothing. It's . . . I'll tell you later."

Lisa Fadden looks terrible. Her leg is swollen and discolored, with angry red streaks spreading from a nasty wound. The pungent odor of infection hangs in the air, making it clear that she needs immediate medical attention. Her face is pale, and beads of sweat dot her forehead, revealing the pain she's enduring. Each time she shifts, a wince crosses her face and emphasizes the severity of her condition. We decide to continue the course of action already started, hoping to pinpoint the source of the infection.

With only three admittances, the hospital rounds take only a few minutes before we grab our jackets and other outerwear and begin the walk to the first long-term care facility. I wonder if we'll see Poppy today as we make our rounds. Surely, she'll at least be at her home, which houses four of the longest-residing patients.

The four are all elderly, and it's a miracle they've not only survived but thrived this long. I have little doubt it's because of Poppy and her diligent care. If the major continues down the path he established this morning, I hate to think about what will happen to the patients who need what Poppy offers.

I don't know Poppy well—not at all, really—but I believe she's the type that won't tolerate nonsense from anyone. Even if he's supposedly her superior.

Outside, the sun radiates its brilliance, casting a warm glow across the landscape. It's a beautiful February day, and my jacket would be too heavy if it weren't for the breeze blowing from the west. I take a deep breath, savoring the smell of the woodstoves burning throughout the district. I fall in by Merissa's side. "What were you thinking about earlier?"

"Have you noticed we've had a lot of repeat patients lately? Not repeat like the Ebright sisters, who tend to come in seeking attention. Of course, that wasn't the case last time they came in." She tilts her head in my direction.

I think about Elaine and Marilyn Ebright—spinster sisters who are frequent visitors at our hospital, often with exaggerated complaints. In addition to the Ebright sisters, there are a few others we've dubbed as frequent flyers. One man in his sixties has his daughter bring him in regularly.

Elaine and Marilyn tend to take turns faking their symptoms. But a recent bout of sepsis caused by a skin infection proved to us we can't just dismiss the claims without further checking. Unfortunately, it's a challenge. Something like the little boy who cried wolf. It's hard to know when to believe them, so we must err on the side of caution.

"You mean people who keep getting sick?"

"Right. But they shouldn't. Why does Lisa Fadden keep getting infections?"

I raise my hands and shake my head. "Not being able to bathe regularly? Her inability to maintain the cleanliness of her clothes? Not having the right type of antibiotics for the particular strain of bacteria?"

"True. All true." Merissa lowers her voice. "Doesn't it seem odd, though? People from the bombings keep having issues. It seems like there are too many people suffering from persistent infections or slow-healing wounds. And when the flu was going around, how many people did we see that would get better and then get sick again?"

"But none of that's unusual, is it? Viruses do that. Bacteria does that."

"You're right. I know you're right. Maybe it's just that prank call that has me seeing conspiracies."

"Because he said there was a biohazard? Do you think Lisa has some sort of pathogen causing these things? How would that even work?"

"Did you know two of the residents at the facility Elliot Tillman was at died the day he left?"

"And?" I ask, my tone harsher than intended. I clear my throat. "Who was it?"

She gives me two names—people who, quite honestly, seemed to be recovering well.

"I know you've been on short shifts since your, um . . ."

"Attack," I offer. "You can call it what it is. I was attacked and left for dead."

Merissa touches my arm. "Sorry. Just forget I brought this up. You're probably right. I'm grasping at straws. With the prank call and the lack of sleep— "

"You're having trouble sleeping?"

"I have a baby doing gymnastics on my bladder twenty-four seven. Speaking of babies, how are Caleb and Zach? Nico?"

My heart swells at the mention of the children's names. "They're good. All of them. Alice and I were talking last night about how fast the babies are growing. The wet nurses, combined with the homemade formula, seem to be giving them what they need. Alice found comfort in the children during this difficult time while she waited to see if charges would be filed. I swear, she picks the babies up when they even squeak. Zach seems to know when she's around, too. I think . . ." I let out a sigh.

"Mrs. Williams is as attached to them as you are. Have any of you made any decisions?"

"Not yet. I'm beginning to wonder if we'll even need to decide, or if the major and his new plans will make the decision for us. Even Leo whispered his concerns to me after the major's bombshell of a meeting."

"You could go home."

"I could. Part of me wants to go home, very much." I notice a patch of ice ahead and caution her to watch her footing before saying, "I've been thinking about what you said the other day about how it doesn't seem like I really want to be in the National Guard, and if I don't want to, I shouldn't do it."

A shadow crosses over her face. "I'm sorry about that, Katie."

"Don't be. I know you meant well. Plus, there was a lot of truth to what you said. When I think about joining the National Guard, I don't think how wonderful it'll be to serve my country . . . um, my state. I felt that way when Leo and I talked about joining the Volunteers. I loved the idea of helping our country get back on its feet. When the Volunteers were booted from South Dakota, I would've gone with them and finished my time wherever they sent me.

"But we were already at the hospital and really liked what we were doing. We liked what Captain Williams was building and believed in it. Staying made sense. Committing to the South Dakota National Guard for a minimum of eight years, though . . . I just don't know if that makes sense for me. Leo, maybe. But now, with the children, I'm really not sure it makes sense for either of us. I don't even know if continuing med school makes sense. Can I be a doctor and a mother to three?"

"Can I be a doctor and a mother to one?" she asks, her hand going to her belly. "Plus, I have Mother Pearl to consider. If things do go bad with the major, I can't move on. The baby needs to be born and old enough to travel. I know we were going to send Kemeera to your family home with a newborn, but I don't know if I'd want to risk it with one so young."

My mouth goes dry as I think about how close we came to unleashing that psycho Kemeera on my family and community. If she hadn't shown her true colors and ended up running off . . . I can't even imagine what she may have done to my family.

If the little girl Abigail, who we called Ivy because she wouldn't tell us her name, hadn't told us Kemeera left to "finish the job," we may not have known who she really was. *What* she really was. She was knee-deep in the murders the preacher and his group committed. She wasn't an innocent bystander as she'd led us to believe.

Thinking of Kemeera puts a thought in my head. "Could Addison be behind the deaths?"

"The biohazard deaths?" Merissa is already shaking her head. "I don't see how. Everyone's on the lookout for her. She's not getting anywhere near the hospital or care centers. No, you're probably right. The prank call was just a prank and I'm hallucinating." She lets out a low laugh as we approach the first care center.

While I join in her chuckle, part of me wonders if Merissa may be on to something. Are more people returning with repeat illnesses? If so, why? It probably isn't some grand conspiracy, but maybe it's something simple we're overlooking. That is definitely worth exploring.

Chapter 13

Merissa

"Merissa?" Mother Pearl calls to me from her bedroom. "Can you come here for a moment?"

I crinkle my brow as I move from our cozy kitchen to her room. It's unusual for her to ask me into her room. Not only unusual, it simply doesn't happen. I stop when I reach the partially open door. "Yes?"

"Come in, dear." Pearl is standing near her bed. She doesn't turn around as she invites me into her private domain.

"Is everything okay?"

"I'm sure it is. I've just got a weird-feeling nodule. Would you mind taking a look at it?"

A weird-feeling nodule? My heart rate speeds up. "Like a lump?"

"Mmm. A bump. Let's just call it a bump."

A bump. Is that different from a lump? The last thing we need is something serious. There's no treatment for things like cancer. "I can look, sure. You can also come by the hospital and let one of the doctors check it."

"Pshaw. I'm sure it's nothing." Her eyes still don't meet mine.

We both know if she was sure it wasn't anything, she wouldn't even be bringing it to my attention. "Let me see."

The bump on her ribcage is obvious. I don't touch it with my unwashed hands, but she does. "It's hard," she says, showing how it doesn't push in.

"Does it hurt?"

She nods. "Not awful, but enough."

Knowing Pearl's high threshold for pain, I suspect it hurts plenty, and she just ignores it. "You find anything anywhere else?"

She finally meets my gaze. "Under my armpit."

"Did you just find these today?"

"The armpit, yes. The other bump was a few days ago. I didn't think much of it at the time."

Keeping my voice even, I say, "You should come in and let a doctor check it."

"Is today a clinic day?"

I consider what day of the week it is. "Yes, it's Thursday. We have clinic days on Tuesday, Thursday, and Saturday. But you don't have to wait for clinic day."

"I don't think this is an emergency, do you?"

I tilt my head and shrug my shoulders. "Want to walk in with me?"

"Don't you have your meeting with Major Whatsit this morning?"

I flick my eyebrows at her. "Major Stone, yes." I'd given Pearl a brief recap of yesterday's meeting with the major. She'd been very supportive, even suggesting I tough it out until my maternity leave. Then, once the baby is born, we move to Opal's farm. My two months of no crew transfer would be up by then.

Because of her age, Pearl has a distinct set of rules as far as crew work. Individuals over the age of sixty-five receive their basic essentials for living, with no need for an official crew job. They ask them to help as they can with things like purifying water and sewing. Pearl also spends time at the daycare down the road and has even visited the orphanage and helped there. It's all really volunteer work, though, as opposed to required.

I shouldn't have any trouble transferring to a position on Opal's farm, but I truly hope it doesn't come to that. I love working in the hospital and have decided I want to be a doctor. A Doctor of the Apocalypse, as we jokingly refer to ourselves. "The meeting is at 8:00. Clinic hours start at 9:00. Why don't you come then? Get there early and you won't have much of a wait."

"I'm supposed to— " She sighs before begrudgingly muttering, "I'll be there."

I arrive at the hospital fifteen minutes before the meeting with Major Stone is set to start. Katie and Leo are already there, but none of the other med students are around.

"Hey," Katie says. "I just heard that Lisa Fadden died overnight."

I shake my head. "That's terrible." In some ways, I'm not surprised. She looked awful yesterday, and her unstable vitals led us to believe her infection was systemic this time.

"Mm-hmm. And someone from one of the care centers, too." She goes on to tell me about one of the men who was there recovering from the flu, his symptoms complicated by something we weren't sure of.

"What? We saw him yesterday. He seemed better, almost ready to go home."

Katie lifts her hands and lowers her voice. "I know, right? Maybe . . ." Her words fade away as she shrugs. "I don't know what to think."

"Does Leo know what we talked about yesterday? Did you tell him about the prank call and my— "

"Your conspiracy theory?" She gives me a wink. "We talked about it. He even asked the captain about the prank call this morning. The captain says Shaw didn't learn anything new. You hear anything from Bowski?"

"Since we spoke yesterday? No, I haven't seen him." I feel heat travel up my neck and land on my cheeks.

"Mm-hmm," she hums.

"Really. I haven't," I insist.

From down the hall, Leo motions that he's ready to go over to the med school building. Katie lifts a hand in acknowledgment. "Ready to go?"

"Might as well get it over with."

The meeting starts at exactly 0800 hours, with the major being even more pompous and condescending than yesterday. Hard to believe that's even possible.

Poppy Gardner and her husband are both in attendance today. At first, the major objects to the husband joining them until Poppy tells him to check his roster for Brad Harmon. "That's my husband."

Major Stone narrows his eyes. "And why wasn't he here yesterday?"

Poppy sighs. "As I attempted to explain then, we can't leave our patients unattended."

The major leans back in his chair and steeples his hands. "And who is with your patients today? Are you neglecting them?"

"I've brought in people I know and trust to cover each of the buildings today. People who are not part of the regular crew. I've arranged for a runner to come get me if I am needed."

"That seems convenient. And you, Captain? Have you left your building unattended?"

The captain shakes his head. "We don't currently have any in-house patients. I have people monitoring the building, and the guard will call me should anyone arrive. I'm sure you know today is our clinic day. That begins at 0900. People will start arriving about half an hour early."

"I fail to see the need for clinic hours when your hospital is open all the time."

The captain dips his chin. "Many people believe the hospital is for emergency treatment only. They treat our clinic day as a physician's office. I'm sure you've gone to the doctor yourself, perhaps for something minor. Did you go to the emergency room or wait until your doctor was open?"

"That is private information and none of your business."

I cover my laugh with a cough. He either doesn't hear me or he ignores me. This guy is something else.

Glancing around the room, the major says, "For those of you who weren't here yesterday, I'm sure your fellow employees have given you the basics of the changes. There will be no excessive days off. You will work your scheduled shifts, no matter what you think you have going on in your personal life." He glares at Kerry before shifting his eyes to Jesse.

"If you physically cannot do the job, we will dismiss you and assign you to a job that you are capable of." He glances toward Leo, and then his eyes travel to Katie, who still has a bandage on her ear, cheek, and fingers. "You will work your full shift. No more of this half-shift business. If you cannot work a full shift, we will reassign you. Don't even think a doctor's note will get you preferential treatment. I know how your ilk sticks together. When that happens, others end up overworked, and it's a downward spiral from there."

I'm surprised he didn't turn to me next and point at my giant belly. Undoubtedly, I'll hear about it in our private meeting. What I don't understand is how he thinks Leo, who's being followed by one of the best orthopedic surgeons in the state, could return to full duty without that doctor's approval.

Major Stone lacks medical experience beyond the basic first aid training received as part of the National Guard. How can he say people must work even with a doctor's note excusing them? I find it interesting he called out both Burnetts. Maybe that's because of having met them at Captain Williams's home the other night?

It almost seems as if Major Stone has it in for them, particularly. Plus, the dirty looks he directed toward Jesse and Kerry, who have both been out for bereavement . . . When I served in the Coast Guard, we could take bereavement leave. I can't imagine the National Guard doesn't have bereavement, sick time, and other paid time off options, at least to some degree, even with the way things are now.

Not to mention, other than the captain—and loosely Katie and Leo—none of us are military. Thinking about bereavement leave makes me think of Mother Pearl. Hopefully, the lumps are nothing. The lump under her armpit could be just about anything. Maybe she's coming down with a cold? Having a second one on her ribcage is concerning, though.

She'll likely prefer the captain to check her today. Even though the lumps are in somewhat private locations, I know she'll prefer an older male doctor compared to a young male or a female at all. That's just how Pearl is. She's been supportive of my pursuit of medical training, but I doubt she'd even want me to treat her. Just having her call me into the room this morning was a tremendous step.

I glance at the captain and wonder if he was able to reach his friend at the governor's office or talk with the general. Katie didn't mention it, and I didn't think to ask until this moment.

"Now," the major says loudly, "if you are currently on shift at the hospital, you may return there. I will interview you last, after I've finished with everyone else. You will meet me in my office at the hospital to help accommodate your schedule." He sends a pious look around the table before settling his gaze on Captain Williams. "See, Captain? I can be reasonable."

"Thank you, sir."

I furrow my brow, wondering exactly where the major's office in the hospital may be. It's not like we have a spare room available.

"If you're on shift at one of the care centers, I'll meet with you first. I have an office set up down the hall. Line up along the wall." He glances at his roster sheet. "Brad Harmon, you're first."

Poppy's husband clears his throat. "I'm not actually on duty today."

"Is that right? Well, you're first anyway. Let's go."

Brad follows the major out of the room, but not before glancing back at his wife and shaking his head. She responds with a nod of her own. I'm sure there was more communication in those two gestures than anyone watching may realize. Sometimes I miss that—having someone who I can talk to without talking at all.

Since I work the overnight shift, which begins at 1800, my turn doesn't arrive for some time. Not that he keeps anyone for terribly long. The meetings seem to be an in-and-out event. Most people come out looking even less happy than they did going in, but no one talks to those of us who are still waiting about what went on.

When Poppy comes out, she looks mad enough to spit nails but says nothing as she motions to her husband and they promptly leave the building. From others, there are headshakes and even teary eyes, but no actual conversation.

When it's my turn, I knock on the door, and then slowly turn the knob when the major bellows, "Enter." I do my best not to waddle as I go into the room. The major is writing something and doesn't look up. I remain standing at attention until he looks up from the paper. I swear, his eyes nearly jump out of his head when he sees me. "You're . . . you're *pregnant*," he spits out.

I keep my eyes forward. "Yes, sir."

He sighs. "And here I had high hopes for you. After seeing that you were part of Homeland Security, I thought . . ." He sighs even louder. "Never mind. Please, have a seat."

I give a curt nod before carefully sitting on the edge of the chair. Although the Coast Guard is under Homeland Security instead of the Department of Defense, I've never had someone refer to my service time in such a manner. The Coast Guard was both a federal law enforcement agency and a military branch. We just fell under Homeland.

Sure, that made us the butt of many jokes, but the major almost sounds like it is some noble posting. I'm not sure I understand that. I'd more expect the good-natured ribbing I receive from other former military people. Not that I think the major would be the type to deliver anything like that.

He stares at me for more than a minute before asking, "When is the child due?"

"Sometime around the end of March."

"How much time will you need off?"

"Assuming everything goes as expected, the captain and I discussed six weeks from my medic job and four weeks from med school. I'll continue to study while I'm off."

"I don't think you need to worry about the med school."

"Sir?"

He waves his hand. "Are you able to perform your medic duties?"

"Most of them, sir."

"Which are you unable to perform?"

"I have a lifting weight limit, and there's some concern about me acting as a combat medic."

"I would imagine. So . . . you're essentially useless as a medic?"

I bristle at his remark and work to keep my tone even. "I do the rest of my duties as needed."

"Other than moving people and being there should someone be shot while on patrol, what are those duties?"

"I clean rooms— "

"The nurses can do that. The janitor."

"Yes, sir. They do, but when— "

"So, you're redundant." He drops his eyes back to the paper and furiously scribbles. Without bothering to look up, he says, "I'm finished with you. You're dismissed."

"Thank you, sir."

He still ignores me as I stand and exit the room as quickly as possible. I slip out of the room with my head down, blinking back tears, the door closing softly behind me.

Chapter 14

Merissa

I enter the hospital and pause at the front door, allowing my eyes to adjust to the shift in brightness. Pearl's distinct voice reaches my ears before she comes into view.

Despite spending most of her adult life in Montana, her slight accent hints at her Oklahoma roots. It's a subtle reminder of her heritage, unlike our friend Walt's deep southern drawl. He, like us, lived in Livingston and initially befriended my husband and me before forming a bond with Pearl after the EMP. Whenever they engage in conversation, Pearl's twang becomes more pronounced, reaching almost comical levels.

After we received a letter from Opal inviting us, we decided to move to South Dakota. Walt helped us move the horses and the bulk of our supplies. He's made his home at Opal's ranch, but we rarely see him.

He's part of the ranch crew that checks the property lines, and he lives in a cabin at the opposite end of the property from the ranch house. When he gets back to the main house, he's busy with the horses. I originally met Walt when we were part of the same mounted archery club.

Mounted, or horse, archery was a passion I shared with my husband. The history of mounted archery dates back to the Stone Age and has now come full circle in today's apocalyptic world.

Not only is Walt an accomplished archer, but he's also a bowyer and makes incredible horse bows, longbows, and more. He even gifted Opal with a bow of her own. I know Opal saw him when he stayed a few days over the holidays, but I haven't seen him for months.

And now, with the baby so close to being due, I've decided not to make the several-mile trek to Opal's until after his or her birth, so I'm not sure when I'll see Walt again. Once the baby's born, I intend to start riding again and brush up on my archery skills.

As Pearl comes into view, I discover she's chatting with the person sitting next to her. My eyes go wide as I realize she's visiting with Bowski. He sees me looking in his direction and gives me a smile.

Pearl turns slightly. "Well, Merissa, there you are."

Discovering Pearl talking to Bowski sends my heart racing. I've purposely avoided mentioning him to her. Partly because it's weird. She is, after all, the mother of my dead husband and the grandmother of my soon-to-be-born child.

The other part is . . . I'm embarrassed. I know it's too soon to have feelings for anyone, but I do. Those feelings are much too complicated to try to explain to Pearl. Plus, the last thing I want is to hurt her.

"Did you get signed in?" I ask Pearl while purposely avoiding looking at Bowski.

"Yes, they said it'd be just a few minutes."

"Okay. Good. I need to, um . . . I'll be back." I turn and take several steps.

"Merissa?" Pearl raises her voice.

I stifle a sigh and turn to face her. "Yes?"

"Come and meet my new friend." She rests her hand on Bowski's arm. "This is Ritchie Kasubowski." She looks toward him. "Did I say it right this time?"

"Perfectly." His baritone voice sends my heart pounding. "But you can call me Bowski. Everyone does."

"I'd rather call you Ritchie, if that's okay? My sons had a playmate named Ritchie when they were in high school. You remind me of him. Taller, of course."

"No doubt." He laughs before glancing at me. "Merissa and I know each other."

A look of surprise crosses Pearl's face before she says, "I'm sure you do. I should've realized that with the job you do, you're in and out of the hospital regularly." She looks at me. "How come you've never mentioned him?"

"Um . . ." I shrug. "I'm not sure. Do I mention many of the people I work with?"

"Well, yes. Some of them. I know about Katie and Leo. Jesse—the poor man. I heard they forced him to come in for a meeting today while he's grieving for his brother. And— "

I raise my hand. "Let me go check in and see if anything's happening with the med school today."

"I'll walk with you," Bowski says. As he stands, he says to Pearl, "It was a pleasure to meet you."

"And you. Perhaps you'd like to join Merissa and me for supper one night?"

"Pearl," I whisper.

"What, dear?" she asks, her voice dripping in innocence. I swear there's a twinkle in her eye. "I think it'd be right nice to have Ritchie over for supper, especially considering you work together and all."

"We don't exactly work together," I say. "He is here when he must be." I look at Bowski. "I'm assuming you're here on Hugo's behalf?"

He dips his chin. "I am. Captain Williams asked me to hold up a minute. He's got some of the med students in with him, discussing the death."

My mouth forms an *O*. "I should be in there." I turn to fast walk down the hall. Bowski is by my side.

When we're out of Pearl's earshot, I whisper, "Why were you talking to her?"

"She sat next to me while I was waiting. I didn't want to be rude."

"Did you know who she was?"

"After she told me. Don't worry, I didn't give away our secret."

"What secret?" I hiss.

He sighs. "Okay, Merissa. I get it. You don't want your mother-in-law to know about us. I understand."

As we reach the patient room Lisa Fadden was in yesterday, I slow and ask, "Do you know if they are in here?"

"As far as I know. I'll wait here."

I nod. "You know it's complicated, right? Braedon just died. I'm— " I put my hand on my stomach. "I don't want to hurt her."

He bends slightly and whispers in my ear, his breath tickling me. "I'm not exactly smart about these things, but I'm pretty sure she wants to set us up." He pulls away and gives me a wink. "Would you mind telling the captain I have another pickup? I can go there first if he'd like."

"The care center?"

He shakes his head. "Already taken care of. There was a home death. Something . . . odd."

My brow furrows in confusion. I want to hear more about this but now is not the time. "I'll tell the captain."

I knock on the door and wait until I hear a faint, "Come in."

Seeing me, the captain says, "Ms. Weaver. Good. I'm sorry we started without you. I'm not sure how much time we'll have before . . ." He tilts his head in the direction of the medical school where Major Stone is still conducting the personnel interviews.

"I understand, sir." I motion toward the hallway. "Bowski has another pickup to make. Should he go to that one and then come back?"

"We're just about finished here. Why don't you come see what we were looking at? Sergeant K. Burnett? Please report on what we've discovered."

Katie gives a brief and concise report that essentially says they've determined that while there was an infection in the leg, they don't believe that's what killed her. They aren't even convinced it was an advanced systemic infection. "She was sick. We know that from our examination yesterday. But the cultures we've been growing are clear so far. And the laboratory tests—the blood slides—didn't have an excessive amount of white blood cells. Her red blood cells seemed a little low but not terribly."

Shaking my head, I ask. "Why did she die?"

"That is the question," the captain says. "Let's move this discussion to my off— " He clears his throat. "We'll move to the break room. As I'm sure you gathered from the meeting with the major, I no longer have an office in this hospital." As we exit the room, he apologizes to Bowski for the delay and tells him to go ahead.

As I pass Bowski, he touches my arm to stop me.

"Yes?"

"I want to take your mother-in-law up on her invite."

I shake my head. "I'm not ready for that."

He pulls his lips into a tight line. "Okay. That's fine. But soon. I planned to find you while I was here to see if you wanted to go to the concert with me tomorrow night."

"The concert?"

"At the orphanage. Did you hear about it?"

"They were talking about it when we made rounds last time. I didn't realize it was tomorrow night."

"Are you working?"

"No, I'm off."

"They're doing a dinner beforehand. Or, as your mother-in-law calls it, supper. Not the orphanage, but volunteers from the district. They'll serve the meal in the cafeteria and then have the performance in the auditorium. At least they're making good use of the school turned orphanage. How about I stop by your place at five thirty?"

I drop my gaze to my shoes. "Can I meet you there?"

"It'll be getting dark. You shouldn't— "

"How about we meet at the corner? Where you wait for me when walking me home?"

"I'll see you there."

In the break room, the rest of the students are taking seats around the table. Even though Kerry Hendricks was at the meeting with the major and had her personal meeting, she isn't with the rest of the group.

"We'll take just a few minutes to finish up our thoughts regarding Lisa Fadden, then we'll begin with our clinic time."

They don't really cover anything new that wasn't delivered by Katie in her recap, but it's clear her death is a mystery even to the captain. Within a few minutes, he says he wants everyone to do a report on what the cause of death may have been.

"Sir?" Leo raises his hand. "Why don't we keep the body and do a postmortem?"

Captain Williams runs a hand through his hair. "Wish we could. I asked the major for permission this morning, considering it'd be an excellent learning experience for you all, but he declined. Said it was disrespectful to Ms. Fadden and her family. The truth is, we don't know her wishes on the subject. And to my knowledge, she doesn't have any remaining family."

Katie raises her hand. "Her husband and son were both killed in the blast at the ration center. There's no one else nearby."

Nodding, the captain says, "I'd planned on having cadavers as part of your training. In the past, your first year of medical school would've had several weeks of cadaver time. People often donated their bodies to science for this specific use. I had intended for you to take part in cadaver training, and we had scheduled it to start as soon as we had the nursing school up and running, allowing you all to train together. Now . . . we'll have to wait and see."

"Do you have people willing to donate their bodies?" Katie asks.

"We have several from the care centers, and even a few elderly from the neighborhood, who filled out the paperwork to do so. Hugo has them stored in a specific place for me. Not being able to bury during the winter has given us that advantage."

As we move to the hallway, I quietly get the captain's attention. "My mother-in-law is waiting to be seen."

"Is she all right?"

"She found a . . . a lump. Two lumps. I was hoping you'd be willing to examine her. I could assist."

"Yes, that's fine. Let's see who else we have waiting for clinic time."

There are a few other people in the waiting area. The captain has Katie and Leo take one of the patients while fellow med students Jeff and Matt take another. The captain and I take Pearl to exam room one.

Pearl's completely matter of fact in describing what she found to the captain. He's wonderfully professional in his examination. "I'd like to have you come back. We'll do a biopsy so we can see what we're dealing with."

"Do you think it's cancer?" Pearl's voice is firm and confident, just as I'd expect.

"It's hard to say without getting a look at the cells."

"Anything you'd be able to do for me if it is?"

"We could operate. Try to remove it all. There's no chemotherapy or radiation."

"And I know you don't like to operate with the way things are. Too much risk of infection."

"That's true."

Pearl motions in my direction. "You know my grandchild is going to be born in just a few weeks."

"I do. We're all very excited for Merissa. And for you."

"If it's cancer, will it kill me before the baby arrives?"

I let out a gasp. "Pearl."

"What? It's a legitimate question." She looks back toward the captain. "What do you think?"

"Unfortunately, we have no way of knowing, without a biopsy, if it is cancer or how advanced it is. Even with a biopsy, I may not be able to know for certain. Some are rather fast moving while others are slower. There don't appear to be any changes to the tissue, so I don't believe we're dealing with an inflammatory variety. Those tend to be rather fast moving."

"So, the biopsy might tell you if I have it and how long I'll live?"

"It might," the captain agrees. "I know you understand things are different now. Even making a diagnosis is more of a challenge. That combined with the lack of specialty physicians. To my knowledge, Rapid City and the surrounding Black Hills don't have an oncologist. We have books and knowledge, but all we can do is what we can do."

"If you had to guess, cancer or not?"

The captain lifts both shoulders near his ears. "I have no way to know for certain. I can tell you that breast cancer risk increases with age. Around a third of females diagnosed are seventy or older."

Pearl makes a face. "And the outcome?"

"Well, these days?" He shrugs. "Before the EMP, the survival rate was lower than that of younger patients, but there's a variety of reasons— "

"I understand," Pearl interrupts. "I think I'll pass on your biopsy. If it was something that could end up making a difference, maybe I'd do it, but as you said yourself, there's no radiation or chemo. I'm probably not going to risk the surgery. At my age, I don't think it'd make sense."

"It may not be cancer," I say, looking to the captain for confirmation.

"It may not be," he agrees.

"How will I know?" Pearl asks.

"Excessive fatigue, night sweats, weight loss, aches or pains that— "

"Come on, doctor. Weight loss and fatigue. Look around. This world we live in isn't exactly the easiest. If they keep cutting our rations, everyone's going to lose weight."

"I understand. How about I see you in a few weeks?"

"All right. Should I just come back on a clinic day?"

"Yes. Three weeks from today. We'll see if there're any changes to the masses or your symptoms."

Even though the captain didn't say anything I wasn't expecting, it's still difficult to hear him put it all into words. Especially considering the tone of his voice and the look on his face. I know he expects it to be malignant. I also know, as does Pearl, there's nothing that can be done.

Chapter 15

Katie

Captain Williams pairs me up with Leo for clinic day. As newcomers to the medical school, transitioning from instructors to official students, today marks our inaugural clinic experience as doctors.

Leo has previous clinic experience, serving as a medic before his injuries and later as the captain's assistant. Similarly, I've worked in clinics as a nurse. However, today brings a new challenge as we're tasked with conducting full patient intakes, gathering medical histories, and performing initial examinations. Subsequently, we'll present our findings and treatment recommendations to either Captain Williams or Dr. Wolff, both of whom are on duty today.

I'm excited about this opportunity but also worried I'll miss something important. It doesn't help that my private meeting with the major didn't go very well. He told me in no uncertain terms that my days of lollygagging were over.

Beginning Monday, they would assign me full nursing shifts and expect me to keep up with medical school for now. He emphasized I had received more privileges than I deserved, and if he had the choice, he would not only revoke my status as a med student but also as a nurse.

Major Stone finished with, "I was against you and the others worming your way over from that useless Volunteer Unit to the proper Guard. If it were my decision, I would've sent all of you packing. At least the only thorns left in my side are you and your husband."

I wasn't exactly sure how to respond to that, so I meekly said, "Yes, sir." Since then, I've thought of dozens of things I wish I would've said. Things that probably would've bought me a truckload of trouble but would've sure made me feel better.

I'm nibbling on my lunch—bread and cheese from our rations— and replaying my meeting with the major in my head when I think about how he said Leo and I were thorns in his side. After taking a sip of water, I turn to Leo. "You know what's odd?"

"Hard telling. What?"

"Something the major said. He said you and I are the only thorns left in his side."

"What do you mean? I'm pretty sure he views the captain as a thorn in his side."

"Probably. But he meant from the Volunteers. Are we the only ones still here? I thought the others were all sworn in?"

"They were, yes." He crinkles his forehead. "You know Tigger and Barnsey died in the Christmas Day blast at Camp Rapid?"

I nod. Leo lost many friends in the explosion. I didn't know as many people from the base, but he had spent some time there. "But there were eight of us who stayed. Tigger and Barnsey died, but there are still four more, right?"

"Maybe they transferred out? The Guard's in charge of the entire state. Before the explosion, they sent some people down to Custer. I didn't hear about them leaving, but I wasn't friendly with anyone but Barnsey, and Tigger somewhat since they were friends. Or maybe the major just means since he's in charge of the hospital, we're the only ones he has to be bothered with?"

"Could be," I agree. "Still, it was an odd thing for him to say."

We're just about finished with lunch when Austin Chambers cracks open the door. "New patient just arrived. She said she's a friend of yours. Opal Maher? She first asked for Merissa, but Merissa and the captain have another patient."

I give him a stiff smile. "Thank you. We'll be right there."

When he closes the door, Leo quietly says, "You don't like him."

"I don't really know him. He's fine, I guess. He just seems a little . . . slick? Maybe that's the word."

"Slick?" Leo laughs. "I'm not sure I follow."

"I can't really explain it. He just seems a little too . . ." I shake my head as I fumble my words.

"Slick?"

"Exactly! I'm sure he's fine. And I don't *dislike* him. He's just not Jesse. Or you. Not like any of the other medics or men that work here." I sigh. "Which reminds me how much I'm going to miss Rand

Hendricks. He was such a good guy. Do you think we'll ever know what happened to him?"

"I don't know. I hope, for Kerry, we do. Shall we go see Opal?"

"Interesting that Pearl was here this morning. And now Opal? Think it's something related?"

"We'll know soon enough."

In the lobby, we find Opal with a young man sitting next to her. It takes me a minute to recognize her companion. "Opal, hello. I see you've brought Jason with you." I hadn't looked at the file when Austin handed it to me as we passed by the nurse's station. It turns out that Jason Wheeler is our patient, not Opal.

"You're looking well, Katie," Opal says. "I'm glad you're healing so well." She turns to Jason. "Do you remember Mr. and Mrs. Burnett?"

He doesn't look up but responds with a nod. I'm not surprised he's quiet. The first day I met sixteen-year-old Jason was under difficult circumstances. Merissa, Leo, and I were at Opal's place for Sunday church services and to share a meal when the alarm went off that there was an issue.

Jason and the two men he was traveling with had trespassed across Opal's neighbor's ranch and the man, Mr. Hayward, sent his attack dogs after the three of them. By the time it was over, one man was dead. Merissa and I treated Jason and the other man. The other man didn't make it, and it's been a slow recovery for Jason. He moved to Opal's ranch just a few weeks ago.

I tilt my head in Leo's direction while quirking an eyebrow. Maybe if he takes the lead, the boy will feel like he can open up to us. "Let's go into exam room three," Leo suggests. "Will you be joining us, Opal?"

She stands. "I think just for a minute. If it's okay with Jason?"

"Suit yourself," he mutters.

Leo leads the way, followed by Opal and Jason. I walk behind. Jason still walks with a limp, which isn't surprising, but it's not nearly as pronounced as it could be, considering the viciousness of the attack. In addition, I notice the bite marks on his cheek have faded quite a bit.

Once we're in the exam room, Leo invites them to take a chair as he and I both sit. Opal sits, but Jason remains standing. He shifts his weight from one foot to the other, his hands fidgeting with the hem of his shirt. There's a tension in his posture, an unmistakable unease that seems to radiate from every fiber of his being.

I glance at Leo, silently urging him to break the silence. He gives me a knowing look, as if he understands the unspoken plea. "Take your time, Jason," he says, his tone soft and reassuring. "We're here to listen whenever you're ready."

For a moment, it seems as though Jason might retreat further into himself, but then something shifts in his demeanor. His shoulders relax ever so slightly, and looks at Leo with a newfound resolve.

Jason takes a deep breath and breaks his silence. "Mrs. Maher said I had to come here," he begins, his voice hesitant but determined. "She thinks there's something wrong with me."

Leo and I look at Opal. In a soft voice, she says, "Tell them why I'm concerned, Jason."

"I told you. It's nothing. Just . . . just accidents. I'm accident prone. That's all." Jason's words come out in a rush. "I've had some accidents. I keep getting hurt." He looks at Opal. "This is a waste of time."

Opal's expression clearly conveys love and understanding. "Not a waste of time at all. If these are accidents, as you say, then we need to figure out why they keep happening." She looks at Leo and me. "Wouldn't you agree, Doctors?"

I'm bewildered by this entire conversation. I wish we would've pulled Opal aside before coming in here. I already looked at the chart, but it just said, "Wound check." Maybe we need to start there.

"Did you have an injury you need us to look at? Your leg, maybe?"

"My leg's fine. Probably as good as it'll ever be. Mrs. Maher, though, she still makes me do the exercises and rub the cream into it." His hand goes to his cheek. "She gives me a cream for here, too."

When he lifts his hand, I notice there's a bandage on it. "Is your hand what we're looking at?"

He quickly drops it to his side. "Look, I know Mrs. Maher means well." He shifts toward Opal. "You've treated me good. I like living at your ranch and helping out, but really, this . . . this is nothing. They're just accidents."

Leo tilts his head. "Can you tell us more about these accidents? How have you been getting hurt?"

Jason hesitates and looks uneasily around the room. "Um, just clumsy, I guess," he mumbles, his words tinged with discomfort. "Tripping over things, getting burned, cutting myself. It's nothing, really."

My eyebrows knit together as I try to understand Jason's hesitant explanation. "Accidents?" I repeat, keeping my voice gentle yet probing. "Can you tell us more about what's been happening? It sounds like you've been going through a lot." My mind races as I search for a medical explanation. Is he having some sort of nervous system issue that is causing these injuries?

Jason shifts uncomfortably from one foot to the other, avoiding my gaze. "It's nothing, really," he insists, his voice wavering slightly. "Just . . . clumsy, I guess."

"Well, since you're here, maybe we should look at the injuries?"

"Your hand? Anywhere else?"

Opal gives Jason a probing look. After a moment, his shoulders drop, and he sighs before moving to the empty chair and plopping down. "I guess, since we're here and already wasting an afternoon of work."

A slight smile crosses Opal's face. "Jason's a hard worker. About the hardest we've got."

As Jason reluctantly takes a seat, a mixture of concern and confusion swirls within me. His avoidance of eye contact and his dismissive attitude toward his injuries leave me puzzled. It's clear there's more to this than meets the eye, but without further information, I'm left grasping at straws.

Leo and I exchange a glance, silently acknowledging the delicate nature of the situation. It's apparent that Jason is struggling, and our priority is to provide him with the support and care he needs, even if he isn't willing to open up.

Leo's gentle voice breaks through the silence. "Let's take a look at that hand, shall we?" he suggests, his expression encouraging.

Jason hesitates for a moment. Finally, with a resigned sigh, he extends his hand for inspection, revealing the bandage wrapped around it. It's a small gesture, but it speaks volumes about his willingness to trust us, even if only begrudgingly.

Leo stands. "Let me go wash."

Before he can move away, Jason plucks the bandage off. "See? No big deal. Just a little burn. Got too close to the woodstove."

The burn on his hand is different from any woodstove burn I've received, and I've had several since our only means of heat is by wood. Usually, my burns are a crease or line. His is a circle. In fact, it almost looks like a happy face.

"I'm going to wash my hands and then take a closer look. Doctor? I'll have you assist me."

Doctor, huh? Usually, when we're at the hospital, he calls me sergeant in front of others. Katie when we're alone. He's never called me *Doctor*. "Be right back." I smile at Jason, who's staring at his hand and doesn't look up. I shift my gaze to Opal. She gives me a barely noticeable shake of her head.

At the sink, Leo's already using the foot pump to activate the container of water. We don't have actual running water, but between the janitors and the medics, they keep us supplied with fresh water in a jug that operates via a pump. It's a decent setup. If we had more solar panels, maybe we could have running water, but for now, we have what we have.

Leo's voice is quiet as he asks, "What do you think?"

I shrug in response. I have no idea what to think.

"Self-inflicted?" Leo whispers.

My eyes go wide as it clicks into place. The perfect burn that looks like a smiley face had to be intentional. All the accidents . . . I remember a girl in high school who did things like that. Not burns, usually, but cuts. She'd cut her arms and legs.

We didn't know for a long time until one day someone saw her arm in gym class. She almost always wore long-sleeved shirts, but that day something happened, and it all came out. She ended up going to a treatment facility for the rest of the school year. I'd heard her family moved away that summer. I don't know what really happened.

As I stand next to Leo and wash my hands, my mind races with a jumble of thoughts and memories. The realization hits me like a ton of bricks—Jason's burn, carefully shaped like a smiley face, couldn't possibly be accidental. It's a deliberate act, a cry for help masked beneath the guise of "accidents."

Memories of the girl from high school flood my mind, her silent struggles hidden beneath long-sleeved shirts until the truth finally came to light. I can't help but wonder what lies beneath Jason's facade of nonchalance.

With a heavy heart, I realize that we're facing a challenge far greater than we initially expected. As we return to Opal and Jason to examine the burn, I straighten my shoulders and give Opal a nod. Tears fill her eyes as she says, "I'm glad we came in to see you today."

Chapter 16

Merissa

"Are you sure you don't want to go with me?" I ask Mother Pearl as I do up my jacket.

She quirks an eyebrow at me. "You go on ahead. I'm sure your friends won't want an old lady tagging along, ruining your fun."

I put my hand on my hip and make sure my belly juts out extra far. "Think we're going to party all night?"

She chuckles. "Maybe not, and I do appreciate the invitation, but I'll be staying home. Go and enjoy your time with your friends."

I didn't exactly lie to Pearl, but I neglected to tell her that my *friends* are really only one friend: Bowski. And it's probably what we could consider our first official date. Or maybe the day he came to my house for lunch was our first date. Perhaps it was one of the many times he walked me home from work. It's all a little murky as to when the dating—the feelings—began.

When I told Pearl I was going out with friends, I asked if she wanted to go along, assuming she'd decline. I'll admit, I feel a little guilty about misleading her. The friends part wasn't a complete lie. There will be plenty of people there that I know. I've visited the orphanage a few times on rounds with the doctors, and I'll likely recognize those who work there.

Still, I do feel a twinge of guilt for not being truthful. Pearl deserves honesty from me. Maybe I should come clean . . . maybe tomorrow, I'll tell her about seeing Bowski.

My heart clenches as it always does when thinking about how many more tomorrows Pearl may have. While I certainly hope—*pray*—her lumps will disappear on their own, I fear that won't be the case. I hate to think if they truly are cancerous, what the months ahead may be like for her. Bracing my shoulders, I give her a smile. "I'll see you later, then."

As I step outside, the cool breeze sends a shiver down my spine. From my porch, I glance toward the corner where Bowski is meeting me. We've spent quite a bit of time on that corner, finishing up whatever conversation we were in the middle of when he walked me home from work.

The manufacturing of the drug Ploy caused an increase in crime in the neighborhood, making it unsafe for us to walk to and from work. As a result, Williams and Shaw created a schedule. It's often the rotating guard walking us, but Bowski is the fill-in person when no one else is available. Somehow, it's always the day I work that he's needed. I don't mind.

As I approach the corner, I can see his smile even in the fading daylight. My heart beats faster, and my stomach does a little flip. I can't help but wonder how he keeps his teeth so white despite our current situation.

"Hey, Merissa. You look good."

"Thanks," I reply, feeling a blush creep into my cheeks. "You do, too." And he does. Even though he usually looks good, it's obvious he's taken a few extra minutes with his grooming and even trimmed his beard.

He offers me his hand, which I accept. We fall into step beside each other, the sound of our footsteps echoing against the silent buildings. The street's bathed in the golden glow of the fading sun, casting long shadows as we go.

We chat as we walk, about anything and everything, the conversation flowing easily between us. "Did you hear there was another death at the care center?" Bowski asks.

"Today? It must have happened after we did rounds this morning."

He nods. "I was already heading out the door when the call came. Hugo took care of it. The death happened at Elaine Ebright's care center. I went to visit her this morning. She was asking me to bust her out then. I'm sure she's up in arms now."

"Because?"

"She and her sister insist there's a murderer on the loose. And it's not just the two of them. Others have also been talking."

I tilt my head to look at him. "A murderer in the care centers?"

He gives an exaggerated shrug. "That's the rumor that has them all riled up. Would you like to guess who they think it is?"

Shaking my head, I say, "I have no—Ohhh. Do they think it's Alice Williams?"

"Bingo. The situation with her former neighbors has now morphed into Alice Williams being an angel of death, killing the elderly and injured to put them out of their misery."

I can't help but chuckle at the absurdity of it. "And when did Mrs. Williams manage this? She doesn't even work at the care centers. In the early days following the captain's partial amputation, she used to assist him with his wheelchair. However, now that the captain is more mobile and Leo's arm is healing, Leo usually takes on the task of pushing him."

"They think the captain might be in on it. Somehow, he's making it so she can get into the buildings undetected. And they know she works at the hospital, too, and there's been deaths there. The lady yesterday, no one expected her to die."

"Well . . . not really. But she has been having trouble since the explosion—assorted infections combined with losing her will to live after her husband and child were killed. It's unexplained, but not terribly surprising."

"Why didn't you guys do an autopsy?"

"We wanted to, but the major wouldn't approve it."

"Hmm. That's interesting. Isn't that a normal thing for med students?"

"That's what the captain said, too. But since she didn't give her permission, and she didn't have any family who could agree . . ." I shrug. "We're supposed to start gross anatomy soon. I think we'd probably already be working with cadavers if things weren't so crazy. The explosions and flu. The captain losing part of his foot. Discovering the illegal activities of Landers and his uncles. One thing after another. It's hard to have an actual med school when we're just doing the best we can to keep people alive."

Our walk is nearing its end as we approach the orphanage. As expected, I see several people I recognize, including Dr. Wolff and Stella Swensen. I'd asked Katie if she and Leo were coming, but she said as much as they'd like to, it's just too much with the children. From the happy look on her face when she mentioned the children, I don't think she minded at all that she'd be staying home with them tonight.

We visit with people standing outside the building before we enter together. As we're filing through the lobby of the former school and heading toward the cafeteria, someone bumps my elbow. I glance over to see a man near me.

"Excuse me," he mutters, before scurrying off.

When we finally reach the cafeteria, I'm amazed by the coziness of the space. Tables and chairs fill the room, while flickering candles softly illuminate the faces of those gathered. On the walls are painted landscape pictures, obviously done by the children living in the orphanage.

"Smells good," Bowski says, inhaling deeply.

I nod, savoring the aroma of baked bread and warm stew. It's nice that dinner was prepared. I don't know how they pulled it off since rations have been cut, but it truly is welcome. We get our food, and then Bowski leads us to a table with two chairs together.

He knows several people here, and I recognize a few faces, including that of Lieutenant David Paul. As we eat, Bowski and I chat quietly about everything and nothing, enjoying each other's company.

After completing the dinner service, the director of the orphanage instructs us to move into the auditorium. Bowski leads me to a seat in the front row with a "reserved" sticker taped to it.

"Oh, someone's already sitting here," I say, turning to look for another pair of seats.

"I asked them to save them for us. I thought you might like the legroom."

Once again, my heart and stomach do that crazy little flip as I look closer at the sign on the chair and notice my name in smaller letters. I smile my thanks and allow him to help me sit before he takes his own seat next to me.

When the lights dim and the children take their places on stage, a hush falls over the room. The piano music begins, filling the air with a melody that seems to transcend time and space. It's a moment of pure magic, a reminder of the beauty that still exists in our broken world.

The children are amazing as they sing and dance. One boy, probably in his early teens, plays a guitar solo while a girl a few years younger accompanies him with a tambourine.

When the last notes fade away, Bowski squeezes my hand. "Thanks for tonight. It was nice to forget about everything for a while."

Warmth spreads through my chest. "It was," I agree as we get to our feet for the standing ovation.

No one appears to be in a big hurry to leave the auditorium. Instead, everyone lingers, chatting and laughing with the other attendees and the children. I love the sense of community present this evening. Lieutenant Paul, who sat in the row behind us, is telling Bowski some funny story about the guard members who are now doing patrol by horse. Dr. Wolff makes a point of coming over to us; Paul gives her a nod and excuses himself.

Lieutenant Paul and Dr. Wolff used to date, but that ended around the time I started working at the hospital. I'm not sure why they ended their relationship exactly, but Katie said it was partly because Paul's a Christian and Wolff isn't.

My husband had issues with me not being a Christian, too. Not when we were first married—it didn't seem to matter to him then—but after his dad died and he started going back to church with his mom, brother, and sister-in-law.

Dr. Wolff touches my arm. "Merissa?"

"Hmm?" I look up blankly, realizing I was so lost in my thoughts that she probably already said my name once.

"Are you okay?"

I smile sheepishly. "Just thinking. Did you ask me something?"

"Just mentioned that it's good to get out tonight. The changes at the hospital have me wondering what Monday will bring."

"I agree. It feels like we're on a temporary furlough and the hammer is about to fall. I'm not even sure Major Stone is going to keep me on." I point to my stomach. "Maybe he'll allow me back after the baby is born. Do you think he'll close the school?"

Dr. Wolff's forehead creases in thought. "It wouldn't surprise me if he did. At the very least, I can't imagine he's going to allow the nursing school to even start. Poppy should've kept her mouth shut, but that's apparently expecting too much of her."

I work to keep the surprise off my face. There's been a considerable change in Dr. Wolff in the months I've been at the hospital. She used to be a lot easier going than she is now. Lately, she's quick to anger and is often making snide comments about people. "I guess we'll know more on Monday." I turn to Bowski, who's talking with a couple of people he knows.

When he sees my gaze, he takes my hand. "Ready to go?"

"I'm ready." I turn back to Dr. Wolff. "Are you on shift this weekend?"

"Days. You're on nights?"

"Starting tomorrow. I'll see you at shift change." I give her what I hope is a kind expression. The last thing I want is for her to think I'm snubbing her or something. Dr. Wolff could make things difficult for me, and Major Stone is already doing his best in that regard.

As we wind our way through the people and out of the auditorium, I notice a man standing in the hallway near the double doors. Glancing at him, I realize it's the man who bumped into me earlier. I dip my chin in acknowledgment, but he quickly looks away.

Bowski and I are still hand in hand as we step out into the cool evening air. It's been a wonderful evening, and I'm grateful for the chance to spend time with him.

Many people are gathered in front of the building, and we stop and talk on our way out. Bowski introduces me to anyone I don't know.

When we finally break away, he asks, "Do you want to get dessert?"

"Dessert? Where?" My stomach tightens, thinking he's going to invite me to his place. I'm not ready for that.

"C'mon. I know a place."

"One of your black-market buddies?"

"Well, let's just say it's unsanctioned."

"Of course it is," I mutter.

"You game? It's a few blocks that way." He motions in the direction opposite my home. "Are you warm enough?"

"I'm game and warm enough. Lead the way to your speakeasy dessert factory."

Bowski flashes me a mischievous grin, his eyes sparkling with excitement. "I promise you won't be disappointed." He grips my hand tighter as we set off into the darkness.

As we walk, anticipation builds inside me. The thought of exploring a hidden speakeasy of sorts fills me with both excitement and trepidation.

Chapter 17

Merissa

We turn down a narrow alley, the walls lined with graffiti and littered with debris. The air is thick with the scent of decay. This is a section of the Guard District I've avoided traveling to. To say it's unsavory would be an understatement. Bowski keeps a tight grip on my hand and doesn't seem at all concerned with our location.

Finally, we come to a nondescript door nestled between two crumbling buildings. Bowski knocks three times, which causes me to laugh. "Is there really a code to get dessert?"

"You never know who may be looking to use cheesecake to incriminate the innocent."

"Oh, I'm sure."

After a moment, the door creaks open, revealing a dimly lit interior. Stepping inside, we're greeted by the sound of laughter and chatter; the room is alive with activity. The space is small and cozy, with mismatched tables and chairs scattered around the space. Old posters and faded photographs adorn the walls, giving the place a nostalgic charm.

Along one edge of the room stands a beautiful oak bar, but instead of liquor bottles, it's lined with jars of homemade jams and preserves. Behind the counter, a grandmotherly figure bustles about, her warm smile lighting up the room.

She sees us as we approach, smiling wide in greeting, and slides out from behind the bar. "Bowski! I was wondering when we'd see you. I have that carrot torte you like."

"Hello, Mary." He leans in close and gives her a kiss on the cheek before whispering something in her ear. She nods knowingly, a twinkle in her eye. "Who's your friend?"

"Mary Millhorn, meet Merissa Weaver."

Mary furrows her brow slightly. "You look familiar."

"Um . . . maybe I just have one of those faces?" I reply.

"Perhaps." She turns to her younger coworker. "Take Bowski to the corner table and get him and his friend the sampler platter." Mary turns back in our direction. "You want tea or chicory?"

He glances toward me, and I shrug. "Tea?"

"The lavender?" Bowski asks Mary.

"You betcha."

The younger woman seats us and returns shortly with a pair of heavy coffee mugs and a small silver kettle, which reminds me of the teakettles from my favorite pre–EMP Chinese restaurant. "Let it steep for a few minutes, and be sure to use the strainer when you pour." She motions to a fine-mesh strainer in one of the mugs.

Even still in the teapot, the light floral scent wafts through the air, invoking memories of summer. I can't help but have a silly smile on my face when I look at Bowski. I drop my shoulders and raise my chin, forcing myself to relax. It should be easy to do in such a lovely location, but old habits are hard to break.

"You okay?" he asks.

I bob my head as the server returns, a wooden cutting board displaying an assortment of items. My eyes go wide as she sets it on the table. "Here you go. Black Hills Sampler Platter." She points to two miniature muffins. "This is sweet corn bread with wildflower honey. These triangle slivers are the flourless carrot cake." She looks up at Bowski. "I know you like this one."

"I do," he agrees as his gaze meets mine. "It's the best, especially the frosting."

The server points to a round pastry-looking thing. "These here are kolaches with apricot preserves. Then we have wojapi and fry bread."

"Wojapi?" I repeat the unfamiliar word.

"It's a Native American dessert dipping sauce," Bowski says. "The fry bread is excellent in it. They used to have something similar at a restaurant near the Crazy Horse Memorial."

The server laughs. "Similar, but not the same. Mary and her bakers put their own spin on things based on what we can get now. It's good, though." She motions to the final item, which looks like some sort of cake. "And here we have the famous kuchen, the official dessert of South Dakota. Do you need your tea water warmed up?"

"Yes, please. Thanks."

After she leaves, Bowski whispers, "Well? Where should we start?"

I snort out a laugh. "I'm not sure. It's been a long time since I've had so many options. Dessert is such a rarity. How does she do it? She can't get enough rations to make this work."

He tilts his head to the side. "We'd have more places like this if they'd do away with the ration chips and let us develop actual commerce."

"I thought you were part of the group that set things up?"

"Yes and no. I was part of the group that said we all needed to work together to survive and that if you didn't work, you'd better have a good reason for it. That was what we needed at the time. We still do, to a degree, but we also need things like what Mary is doing. She and her friends work their crew jobs and bake in their spare time. They put this place together, decorating it and making it comfortable."

He lifts his chin toward the door and gives a wave. Another couple I recognize as having been at the concert is coming in and returning Bowski's greeting. As I watch them head toward an empty seat, I notice the man who bumped into me at the concert sitting at a small table in the corner. He sees me looking in his direction and quickly averts his eyes.

"Being able to come here after the concert at the orphanage," Bowski says, garnering my attention back to him, "to be able to share this with you, it makes me feel like we can get things back together again. It also helps me forget for a little while just how difficult things still are out there."

Bowski and I decide to eat the same desserts at the same time. "Maybe we start with the corn bread?" he suggests. "It's the least sweet on the board."

While it may be the least sweet, it's still delicious. The honey has a mild flavor to it that I can't place. "What kind of honey is it?"

"Not sure. Maybe some kind of wildflower? Do you like it?"

"Love it."

Next, we try the kuchen, which is a little like a cake and a little like a pie with a creamy custard topping. "Is this apple?"

"Dried apples, I think. She makes other varieties during the summer with whatever produce is fresh. The zucchini kuchen she made was pretty good. She makes a pie out of pinto beans, too. It's a little like a pecan pie. Too bad she doesn't have that tonight."

I make a face. "I'm okay with missing it. My baby doesn't care much for beans."

The wojapi and fry bread are amazing, as is the kolache with apricot preserves. We save the carrot torte for last. "I don't know, Bowski," I say, shaking my head. "I might be too full to try the carrot cake."

He puts his hands to his chest and shakes his head. "Try it, you must. All the others are good, but this is the absolute best." He cuts into one of the pieces with his fork and leans across the table, offering me a bite with a playful smile. "Trust me, Merissa," he whispers, his eyes twinkling with warmth and affection.

I take the bite he offers, savoring the flavors as they dance across my palate. The tender gesture makes the sweetness of the dessert even more delightful. As I chew, I can't help but feel a warmth spreading through me, a feeling of closeness and intimacy that's both unexpected and welcome.

Bowski watches me intently, his eyes never leaving my face. There's a softness in his expression, a vulnerability that speaks volumes without a single word. It's as if the world around us fades away, leaving only the two of us and the simple pleasure of sharing dessert together.

"You were right. This is amazing."

A look of satisfaction crosses his features. "I told you," he says, his voice filled with pride.

Our eyes lock in a shared moment of understanding, the unspoken connection between us growing stronger with each passing second. It's as if we've entered our own private world, where only the two of us exist, cocooned in a bubble of warmth and affection.

At this moment, I realize how much I've come to rely on his presence in my life. Bowski reaches across the table, his hand finding mine in a gentle, reassuring grip. His touch sends a shiver down my spine, igniting a spark of something deep within me.

"I'm glad you're here." His voice is barely above a whisper.

I squeeze his hand in response, a silent acknowledgment of the bond that exists between us.

We finish our dessert and linger over another cup of tea. Seated together, lost in conversation, I have a rare feeling of contentment and belonging. Surrounded by the cozy atmosphere of the dessert speakeasy and the gentle buzz of conversation, I find myself not wanting this night to end.

Eventually, we've stalled as long as we should. The speakeasy is clearing out, and I'm sure Pearl is wondering where I am.

Bowski sighs. "You need to go home."

"I do. Tonight . . ." I look at the table as my shoulders go up near my ears. "It's been amazing."

He helps me into my jacket before going up to talk to Mary. I'm sure he's settling the bill, and I want to offer to help with it, but I'm not even sure how to do so. Do I offer a few of my ration chips? When Bowski returns, he reaches for my hand. "Ready?"

"Do you need some of my chips?"

"Nope. Everything is good."

As we stroll through the streets, a sense of peace settles over me. The events of the evening remind me of the beauty and strength that still exist in our world, despite the challenges we face.

As we round a corner, Bowski pulls me closer to him. "Don't look around, but I think we're being followed. Do you have your gun?"

My heart rate speeds up as I nod. "Who is it?"

"Not sure. I can't get a good look at them."

"Them? More than one?"

"Mm–hmm. Three, I think." He lets out a breath. "I don't want to lead them to your house. Let's go to the hospital. We'll see if we can lose them."

I quicken my steps, but he holds me back. "Act natural."

"Not sure I can," I mutter, my pulse racing.

We continue down the dark streets. Every shadow seems to conceal a potential threat, and I can't shake the feeling of unease that grips me. We're about half a block from the guard shack at the hospital when I steal a glance over my shoulder. A single figure trails behind us at a discreet distance, but there, nonetheless.

Bowski's hand tightens around mine. "We're almost there. We're going to stop at the guard station and let them know what's happening."

"What *is* happening?"

"Wish I knew. This wasn't quite how I expected our date to end. It was perfect up to this part."

I can't help but laugh. "Other than that, how was the play, Mrs. Lincoln?"

As we near the guard shack, Bowski releases my hand, making sure both his hands are visible. I follow suit. The guard probably won't shoot first and ask questions later, but we've had more than enough issues around the hospital to be cautious.

"Do you recognize the guard?" I ask, squinting to make out his features. For a moment, I think it might be Josiah Talbot, but then I remember the awful truth of his loss.

"Yeah. He's from the Citizen Patrol."

The guard steps out and greets Bowski by name. I recognize him as someone who's often a guard at the back of the building or one of the rotating guards. In a low voice, Bowski explains that we're being followed. I glance at where I saw the single man before, but he's no longer there.

"Why don't you take the lady inside?" I dart my eyes in his direction. "Oh, uh, doctor, um, Ms. Weaver. I'm sorry. I didn't recognize you. Sorry, ma'am." I give him a nod as he says, "Take Ms. Weaver inside. I'll get on the radio, and we'll see if we can find them. The roving patrol is out and about."

As we reach the hospital, a surge of relief washes over me. The familiar sight of the building offers a glimmer of hope during uncertainty. But as we step through the doors, I can't shake the feeling that our troubles are far from over. It seems danger lurks around every corner, and tonight we've stumbled right into its path.

Chapter 18

Katie

Alice and I sit in the family room, going through the children's clothes she picked up today while Gerry sleeps by my feet. We already sorted everything by size and set aside the pieces needing repairs and mending. Alice's nimble fingers are deftly sewing a button on a shirt for Nico. I'm a lot less coordinated as I attempt to reattach a snap that's loose on one of the baby outfits.

Across from us, Leo and the captain huddle over the coffee table, their focus intent on the task at hand—sharpening knives. Not just pocketknives, but also kitchen knives. For Leo, one-handed knife sharpening isn't easy, but he's become adept at it.

I'm struck by how normal this feels. As we discuss the latest news from the community and the changes in our hospital, we feel like family. Even though I miss Jake and the rest of my family in Bakerville terribly, and I'm sure I'll always miss my mom, being with the captain and Mrs. Williams is nice. Comfortable.

Leo and I have discussed moving back to our house, and we even brought it up to the Williamses earlier this evening, but we all agree it makes more sense for us to stay here. Alice loves helping with the children, and with work and school, we welcome the help.

Things may change next week. If Major Stone does what we fear and closes the med school, I'll only need to worry about my nursing shifts. It'll lighten my load and give me more time with the children. Although the idea of more time with them is appealing, I don't really want him to close the school. If he did, I wouldn't be the only one affected. Leo, Merissa, Kerry, and the others have all put a lot of time and effort into med school.

Leo may have only become an official student a short time ago, but he's been the captain's assistant since the classes began. I've been involved, too, as an honorary instructor. I used to think the captain was using me as an example of what not to do if you wanted a career in medicine. But now, I think maybe he thought I truly had something important to offer.

"Maybe we should've gone to the concert tonight," Alice says with a quiet sigh.

"We could've taken the kids," the captain agrees.

At that moment, Caleb lets out a cry. His wail carries from his bassinet in our bedroom to the living room. A softer whimper follows as Zach also awakens.

Leo chuckles. "Yeah. I'm sure we'd have a great time."

"I'll get Zach." Alice bounces to her feet.

I'm right behind her as I say, "And I'll take Caleb."

When we're both home, that's the normal division. I know Alice is becoming attached to Zach. To Caleb and Nico also, but Zach is special to her. When she was picking him up earlier today, I heard her mutter, "Come to Nana."

I understand her feelings. We've had the boys for only a week and a half, and I already love them. Even though Leo and I tell people we haven't decided, I have. I want to be their mom. I know Leo feels the same, but he questions how we can make it work.

As I scoop Caleb into my arms, his cries subside, replaced by soft whimpers as he nestles against my chest. I rock him gently, murmuring soothing words to calm his restless slumber. Beside me, Alice gathers Zach into her embrace, her maternal instincts kicking in as she whispers words of comfort to the infant.

I steal a glance at Nico, sleeping soundly in his twin-sized bed, before whispering, "We should take the babies to the living room so we don't disturb him." Alice dips her chin in agreement and follows me out.

"Are they hungry?" Leo asks.

"Probably not. Caleb is already calming down." In Leo's eyes, I see a flicker of doubt and hesitation, but also a deep-rooted love and commitment to our newfound family.

"Zach, too," Alice says.

"Want me to rock him?" Captain Williams asks, putting the whetstone on the table.

"No, no. I'll do it. You finish what you're working on. Did you get my knife out of my purse?"

"You gave it to me."

"The one in the drawer of my bedside table?"

"Yep. And the one you usually keep in your boot, plus the one that hangs from your pocket." He gives her a wink. "I'm thinking you have a knife fetish, my dear."

She snickers. "I'm thinking I need to find another knife. Winter will be over soon, and I'll start wearing dresses. Do you think a garter could hold a knife?"

He rolls his eyes in mock exasperation. "I think it might get in the way of your gun."

"Oh." She shrugs. "That's true."

I meet Leo's gaze and give a slight shake of my head, along with a wide smile. The banter between the Williamses is often lively. Alice is certainly different from what I'd originally believed. When we first met, her put-together appearance left a strong impression on me, especially considering our circumstances. Nicely dressed, she always had her hair done and makeup on. She was exactly what I would expect a doctor's wife—an officer's wife—to look like.

She still maintains a very polished appearance in public. But those public clothes hide two pistols and several knives. At home, she's much more casual and comfortable, and still able to defend herself properly should the need arise.

As Captain Williams returns to his task, Alice settles into one rocking chair and I take the other. The gentle motion lulls Caleb back into a peaceful slumber, his tiny breaths steady against my chest. Beside me, Alice mirrors my actions with Zach, her soft hums filling the room as she rocks him back and forth.

"I'm concerned about the boy Opal Maher brought in today," the captain says as he observes the blade he's working on.

"Same, sir," Leo agrees. "I'm not sure what we can do to help him."

"He'll have to want our help."

"What's this?" Alice asks, as she gently rocks Zach.

The captain gives a brief accounting of Jason Wheeler's visit. We're careful about keeping patient information private, but I've noticed the captain will often bounce his tougher cases off his wife. She used to work in his private practice and helps at the hospital, too, so it's probably not a breach of confidence. Not that HIPAA laws exist in today's world.

Alice clucks her tongue. "The poor dear. With all he's been through, it's no wonder. I'm sure your journals have articles on NSSI, right, Chris?"

"Some, yes."

"And what's the treatment?"

"Therapy, either inpatient or outpatient, along with self-help groups."

"None of which we have right now." Alice clucks again.

"Some people who have these behaviors are able to stop on their own," the captain adds. "Maybe the boy will understand the dangers and move past the crisis he's having."

While I certainly pray that's the case with Jason Wheeler, Leo and I spent quite a bit of time scanning books and articles today on self-injuring. Most of what we learned is that acute symptoms need to be brought under control with either medication or behavior modification. And we don't have the meds or the therapist to do either.

There are very few therapists working in the Rapid City area, but none in our district. Captain Williams contacted the main hospital today to see if we can have a consult with the psychiatrist still working there. I've also suggested we contact Kelley Hudson from Bakerville, who's a psychiatric nurse practitioner and was a tremendous help to Sheila, my sister Calley's sister-in-law, when she had a mental break following the murder of her mom.

Captain Williams suggested I write to her, but chances are good she won't even receive the letter until the snow melts. Then it could still be months before she replies. If Jason ends up in a crisis before we can find local help, the captain said we could try contacting Bakerville by radio again. The prospect of being able to talk to people from home almost makes me wish we could admit Jason to the hospital and call Kelley to have help treating him.

With the babies back to sleep, we decide it's time for us to go to bed, too. I'm on an overnight shift for the next three days, which means I can sleep in tomorrow. Upon Major Stone's orders, there are not to be any rounds done by med students over the weekend, either.

As a result, both Leo and Captain Williams have a rare day off tomorrow.

I know Leo's looking forward to spending time with Nico and Gerry. I think he's also a little concerned about being the primary caregiver for the babies, but I am completely confident Alice won't be terribly far away most of the time.

Alice brings Zach to my bedroom and gently places him in his crib. In the days since we brought the children here, she's taken great pleasure in finding them the things they need to be comfortable, from clothes to bottles to beds.

We'd discussed letting the three of them share a room, but all the guest bedrooms are on the second level. With two main-level masters, they'd be up there all alone. Since we're in one master, which isn't much smaller than the house we previously lived in, it only made sense for us to bring them into our room.

Even with a twin bed for Nico, a crib for Zach, and a bassinet for Caleb, we still have plenty of space. In a few months, when two-month-old Caleb outgrows his bassinet, even adding a second crib will still be fine.

The Williamses' master is on the other side of the house from ours, with all the public spaces between the rooms, giving us what feels like our own private sanctuary. We even have a door that leads to the backyard. Our cozy space, along with the camaraderie we have with the Williamses, makes staying here easy.

After brushing my teeth and changing into my sleeping clothes—a T-shirt and a pair of heavy sweatpants without elastic at the legs—I climb into bed.

As Leo finishes tending to the fire, I watch him with a soft smile. His silhouette against the flickering flames paints a picture of domestic comfort, a scene I could never tire of.

"Need anything?" he asks, turning his attention back to me.

"Nope. I'm good." I pat his side of the bed, inviting him to join me in its warmth.

"Let me just make sure Nico's covered."

"I already did. And the babies are in their sleep sacks, so they'll stay warm."

Leo joins me, the mattress dipping slightly under his weight. I pull the covers closer around us, reveling in the shared warmth of our bodies.

"Let's hope for warmer nights soon," Leo muses, his voice carrying a hint of anticipation for the changing season.

I chuckle softly and lean into his side. "Definitely. I can't wait to trade these heavy blankets for something lighter."

Leo wraps an arm around me and pulls me close. "Me too," he agrees, his breath warm against my ear.

"It's only the middle of February, so we've still got some weather ahead of us."

"Don't worry. I'll keep you warm."

Time passes in quiet intimacy before sleep finally claims us.

A sudden, jarring noise shatters the stillness of the night. It echoes through our bedroom, jolting me from sleep and causing a shriek from one of the babies and panicked barking from Gerry.

"What's happening?" I ask, throwing the covers back. Panic rushes through me as I scramble to sit up, my heart pounding in my chest.

Leo stirs beside me, his eyes snapping open with alertness. "I don't know," he mutters, his voice steady despite the surprise. He swings his legs over the edge of the bed.

The baby's cries intensify, mingling with the growing chaos that surrounds us. My mind races as I try to make sense of the situation. Is someone at the door? Is there an intruder?

I glance at the bedroom door, my instincts urging me to protect the children at all costs. "Leo?" I whisper, my voice trembling with fear. Gerry's bark has turned into a low growl.

"I'm going to go check. Stay with the children." He lifts his chin in the direction of my nightstand, where my pistol is in the top drawer.

He slips on his shoes and quietly exits the room, shutting the door behind him. Swiftly, I fasten my belly holster and tuck my gun into place before heading toward Caleb. "Hey, hey," I croon, lifting him from his bassinet to comfort and quiet him. Zach whimpers in his sleep.

As I hold Caleb close, his tiny body trembling in my arms, the acrid smell of smoke seeps into the room, assaulting my senses and jolting me into action. With a surge of adrenaline, I realize the gravity of the situation—our house is on fire.

"Gerry, come," I command. With a look at the door and a whimper, Gerry moves to my side. "Stay with me." I raise my voice as I move to Nico's bedside. "Nico, wake up. We have to go. Nico."

"Huh?" he mutters, his voice heavy with sleep. The distant sound of Leo's voice echoes through the darkness.

"Slide into your slippers." I move the slippers next to his bed. "We have to get out of the house. Here. Wrap your blanket around you."

"Katie, we need to go," Leo shouts, his voice strained with urgency as he appears in the doorway, Captain Williams behind him, their faces illuminated by the flickering glow of flames. They move into the room and shut the door behind them.

"The entire front of the house is on fire. We need to go out the back. Alice is already outside," the captain says. "She's waiting to help you with the children."

Nico is now standing beside his bed. I reach for his hand. "Let's go, buddy."

"I'll get him," the captain says, swooping down to pick up Nico as I move to grab Gerry's leash.

"Why's our house on fire?" Nico asks, his voice tiny and scared.

Leo is at Zach's crib, gently pulling the baby into his uninjured arm. "I've got Zach. He's still in his sleep sack, so he should stay warm enough."

"Caleb, too. We're ready," I say, stooping to fasten Gerry's leash while I cradle Caleb close to my body. "Is . . . is the backyard safe? The fire didn't start on its own, did it?"

Leo scrunches his forehead.

"She's got a point." There's panic in the captain's voice. "I didn't even think about that before sending Alice outside."

Nodding, Leo motions toward me. "Can you take both babies?" He glances at Gerry. "And the dog?"

I adjust Caleb so I can take Zach, too. "I've got them. Captain? Nico could hold my shirttail so you can, um, help keep us safe." My eyes are beginning to water from the smoke coming in under the door.

"All right. That's a good plan." He puts Nico right next to me. "Use one hand to hold on to Katie and the other to keep the blanket around you, okay? You've got your shoes on, so you're ready to go."

"They're slippers," Nico mutters, then coughs. "I can't breathe right."

"Let's go," Leo says. "I'll take the lead. Captain?"

"Yep. I'll be right behind Katie and the children. We're going to move as fast as we can."

As Leo leads the way, his sidearm held firmly in his grasp, we step out into the darkness of the backyard; the flames casting eerie shadows across the winter-worn grass. The acrid scent of smoke hangs heavy in the air, making it difficult to breathe as we make our way toward the guest house.

Nico clings to my side, his hand gripping my shirttail tightly as we navigate the darkness. Caleb and Zach whimper softly in my arms, their tiny bodies pressed close to mine as we follow Leo's lead.

With each step, my heart pounds, the fear of the unknown driving us forward as we inch closer to safety. The crackle of flames grows louder behind us.

"Chris! Chris!" Alice cries from near the guest house. "Thank God. Thank God. You got them. Thank you, Jesus. Thank you."

I rush toward Alice and hand off Zach to her.

"Hurry!" The captain ushers us toward the smaller house. "Get inside. Stay away from the windows but try to keep watch. The fire shouldn't be a problem here, but if it is, go out the back and get to the hospital."

"What are you going to do?" Alice asks, her voice trembling.

"Save what we can," he responds, giving her a quick kiss. He also drops a kiss on the top of Zach's head.

"I'll be back soon," Leo says. "Keep watch for . . ." He shakes his head. "For anything out of the ordinary. I'm going to go help the captain. Maybe we can get the fire out."

From what I saw in the brief moment Leo had our bedroom door open, my guess is there's zero chance of putting the fire out. The fire will destroy the Williamses' beautiful home.

"Nico, please go sit on the couch." I motion to the sitting area before turning toward Alice. "Do you want to take both babies and I'll stand guard?"

"I'm armed, too. I'll take them to one of the bedrooms and see if I can get them comfortable."

As Alice takes the babies from my arms, I give a nod of acknowledgment. "Take Nico, too?"

"Of course."

After watching them disappear into the bedroom at the back of the small house, I turn my attention to the big house. The flames are now clearly visible from my vantage point.

I pray that Leo and Captain Williams will be smart about going inside. Although they want to salvage whatever they can, the importance of their lives surpasses any of our material possessions. I also pray there's enough distance between the two houses that the fire won't be a threat to our safety.

Chapter 19

Merissa

As we reach the front door of the hospital, Nurse Jacquie Haley cautiously opens it, a disapproving smirk on her lips as she shakes her head. Once we're inside, she relocks it. "Going on lockdown is always a pain," she mutters.

Bowski's grip on my hand tightens as we move down the corridor; Jacquie plods along behind us. I cast furtive glances over my shoulder, half-expecting to see our pursuers come through the door behind us. But the hallway remains empty.

When we reach the nurse's station, Jacquie points to the handheld radio on the desk. "I'd like to say someone following you surprises me, but it doesn't. Seems trouble follows you around."

Scrunching my forehead, I try to decipher her meaning before deciding to let it go. I mean, sure, there have been a few incidents lately, but it's more like I'm in the wrong place at the wrong time.

"Who is it this time?" she asks.

I shake my head. "We don't know. Didn't get a good look at them. Who's on duty tonight?"

"All the new guys."

I decipher that to mean Dr. Murphy, Austin Chambers, and the new janitor brought on after Rand Hendricks disappeared. I point to the radio on the desk. "Why do you have the radio? Chambers should have it on his belt."

"Seems he has a bit of a tummy bug and keeps running to the toilet." She jerks her thumb toward the bathrooms down the hall. "Murphy's in the sleeping room, and the janitor's dinking around in the wood storage room." She places a hand on her hip. "What do you think they want? The people following you."

Bowski's brows furrow in thought, his gaze distant as he weighs the possibilities. "It could be anything. Supplies, information, or maybe they're just looking for trouble."

Jacquie snickers. "Looking for trouble, huh? Why not? I've heard of crazier things."

I exchange a glance with Bowski. Her words echo the unease gnawing at the edges of my mind. Why were they following us? It doesn't even make any sense. Maybe if we could have at least seen their faces, we'd know more.

"You might as well have a seat," Jacquie motions to the empty chairs next to her. "I was just going to go get a cup of tea. You can monitor the radio for me while I'm gone. If that Chambers gets out of the bathroom, tell him to take his radio back."

She doesn't wait for a response before she stalks off.

Bowski and I exchange a look as I shake my head. "Jacquie's something," I whisper.

"I've known Jacquie for years. She's actually mellowed quite a bit."

"That's hard to believe."

We sit in silence for many minutes, our chairs angled so each of us has a full view of both doors. While we're probably safe inside the hospital, there's always a chance something could happen. Better not to let our guard down.

"Chambers must be in rough shape," I whisper.

"Doubtful. He's probably faking it."

"What exactly happened between you and him?" I've heard plenty of rumors about the trouble between the two, but now seems like a good time to get the facts. Or at least the facts as Bowski sees them.

"Between Chambers and me? Not a thing."

I tilt my head in his direction. "Is that so?"

"Mostly. I mean . . . there's some history there. I'm sure you've heard."

"I'd rather hear it from you."

He runs a hand through his hair and leans back in his chair. "My wife and I were having trouble. Separated. I thought we were trying to work it out. We had a child together, and we'd both agreed our daughter needed both parents. In my mind, that meant both parents living together. In my wife's mind, it meant I supported them both financially, but she did what she wanted. Chambers was always a womanizer. I've never really understood what they see in him. I mean, is he good looking?"

I bite my upper lip as I consider the question. Chambers is undeniably handsome, with his chiseled jawline, warm hazel eyes, and effortlessly confident demeanor. I think he fancies himself as a ladies' man, and some women seem to agree.

I've noticed it with Dr. Wolff. More than once, I've caught them in a flirty exchange. And when Chambers was first brought on to the hospital, she had him come in and fill out paperwork, which was interesting because paperwork doesn't really exist these days.

But there's also something else about Chambers. Something that isn't quite real. I've noticed that his mannerisms often seem rehearsed, as if he's responding to how he thinks people expect him to respond and not how he really thinks.

When the radio on the desk goes off, I grab it. Shaw's on the other end, saying he'll be at the front door of the hospital in a few minutes.

Bowski stands. "I'll let him in."

Instead of staying at the nurse's station, I follow Bowski to the front door. Memories of another time race through my mind—not many days prior, when I unlocked the front door to let Shaw in, only to discover he was being held at gunpoint by his then boss, Sheriff Cabal. Surely, the same thing couldn't happen again.

Even so, I stop at the edge of the corridor and slide up against the wall. Bowski must also be concerned. He unlocks the door with one hand while keeping the other on the butt of his pistol as he takes several steps backward.

Shaw opens the door slowly, saying, "I'm alone."

"Good enough," Bowski responds.

"Did you find them?" I ask, still staying in my semi-concealed location.

"Sorry, no. My guess is that as soon as they realized you were on to them, they skedaddled. We can lift the lockdown."

Bowski runs his hand across the nape of his neck. "I should've played it differently. Figured out how to turn the tables."

"You got Petty Officer Weaver out of harm's way." Shaw motions toward me.

I purse my lips and shake my head. Even though I've said he shouldn't, he still insists on referring to me as my former Coast Guard rank. He said I should wear the rank proudly. His dad was also a Petty Officer, and a DC 2—or Damage Controlman 2—just like me. There aren't a lot of former Coasties in landlocked South Dakota, so maybe that's why it tickles him so much to acknowledge my rank.

"Are you ready to head home?" Shaw asks. "I'd like to walk with you. I assume you're going to get Weaver home before heading to your own place, Bowski?"

"That's right."

"Let me tell Jacquie we're leaving," I say. "She'll want to monitor the radio." I'm surprised Chambers hasn't come out of the bathroom in the ten or fifteen minutes we've been here. He must be in the middle of some serious business.

After notifying her that the lockdown is lifted and the radio is still at the nurse's station, Shaw proposes we use the back door to leave. I'd already figured we would since it's a more direct route to my house and is my usual method of traveling back and forth.

Unlike when we were alone, Bowski and I don't touch each other. While I'm adapting to the idea of us dating, I'm not sure I'm ready to advertise it yet. Of course, just showing up at the hospital together with Jacquie on duty is probably about the equivalent of announcing our relationship status on the now-defunct Facebook. To say she is a gossip is an understatement.

Stepping outside, the smell of smoke assaults my senses. "Whoa. What's that? Is something burning?"

Shaw and Bowski both sniff the air.

"Woodstoves." Shaw shrugs.

"I don't think so." I shake my head. "It's too much and isn't quite right."

Shaw looks skeptical as Bowski takes another sniff. "I think she's right. Wouldn't hurt to check it out."

"I'll have the patrollers check-in." Shaw uses his radio and asks if anyone smells the smoke or sees anything out of the ordinary. It's only a few seconds before someone responds that they think there's a fire. They smell it and can see a glow. They're on their way to investigate.

Shaw shakes his head. "That's all we need. At least there's still snow on the ground in some places, and there isn't any wind. Maybe it won't spread too much."

"If it gets in some of these tight neighborhoods, even without wind, it could be trouble," Bowski adds.

I nod, thinking of my little house and the houses on either side. There's only about fifteen feet between them.

"I'll walk with you for now," Shaw says, "but once the report comes in— "

"Understood," Bowski interrupts. "I'll get Merissa home and help you."

"They may need a medic," I offer.

Bowski tilts his head in my direction. "You're sure?"

"I'm sure."

"My man who responded is nearby. Let's head— " The radio interrupts Shaw.

"I've found it! It's Captain Williams's place."

"The children!" I cry, picking up my pace.

"Slow down," Bowski cautions as he reaches for my hand. "There are still slick spots, and . . ." He motions toward my stomach.

Ignoring him, I keep moving. I'm not running but am moving fast. Bowski's long legs easily keep up.

"I'll see you there!" Shaw says as he jogs ahead of us.

The closer we get to the street the Williamses live on, the stronger the smell of smoke. As we turn the corner, the glow of the fire comes into full view. I gasp. "It's worse than I imagined."

Please, God. Please help them, I silently plead.

As we approach Captain Williams's house, the intensity of the flames becomes starkly apparent. An inferno engulfs the once beautiful structure. With their large lot, the fire doesn't appear to be threatening the neighboring homes, but that could change if the wind comes up.

My heart clenches with fear for the safety of the captain and Mrs. Williams, along with Katie and Leo, not to mention the children. Did they get out?

Bowski squeezes my hand reassuringly, his expression grim with concern. "It looks bad."

I take a deep breath, trying to steady my nerves. The crackling of the flames and the shouts of those who have shown up to fight the fire amplify the tension. With each step closer to the blaze, the heat becomes more intense, searing against my skin, even in the cold winter air.

"Look!" Bowski points. "There's Leo."

Tears of relief fill my eyes. "Do you see Katie? The children?"

"I'm sure they're fine." Bowski tries to sound confident, but I hear the question in his tone. "Stay back here. I'm going up to help."

"They can't save the house."

"No, I don't think so. It looks like they're just making sure it doesn't spread. Try to stay out of the direct smoke."

I reach for his arm. "Ask Leo where Katie is, please. I need to know." In the time since I've arrived in Rapid City, Katie and I have become friends—genuine friends, which is a rarity for me.

The dynamics of female relationships can be complicated, so much so I've often wondered if women can truly be friends. The petty jealousies and continual competitions have always been more drama than I want to engage in. This hasn't happened with Katie. Although she sometimes struggles with her own self-esteem and choices, she never makes me feel like we're in a competition.

"I'll find out," he assures me.

Bowski heads toward Leo, who's frantically coordinating with the other responders. I watch anxiously, my heart pounding with each passing second. The acrid smoke billows into the night sky, shrouding everything in an ominous haze. I fight against the urge to rush forward, knowing that any misstep could put both myself and the unborn child I carry in danger.

Leo spots Bowski approaching and gestures for him to come closer. They exchange hurried words, their voices inaudible from this distance, especially with the roar of the flames. My breath catches in my throat as I wait for Bowski to return with news of Katie and the children. Every second feels like an eternity, each flicker of the fire casting long shadows of doubt and fear.

Finally, Bowski makes his way back to me, his expression somber. I hold my breath, bracing myself for the worst. "Katie and the kids are safe," he says, his voice tinged with relief. "They got out in time. They're in the guest house with Mrs. Williams. Leo asked if you could go check on them."

A wave of gratitude washes over me, overwhelming any lingering anxiety. Tears of relief blur my vision as I wrap my arms around Bowski and hold him tightly, uncaring that there are so many prying eyes. "Thank you," I whisper, my voice choked with emotion.

Bowski holds me close. "I'll take you to the guest house. It's— "

"In the backyard. I know," I say, releasing my grip. My cheeks are warm, and not just from the heat of the fire. "Stay and help with the fire. I'm fine."

With a nod, Bowski acknowledges my request, his eyes reflecting a mixture of concern and determination. "Be careful," he whispers, his voice laden with unspoken worry. "I'll come for you when we've done all we can."

Turning away from the blaze, I plunge through the chaos, dodging debris and people. My only goal is to reach the guest house and make sure Katie and the children are safe.

Chapter 20

Katie

Nico is still asleep in one of the bedrooms, while the rest of us sit in the cozy living room. Merissa stayed with us until almost dawn when Leo and the captain, along with Bowski, finally returned.

Merissa surprised me when she knocked on the door, since I figured she would've long been home and in bed. I was even more surprised when she told me about the difficulties she had near the end of her date when she and Bowski were being followed.

"This house will be fine," Alice says with a strained smile. "I've always thought it was adorable."

Leo clears his throat. "If we can use one of the trucks, or even the horse and wagon, I could start moving the things we salvaged to our place."

"No, no." Alice shakes her head. "Please. It'll be so much easier if we're together. You need help with the children."

Leo looks at me, motioning that it's my choice. "With four adults and three children, not to mention Gerry, it'll be too tight in this cottage." Hearing his name, Gerry thumps his tail while looking at me with big brown eyes.

"There's a house on this block that came available during the flu," the captain says. "It'd be closer than the place you lived, so Alice could still help with the children."

She turns to the captain with a stern look. "I'm sure we can all stay here."

Using his index and second finger, he massages the spot between his eyes. "For a few days while we make arrangements for the other house, yes. But long term, Katie's right. It'll be too tight."

"Will there be any trouble with that, sir?" Leo asks. "With us being allowed in the house on this street?"

"As long as you two are okay giving up your original home, we could propose it as a swap." His eyes darken. "The only issue is that

Major Stone will have to sign off on it. If I was still in charge of the hospital, it'd be up to me, but now . . ." He raises his hands.

"Understood, sir."

As they continue discussing the process of getting approval for a new house, I consider the house we used to live in. I don't wish to return there. While the house is adorable and was, at first, perfect for Leo and me, it holds too many hard memories, after being held hostage there and then being attacked in my own backyard.

I lift my stockinged foot to rub Gerry across the back. There are some wonderful memories, too. It was the first home Leo and I had, unless you count the camp trailer we lived in with another couple. Talk about tight quarters. This guest cottage is nearly palatial compared to that place. Of course, we didn't have three children then, with two of them under the age of six months.

"Can we see it first? I'm sure it's fine, but . . ." I tilt my ear to my shoulder.

"I suppose you're right," Alice agrees with a sigh. "That house will give everyone their own space. And it's nearby, so . . ." she pulls Zach closer to her. "I'll miss our evenings together."

Leo leans forward and rests his elbows on his knees. "Have you been inside the house, sir?"

The captain responds with a shake of his head. "I just know it's empty. I believe it's a nice place. Not as large as my sister's house." The captain motions to the now-destroyed house he and Alice had been living in since a few weeks after the trouble started. "It's one of the original homes on the street. From before they built the larger places."

"It's the blue one?" I ask.

"Yes, exactly."

I let out a breath and drop my shoulders. "I noticed it the other day when I was taking Gerry for a walk. It is cute. It didn't look that small."

"It's still too early in the day to start the process of permission to move you into it. But we could go see if it's unlocked. I'm sure Alice will be happy to keep the children."

"Caleb should sleep for a while longer." I motion to the bassinet. Leo and the captain were able to pull Caleb's bassinet out of the house before it got too smoky. They were also able to save Zach's crib and the mattress on Nico's bed. The plastic-covered crib mattress seems fine, but Nico's fabric mattress has a slight smoky odor. It's propped up outside against the house to air out. Most of ours and the Williamses' clothes were also salvaged, but nothing from the front rooms was able to be saved.

Putting my coat on, I realize just how blessed we were to get out with not only our lives but warm clothes and boots. I reach for Leo's hand. "God will turn this into something good, right?"

Leo pulls me close. "He already did. We're together and safe."

"I don't know," I mutter. "I'm beginning to feel a little like Job."

"We'll come out as gold. Tested, tried, and true."

"Thank you for thinking of grabbing our Bibles. I was so flustered, I don't think I would've remembered."

"Well, I can't take full credit. I took both of the nightstands. Your Bible was sitting on top, so I put it in the drawer."

I lift my chin to gaze into his green eyes. "Let me guess, even though you read your Bible before bed, yours was in the drawer."

He shrugged before kissing me on the nose. "That is where it goes."

I have little doubt that Leo had a considerably easier time gathering his things than he did mine. His dirty laundry was in the basket, and his clean clothes were in his dresser. My dirty laundry was in a pile on the floor of the closet, and I had things hanging in various places in our room and bathroom since I wanted to wear them again. This fire was a good reminder that I should do a better job tidying up.

At least the children's clothes were where they should have been, in a cute antique-looking dresser with wheels. Leo was able to roll it out to the deck and then have the captain help him get it to the guest house. He also saved our archery equipment and all of our sidearms and rifles, along with various items that will help as we rebuild our lives from this newest setback.

I wasn't lying when I told him I felt like Job from the Bible. I hope Leo's right and we'll come through this stronger. It seems it's been one thing after another ever since we moved to Rapid City. It's not just since then, but since someone deliberately crashed those first planes almost two years ago and plummeted our world into chaos.

"C'mon, Gerry." I pat my leg. "Want to go for a walk?"

Gerry wiggles and gives me a doggy smile, his excitement making it difficult to get his leash snapped into place.

As we make our way to the blue house, I notice today feels considerably warmer than yesterday. If I didn't know better, I'd think it was nearly spring. But since it's only February 13, I know there are still many weeks—maybe months—of winter weather remaining.

At least the weather seems more average this year compared to last, when winter was over-the-top difficult, with too much snow and freezing temps. Many people suggested it was because of the ground detonations on the East and West Coasts. Nuclear winter.

I don't know if that was the case or if it was just a hard winter, as can happen even without nuclear warfare. Whatever it was, I'm glad this year has been milder, and I hope the weird weather patterns have subsided.

The temps may be warmer but the change in weather has done nothing to improve the smoky smell. Seeing the front of the house for the first time since the fire takes my breath away. The roof is gone, as well as part of the second floor, but the entire front of the house is nothing but a gaping hole. There are about half a dozen people standing around with rakes and shovels, making sure there's nothing that will spark and restart, then spread to the adjacent homes.

"Why didn't the house burn to the ground?" I ask.

"It pretty much did," Leo replies.

"But most of the back wall is still standing."

"Ran out of fuel, I guess," the captain responds. "It started out front . . . I'd sure like to know how it started."

"Agreed." Leo's jaw tightens, and his right hand clenches into a fist. "What's our next move?"

"Shaw will look into it, but it might not lead to much."

The blue house is on the other side of the street and down two places. It'd still be convenient for Alice to watch the children; although I'll admit, I already feel a bit of a loss at the thought of not having her company. I've truly enjoyed staying with the Williamses.

I remain on the walkway with Gerry while the captain and Leo check the front door.

"It's locked," Leo confirms as he peers in the window next to the door. "There're no curtains, so we can see in. Come on up, Katie. It's bigger than I expected it to be."

"I'm going to go around and check the back door," the captain says.

Gerry and I join Leo on the porch. Not only have the curtains disappeared, but someone has removed all the furniture from the front room. The floors are dark hardwood, and there's a fireplace in the living room. "No woodstove?"

"Doesn't look like it. Not here, anyway. The captain thinks all the woodstoves from the burned-out house are salvageable. We might be able to take the insert from our room and move it over here. It looks like there's a dining room and then the kitchen. Maybe a second family room? It's hard to tell from here. Want to go around back and see— oh, hey. It looks like someone left the back door unlocked," Leo comments as the captain emerges in one of the doorways.

As the captain opens the front door, we step inside, and Leo mentions his surprise at the captain gaining entrance.

"Well . . ." He gives a sly smile. "I found a key underneath the birdbath. Seemed like a place the former owners might put it."

The home, devoid of occupants for weeks since the owners succumbed to the flu, exudes a musty, stale odor. Leo moves to crack open a window in the living room, while I proceed toward the back of the house. As anticipated, a family room adjoins the kitchen. I pause to unlatch windows in each room, allowing a welcome influx of fresh air.

"It's pretty nice," the captain says as he motions toward the hallway. "There's an office and the master bedroom down here. My guess is there are three bedrooms upstairs. It's bigger than I expected. And the yard is great, too."

Looking out the window from the family room, I agree with a nod. The covered patio looks like a perfect spot for summer barbecues, and the garden beyond seems ready for planting vegetables or flowers. If only barbecues and flower gardens were commonplace in our world. A vegetable garden is a given, and it's nice the ground is already dug up.

I'm sure Nico and Gerry will both love running and playing out there. It won't be long until Zach is getting around, too. I can almost see him toddling in the grass with his tiny steps, giggling as he explores the world around him. Caleb will be only a month or two behind him. Moments like those are what would make this empty house feel like a home.

I turn to Leo. "I love it!"

"Do you want to see the bedrooms?"

"I don't need to, but we can if you want."

The tour of the bedrooms doesn't take long. The layout is exactly as the captain said: master bed and bath, along with a separate office and half bath on the main level, and three bedrooms and two bathrooms upstairs.

The sewer system to the house, as with all the Rapid City homes, has been shut off, so there's no sewage backup, but only the master bath has been converted to a compost toilet. Whoever cleaned out the house after the previous owner's deaths did a thorough job, even emptying and sanitizing the compost toilet.

"Do you think Major Stone will sign off on this?" I ask the captain.

"To be honest, I don't know. In theory, there's no reason for him to deny it. In reality, he'll do whatever he wishes."

I deflate slightly. "You really think he'll say no?"

The captain shakes his head. "Hard telling. The major does seem to have a point to make concerning our hospital and our staff. A point that is likely directed at me more than anyone else. Unfortunately, you all get dragged through the mud alongside me."

The four of us have discussed the major and his apparent trouble with the captain and the hospital, but the captain insists he has no idea what the issue may be. He didn't even know the major before the EMP.

Major Stone was new to the Guard, having left the regular Army to finish his time until retirement in the Guard. The rumor was the major needed the flexibility of the Guard because one of his relatives was sick. Who that was, the captain didn't know for certain, but he got the impression it may have been his child and she or he died in the early days of the attacks, even before the EMP.

"Katie and I will talk with the major, sir," Leo says. "I'm sure he'll be reasonable."

I glance over at Leo just in time to see the cloud of skepticism pass over his face before he quickly clears it. The captain says he'll lock it up and put the key back where he found it. As Leo and I head out the front door, I give one last longing look at the house, doubting it'll ever be mine.

Chapter 21

Katie

"I need to get a nap in," I say as we walk back to the guest house. "Tonight is going to be a rough one."

"I wish you could call in sick." Leo gives my hand a squeeze.

"Pretty sure I used all my sick days when I was recovering from hypothermia."

Gerry releases a low-throated growl, alerting us of someone down the street walking toward us. "Is that David Paul?"

"Looks like him," Leo agrees, while the captain says, "I believe it is."

We stop walking and wait for him to approach. When he's near enough, he says, "Heard about your troubles. Thought I'd drop by and check on you all."

The men exchange handshakes before the lieutenant gives me a nod and drops to one knee to greet Gerry. "You're looking good, little guy."

Gerry wiggles in response. The lieutenant gives him another pat before standing upright. "Heard it was arson."

"Most likely," the captain agrees. "We didn't see anyone, but we heard a noise before smelling the smoke. I'm guessing some kind of Molotov cocktail."

"More than one," Leo adds, motioning to the house and the massive destruction.

"Yeah." The lieutenant sighs. "Shaw said he thought they probably used an accelerator across the front. Looks like they knew how to inflict the most damage. This is another reason we need to get a fire wagon set up. We talked about doing it last summer, but it didn't happen."

"A fire wagon?" I ask. "What's that?"

"We have large water barrels, each holding several hundred gallons. We'll set them up on a trailer and haul it around as needed to bring water to the source. I'm sure we'll also discuss adding additional wells.

It'd be great to have a well on every block. Those would help our water supply, too. Any idea who it was?"

"Melvin Cabal? Any chance you can find out if he's had any visitors? Maybe he sent them."

"Doubtful. The governor was insistent no one would get in to see him."

At the mention of the governor, the captain's mouth moves into a tight line. While he used to be a fan of the office, and the person holding it, things have changed since the governor removed the captain's command over the hospital. Especially considering Major Stone has zero medical experience. I'll admit, I don't understand it. I also suspect the captain wouldn't share those feelings with the lieutenant.

Even though Leo and David Paul are friends, questions remain about where Paul will draw the line between personal and professional matters. If Leo or the captain expressed concerns about the captain's removal and the major's assignment, would David Paul inform the general and worsen the situation at the hospital?

Truthfully, I was surprised Captain Williams told Leo and me about his worries. He typically avoids saying anything remotely critical of the National Guard or the governor.

There are several beats of awkward silence until I clear my throat and all eyes turn in my direction. "What about Landers? I know they decided moving him to the jail and bringing in round-the-clock nursing staff was the best choice."

"Yes," David Paul agrees. "He's stabilized, at least to a point, but he still isn't coherent. I believe there may have been some brain damage. He isn't talking or able to provide any of his own care. Other than the nursing staff and a doctor that comes in occasionally, he's not allowed visitors either."

The lieutenant takes a few steps closer. In a low voice, he says, "I think it's about time you read the letter the preacher wrote."

As David's words hang heavy in the air, a shiver runs down my spine.

In a guarded tone, the captain responds, "You could get in trouble for that, son."

"Perhaps. But if you remember correctly, I was supposed to share the letter with you originally. It was my decision to withhold it until the . . ." He clears his throat. "Until we sorted out the other issue."

The other issue was the situation with Alice and her neighbors, along with the captain being blackmailed by Melvin Cabal. When everything came to light, it was highly possible the captain could lose his commission and either one or both could have charges brought against them. It really was a blessing that, other than losing command of the hospital, nothing else happened. Of course, Major Stone taking over the hospital sure doesn't feel like a blessing. It feels more like a curse.

The captain quirks an eyebrow. "And has anyone given you permission to read me in?"

"No, sir, but no one told me I couldn't give you the information either. I think once you read it, you'll understand why I believe you should."

"Alice and the children are in the guest house. Should we— "

"That will be fine. The Burnetts might as well read it, too. My guess is, you'd probably give them the general gist of it, anyway."

The captain doesn't try to deny that he would. Leo's hand tightens around mine, a silent reassurance amid the growing tension. Sensing the shift in mood, Gerry emits a low whine, his eyes darting between us.

We make our way back to the guest house in silence. My mind is reeling as I wonder just what the note could have to do with Captain Williams. As far as I know, he didn't know the preacher.

We'd first found out who the preacher was a few months prior when Bryson Young and RJ Kittleson took me hostage. After RJ died, Bryson said they thought they knew who was behind the explosions. He said it was a street preacher who was always going on about how God brought on the original attacks and the nukes to teach us to turn back to the old ways. He'd preach about how rebuilding would put us back where we were, and that isn't God's plan for us.

As Bryson Young described the man, I realized I'd heard him preaching outside the festival where, what we believed at the time, the first attack took place. It seems RJ Kittleson, who was Bryson Young's half-brother, knew the preacher from before the EMP when the man worked with computers and Kittleson, a lawyer, had helped him with a contract dispute.

How the man went from working with computers to preaching about God not wanting us to rebuild was beyond me. We found out later that the festival attack wasn't the first orchestrated by the preacher and his followers.

Before Leo and I even moved to the Black Hills, someone set multiple fires in the small town of Black Canyon and shot people as they tried to escape. We didn't know for sure why the attack happened until Kemeera and Mindy identified the preacher as the mastermind. He had targeted the town because of the edict put in place to euthanize all pets to conserve food for the townspeople.

We believed Kemeera was probably truthful about the preacher being behind that attack, plus the attacks at the festival, on the ration centers throughout Rapid City, and on some of the hospitals. But she'd proven herself a liar, so the full truth was still in doubt.

Kemeera had also insisted the preacher had nothing to do with the Christmas Day attack on Camp Rapid. Maybe this note would reveal the truth about what really happened.

When we reach the small guest house, Alice gives the lieutenant a less-than-warm greeting. She'd mentioned several times that she wasn't at all happy with David Paul and believed he was part of the trouble with Major Stone taking over the hospital and schools.

Even though both Leo and the captain wanted to defend Paul, they couldn't deny there was probably more going on than they realized.

Especially considering Captain Williams hasn't been able to speak with the general since losing oversight of the hospital and schools. He was not only denied the opportunity to visit with the general but was also unable to reach his contact at the governor's office. He'd reached out by radio and left messages, but there'd been no response.

The babies are asleep, but Nico is up and roaming around. Before we get started, I take him to the bedroom the five of us are currently using and set him up with a coloring book. "We'll just be out in the living room, okay?"

"Mm-hmm. Did you find us a new house?"

"Maybe. That's probably one of the things we'll talk with the lieutenant about. He might be able to help us get permission to move."

"Will Nana Alice move with us? How about Pawpaw?"

I'd heard Alice say he could call her nana if he wanted, but I missed the whole pawpaw thing. I wonder when that started. "They'll live in this house, but we'll still see them all the time. You'll still stay with Alice, erm . . . Nana Alice, while Leo and I work or go to school."

"How come someone burned our house down?"

I work at keeping my face neutral as I consider his question and my response. When we're around Nico, we've avoided discussing our belief that the fire was purposely set, but obviously, we've failed. "Can we talk about this later, Nico?" I ask, mustering a smile. "I promise you, I'll do my best to answer all your questions when I can. For now, though, you're safe and sound."

"I guess." He sighs as he turns his attention to the coloring book.

"Hey." I touch his hair. When he looks up at me, I say, "We're all okay, and we're together. We're going to be fine."

Dropping his gaze, he gives me a brief nod. As Nico colors, I take a deep breath, trying to push away the memories of last night and our home going up in flames. It was a terrifying ordeal, but thankfully, we all made it out safely. Still, it's obvious the emotional scars will linger.

Poor Nico.

He's been through so much in his short life. What I want more than anything is to change it all. To give him a safe and secure home full of plenty of love and laughter. So far, that isn't going quite as I'd envisioned. In the days since Nico, Zach, and Caleb have come under our care, we've had one trouble after another. Is there any way to give the boys the kind of life they deserve?

Chapter 22

Katie

When I enter the living room, Leo's eyes meet mine, concern etched across his face. "Is he okay?"

I force a smile, trying to reassure him. "Nico just had a question about the fire. I think we need to have a chat with him after we're finished here."

"Leo was just telling me about the house across the street. It sounds like it'd be perfect for the two of you and the children," David Paul says.

"It's very nice," I agree as I sit on the loveseat next to Leo. The Williamses are on the couch, while the lieutenant is sitting in the side chair.

"I suppose the next hurdle will be with Major Stone?" David Paul asks.

Captain Williams clears his throat, and Leo drops his gaze to the area rug. Feeling a burst of feistiness, I say, "Is that something you can help us with?"

"Katie," Leo cautions.

"It's a good question, Lieutenant," Alice chimes in. "Do you realize the trouble Major Stone is causing for everyone at the hospital? My guess is, he'll go out of his way to make sure Katie and Leo have a hard time."

The look the captain sends his wife is the equivalent of the verbal warning Leo gave me. She pulls her lips tight and shakes her head.

I think she's going to let it go when she says, "I understand there should be repercussions for my actions. Possibly even for my husband trying to keep what I did quiet. However, appointing someone with no medical expertise to oversee a hospital, where lives are on the line, is utterly nonsensical to me. Does that make any sense to you, Lieutenant?"

Lieutenant Paul has the grace to look apologetic as he says, "It's not really my place to question orders, ma'am. I'm also not a medical person, so I'm doubly unqualified to offer an opinion."

"Well, at least you're smart enough to realize that," Alice mutters.

The captain reaches for her hand as he shakes his head. "I'm sure you understand, Lieutenant, it's been a difficult several days, culminating in a night of losing our home and barely escaping with our lives."

"Understood, sir." As Lieutenant Paul nods in acknowledgment, I feel a mixture of frustration and gratitude. Frustration at the seemingly insurmountable obstacles we face, yet gratitude for the support we've found in unexpected places.

"I appreciate your understanding, Lieutenant," I say, trying to steer the conversation back to our immediate concerns. "But is there any way you can help expedite the process of getting us approved for a new place to live? It's going to be difficult for the five of us to stay here with Captain and Mrs. Williams."

Lieutenant Paul considers my request, his brow furrowing with concentration. "I'll see what I can do. Surprisingly, one thing that hasn't changed in the apocalypse is the bureaucracy." He gives a light chuckle. "Bureaucracy and red tape."

There's an awkward moment of silence until Captain Williams says, "Did you bring a copy of the letter with you?"

Pulling the paper out of his shirt pocket, the lieutenant hands it to the captain. As Mrs. Williams reads over his shoulder, Leo and I watch their faces. The captain reveals little, but Alice doesn't hide her thoughts. She's shaking her head and clicking her tongue as she reads. When they're finished, the captain passes it across the coffee table to Leo and me.

My dear brothers and sisters,

As I inscribe these last words, entrusted by the Almighty with the weight of our collective burdens, I am compelled to reveal the perilous path we now tread. Chosen as a prophet by the divine, I bear witness to the aftermath of the calamitous event that cast our world into darkness, where a malevolent force masquerades as the herald of progress.

Beware, for these wolves cloak themselves in robes of righteousness, their tongues dripping with honeyed lies and false promises of salvation. They seek dominion over our bodies and souls, weaving a web of deceit that ensnares the unwary.

I implore you to remain vigilant, to resist the siren call of power wielded by those who would exploit our suffering for their own gain. The very fabric of society unravels beneath the weight of their avarice and ambition.

Know this: corruption seeps even into the sanctuaries of healing. The medical fraternity, once a bastion of compassion, now finds itself ensnared in the machinations of the wicked. Do not be deceived by their false benevolence, for they are but pawns in a larger game of manipulation.

Given knowledge of the divine, my swords of righteousness attempted to cut out this corruption. To eliminate the cancerous tumors festering within the hallowed halls of hospitals, desecrating the sacred grounds where promises of healing once blossomed like fragile petals amid the chaos of illness and despair.

In the ashes of our shattered world, hope flickers like a beacon, a flame to be nurtured and protected from the encroaching darkness. Let not the shadows of tyranny obscure your vision, but instead, let the light of truth and justice be your guide.

May you find the fortitude to stand against the tide of oppression, and may the spirit of righteousness embolden your resolve in these dark times.

In the name of the Divine, I remain,
Prophet Justin Zadok

As I finish reading it, like Alice, I'm also shaking my head. I point to the word avarice and whisper Leo's name.

He lets out a breath through his nose. "Do you think he used a thesaurus to write this?"

"I don't even know what some of these words mean." I jab at avarice again.

"Greed," Leo says before clarifying, "being extremely greedy."

"Plain English would've been nice," Alice says. "I like to think of myself as fairly intelligent, but some of those words . . ." She lifts her hands.

"And that's not really his name." I point to the signature. "Bryson told me his name was Norman Smith. I know everyone calls him the preacher now— "

"Not his followers," the captain corrects. "Kemeera and Mindy referred to him simply as Preacher. But yes, he was Norman Smith before he decided to be a self-proclaimed prophet and murderer."

"We're not sure when he took the name Justin Zadok," David Paul says. "We've had this note analyzed by dozens of people—the original note, I mean. His handwriting and interesting use of words, along with the fact he calls himself a prophet and says he's chosen by the divine . . . Even the name has meaning. Justin and Zadok both mean righteous."

He angles his body toward the captain. "I'm sure you noticed the jab at doctors, too, which is why I thought you should read it. That and the mention of destroying hospitals. The perpetrators targeted your hospital, but we stopped them. From the sound of the note, it's almost as if he knows about the various internal conflicts that were happening."

"Well, that would make sense," Captain Williams agrees. "Especially considering Melvin Cabal and Geoff Landers were going to his preaching services. Remember? Kemeera called Landers Dr. Loving?"

"I'm not sure we can trust much that woman said." Alice leans back on the sofa. "Anyone who would abandon her own child . . ."

While I agree with Alice that Kemeera was feeding us lies, my heart swells thinking of Caleb. The day I met Kemeera was the day Caleb was born. I remember the warmth of her smile as she cradled him in her arms, a picture of maternal bliss. Then, as we took her in, hiding her and fellow cult member Mindy along with the children, things began to unravel. I didn't really notice at the time, but some of her stories didn't add up.

The day Mindy died from what we believe was hemlock poisoning, supposedly supplied by herbalist Addison, the cracks in the carefully constructed lies began to show. When Kemeera assaulted Stella Swensen, and then ran off with her daughter, leaving her newborn son, Nico, and baby Zach behind, it became clear that Kemeera wasn't who I thought she was.

"While I agree we can't trust much of what she said," the captain begins, "we know Cabal, Landers, and that Addison woman were involved with the preacher . . . or prophet, whatever we're calling him today, at least to some degree. We believe Addison and Landers delivered the poison that those in the jail took. We believe the two of them also left the poison for Mindy and Kemeera. Why only Mindy took it and not Kemeera is unknown. Frankly, I'm not sure it matters. If she's gone, all the better."

Captain Williams shakes his head. "My only wish is she would've left her little girl behind, too. I can't imagine the life she may have with a mom like that." He lets out a sigh before continuing. "The inclusion of the medical community in the note is disturbing. Can you read that section again, Leo?"

Leo finds the section in the letter and reads it aloud.

"*Know this: corruption seeps even into the sanctuaries of healing. The medical fraternity, once a bastion of compassion, now finds itself ensnared in the machinations of the wicked. Do not be deceived by their false benevolence, for they are but pawns in a larger game of manipulation.*

"*Given knowledge of the divine, my swords of righteousness attempted to cut out this corruption. To eliminate the cancerous tumors festering within the hallowed halls of hospitals, desecrating the sacred grounds where promises of healing once blossomed like fragile petals amid the chaos of illness and despair.*"

"Goodness," Alice exclaims. "It sounds like he thinks he knows something, doesn't it? Something that involves the hospitals and doctors. Do you think it's as simple as the push to get the National Guard out of the hospitals?"

"If it is, then that has flipped completely backward, hasn't it?" the captain asks. "Cabal and a few others were behind that, not wanting the hospitals to be under military control. Not that they were."

"Until now," I add, remembering how Chastity Morrow had been part of the group who wanted to get the military out of the hospitals. At the time, I thought it was simply because she was dating Geoff Landers. Then, during a conversation with Mindy and Kemeera, Mindy described visiting Chastity's house for medical care. Someone from the cult had taken her there and said they had a friend who was a doctor. But Chastity wasn't home, so Mindy never saw her.

If Chastity was feeding information to the preacher about the push to get the National Guard out of the hospitals, then that might be the reference being made in the letter. But really, why would the preacher care? What did it matter if the National Guard oversaw the hospitals or if civilians ran them?

Even as I consider it, I realize it does matter. In the days since the preacher died and left this letter behind, the governor has put the National Guard in charge of all the hospitals. Why did the preacher warn against this? Is there something more happening?

Chapter 23

Merissa

"Well, hello, Merissa," Opal greets me with a hug and a kiss. "You're looking lovely."

"Humph," I snort. "I'm huge."

"You're beautiful. Are you feeling well?"

"Well enough. Looking forward to . . ." I tilt my head to the side.

"You're getting excited to meet him or her, I suspect."

"We both are," Pearl says, stepping toward the front door. "Are you going to come inside or just keep letting the heat out?"

"Hello to you, too, dear sister." Opal steps inside, followed by one of her ranch hands, a young man of sixteen who has had a rough time of things.

"Hello, Jason," I say with a smile. He answers with a minuscule dip of his chin.

Opal chuckles and pats Jason's shoulder. "He's a bit shy, but he's a hard worker. Been helping out around the ranch a fair bit, haven't you, Jason?"

Jason nods, his eyes fixed on the floor.

Pearl ushers us into the cozy living room, where a fire crackles in the rocket stove heater. "Want to warm up for a minute before we go? I'm not quite finished packing. Make yourselves comfortable." Pearl gestures to the plush armchairs arranged around the fireplace. She sends me a pointed look before leaving for her bedroom.

That look is a warning, a reminder that I'm not to say anything about her possible medical issues. Pearl already made it clear she didn't want Opal to know until she has another exam and maybe some better answers.

My eyes fill with tears. I blink a few times before turning back toward our guests.

As we settle in, Opal leans forward, her eyes twinkling with curiosity. "So, any guesses on whether it's a boy or a girl?"

"I've tried to guess, but honestly, I have no idea. Pearl is sure it's a boy. I'm not sure at all. We'll just have to wait and see."

Opal nods thoughtfully. "I guess this is a time when you must really miss the medical advances we had. Why, by now, you'd have had who knows how many ultrasounds."

"Mostly I'm just glad we have several doctors and nurses who know what they're doing."

Pearl steps out of her bedroom and into the hallway. No doubt she overheard the conversation. "It's still nerve-racking. I'm just glad Merissa's healthy. She's had a little swelling in her feet, but her blood pressure and everything else are still fine. They've been monitoring her. Of course, all the stress of work and everything else . . ."

"I'm so glad that nobody got hurt at Captain Williams's place last night. Is it true the house was completely destroyed?"

"Pretty much, yes."

Pearl makes a tutting noise and returns to her room to finish packing. She's planned a few days at the ranch. I didn't tell her about the suspicion Bowski had last night that we were being followed. There's no reason to worry her, especially considering we don't really know who it was. I never got a good look at them, and since Shaw didn't find them, it's best to let it go.

I'll admit, Bowski and I wondered if whoever was following us had a connection to the fire at the captain's house, but that doesn't make much sense. Besides our shared workplace and my friendship with Katie, I have few similarities with them.

"What happened?" Jason asks, his curiosity suddenly piqued.

Opal turns to him. "I'm so sorry. I thought you were there when the drayers came by this morning. Captain Williams's house caught fire last night. I'm sure you remember him from when he cared for you at the hospital."

"I do," Jason agreed. "The other couple, they're the ones we saw at the hospital last week. They live with the captain, too, right? Isn't that what I've heard?"

"Katie and Leo Burnett, yes. They, along with three children recently entrusted into their care. They're all okay, though." Opal looks toward me for confirmation.

"Yes, they're fine. Everyone got out. The fire started at the front of the house, so they were able to retrieve many of their personal items from the bedrooms."

"What do you mean *started?*"

I glance at Opal, who gives a nod of permission. "It seems the fire was a deliberate act," I tell Jason.

His eyes go wide. "Someone tried to burn the doctor's house down on purpose? Were they trying to . . . to kill them?"

I lift my shoulders while I shake my head. "We don't know, not for sure. But most people that were there last night thought it was probably a warning of some sort."

"Were you there?"

"I was. I stayed with Katie, Mrs. Williams, and the children while a bunch of people kept the fire from spreading to other houses. There wasn't anything they could do for the Williamses' house."

"Where will they live?" Opal asks.

"There's a guest house at the back of the property. You know the place was the captain's brother's home?"

"Yes, I know the story. Knew that family, too. I hope they're safe where they are. Who would've ever thought they'd go to do important work in a developing country, and now here we are? Our own beautiful town—beautiful state and country—is a third-world nation."

Jason listens intently, his expression a mixture of concern and disbelief. "It used to be hard to imagine something like that happening here," he murmurs, his voice barely above a whisper. "When I studied about other countries in school, places that didn't have enough food or electricity—or the places where children were used as soldiers—I never thought it'd be like that here."

He glances around my tiny house. The only light is coming in the windows on this sunny February afternoon, and the only heat is from the homemade wood-burning stove. While there is food in the kitchen, it's a meager amount, barely enough to get us through until our next ration chips drop.

"Indeed," Opal says. "Very few of us believed something like this could happen right in our own backyard."

Pearl returns to the living room, her bag packed and gripped tightly in her hand. "I'm ready," she announces in a firm tone. "Let's head out before it gets too late."

"A moment, please?" Opal smiles at Pearl. "Can you sit?" She waits until Pearl is seated before continuing, "Jason and I were hoping we might . . ." She glances toward the boy, who's again studying his shoes. "Jason? Would you like to talk with them?"

He shakes his head in response.

"Have you changed your mind?"

"No," he whispers. He clears his throat before lifting his gaze. "We planned to talk to the doctors again today." His words come out in a rush. "Then Opal said maybe we should talk with you instead. I didn't understand it was because the doctors had the fire, but now that makes sense why she said to talk to you. You lost your husband." He glances from me to Pearl. "Your son. Maybe . . . maybe some of my trouble is from everyone around me dying."

Confusion paints Pearl's face. I have the advantage of knowing Opal brought Jason into the hospital a few days ago for clinic day. At the end of the day, we went over the charts and discussed treatments and diagnosis. Leo and Katie had seen Jason and suspected NSSI, or nonsuicidal self-injury.

NSSI refers to the intentional destruction of one's own body tissue without suicidal intent and for purposes not considered socially acceptable. Examples include cutting, burning, scratching, and hitting oneself. Most individuals who engage in self-injury have experimented with various methods.

From Katie and Leo's examination of Jason, they discovered physical evidence he was burning and cutting himself. He also admitted to hitting himself but told them he didn't do that very often.

"You have lost a lot," I say.

"Everyone. I'm beginning to think . . ." He glances at Opal. "I think I may be cursed and Miss Opal and her family were stupid to take me in."

Opal shakes her head. "I've told you not to talk like that."

With empathy, Pearl's expression softens as she gently reaches out to touch Jason's shoulder. "Jason, listen to me," she says, her gravelly voice gentle yet firm. "You are not cursed; you are blessed by God. You are certainly not a burden. Opal's told me much about you.

About what a hard worker you are and how you're a part of their family. Why, she says she sometimes forgets you're not one of her own! I know she wants to help you through whatever struggles you're facing. Merissa and I are happy to help, too, if we can."

"That's right, Jason," Opal says. "We're here to support you, no matter what."

I add my voice to theirs, wanting to reassure him. "And you're not alone in this. We'll figure out a way to help you heal."

Jason's eyes glisten with unshed tears, and he sniffles, his emotions raw and vulnerable. "But what if I can't change? What if I'm just broken?"

Pearl squeezes his shoulder gently. "You're not broken, Jason. You're just hurting right now, and that's okay. But with time and support, you can heal."

Opal nods in agreement. "You know that Merissa's training to be a doctor just like Katie and Leo Burnett? That's one of the reasons I thought we could talk with her today." Opal turns to me. "Jason had a rough spell last night. But he came to me and told me about the trouble he was having. Said he really wants to get help."

Pearl, obviously still confused about the full situation but understanding that this boy is hurting, says, "Merissa is going to be a great doctor. She's already learned most everything she needs to know."

I look at her with wide eyes and fight the urge to laugh as I explain to Jason, "I'm a student in the med school. While it's true, it's an advanced program compared to med schools before the EMP, I still have much to learn. I was on shift at the hospital when you came in last week. I know you met with doctors Katie and Leo Burnett and then you saw Captain Williams—he's the doctor in charge."

Jason nods.

"One of the things we do, to help us learn how to become doctors, is talk about the patients we see in the clinic."

His voice is quiet as he says, "So, you know about all the stuff?"

"I read the reports and talked with Katie and Leo."

"Do you think I'm a freak?"

"Not at all. Captain Williams has some medical journals that talk about your condition. The most recent journal showed that approximately seventeen percent of adolescents—that's people in your age group—self-harm, and that was before the EMP."

He furrows his brows. "That seems like . . . a lot."

"The captain has some great information on how we can help you. It sounds like, since you went to Opal, you want to help yourself, too."

"I just don't want to hurt anymore. Sometimes . . . sometimes the only thing that makes it go away is the physical pain. But then I have the cuts and the burns, and I might get an infection working around the cattle. It's risky. And even though it might seem like I don't care what happens to me, I do. I don't want to die or anything, I just want to . . . I don't know. Feel something different."

As Jason speaks, his words resonate with a raw honesty that tugs at my heartstrings. I can sense the weight of his pain, the burden he carries with each self-inflicted wound. And yet, beneath his anguish, there's a flicker of hope, a desire for healing that shines through the darkness.

"You're not alone in this, Jason," I say, softly. "We're here to help you find a way through the pain, to support you every step of the way."

Opal's expression is filled with compassion. "That's right. We'll work together to find healthier coping mechanisms, to help you manage your emotions without resorting to self-harm."

Pearl reaches out to squeeze Jason's hand, her touch silently reassuring him of her support. "And we'll make sure you get the medical care you need to treat any injuries and prevent infections."

Jason's eyes glisten with tears. "Thank you," he whispers, his voice choked with emotion.

I look at Opal, whose eyes are shining, before glancing at Pearl. My mother-in-law, who's usually the stoic one, surprises me with her own sheen of tears. Jason's story sits heavily in our hearts. But with shared commitment and support, we'll find a way forward and help him as best we can.

Chapter 24

Merissa

"Did you get much sleep today?" I ask, noticing the dark circles under Katie's eyes.

"Not much," she replies, shaking her head. "With the fire and Nico being so upset, he didn't fall asleep until daylight. Then we went to check out a house we hope to get permission to move into. You? I feel terrible about keeping you up so late. I know— "

"I'm fine," I assure her. "I didn't get out of bed until nearly lunchtime. Feeling good and all set for our shift."

We're five hours into our twelve-hour shift—me as a medic and Katie as a nurse. Kerry Hendricks is on her first shift since her husband's disappearance, working as a janitor but able to assist with medical issues, thanks to her med school training. Dr. Murphy, the overnight physician, is currently napping in the call room.

Katie quirks her brow at me. "So, Merissa, we didn't get a chance to talk about your date—I mean, the details of the actual date before things went awry."

"I guess not." I shrug, trying to play it cool, but my heart quickens at the mere mention of it. The memory of the date sends a flutter through me, reminding me of last night's whirlwind of emotions. "I'd rather talk about the house you looked at."

"That'll wait." Katie leans forward, her eyes sparkling with curiosity. "So, spill. How was it? Was it all romance and roses?"

I can't help but grin, feeling the warmth spread across my cheeks. "No roses, but he was . . . unexpectedly charming, actually. The dinner before the concert was good. Everybody knows Bowski, so we weren't alone, of course. He somehow managed to set up reserved seating for us at the concert. Right up front. There were even little signs on the chairs that said saved for Merissa. It kind of reminded me of the limo drivers who'd be at the airport holding up the signs for the passengers. Silly, huh?"

Katie's smile mirrors mine, and I can tell she's hanging onto every word. "Wow. No, not silly. That is romantic, considering the world we live in."

"No kidding." I step nearer to her and lower my voice. "Have you heard anything about a restaurant operating?"

"A restaurant? Here? In Rapid?"

I tilt my head and widen my eyes while giving a slight nod. "Mm-hmm."

"No . . . but that'd be something if there was."

"There is," I mouth.

"What?" she almost shrieks.

"Shh." I motion with my hand for her to be quiet. "I didn't know about it either. It's— "

"Don't tell me, it's one of Bowski's black-market things."

"More like a speakeasy."

Katie furrows her brow.

"You know, from during prohibition? A secret bar or club that operated outside the law."

"Oh, yeah, sure. Seems weird a restaurant would need to be a secret," she whispers.

"Indeed. It's not a full restaurant. More like a coffee and dessert bar."

"Coffee?"

I shake my head. "Not real coffee. Different herbal teas and chicory. It was still pretty amazing. And the desserts . . ." My mouth is almost watering as I recall the amazing, sweet treats. "It was pretty great. I thought maybe, when things calm down, we could talk about a double date?"

"Yes, please! Leo and I would love that. Is that when they followed you? The men? After you left the dessert place?"

"Yes, but I think maybe they'd been following us all night."

"Really? Why?"

"There was a man at the concert, and he bumped my elbow. I thought he seemed familiar, maybe a patient. Then I saw him again when we were leaving the auditorium. That time, he seemed to pretend like he didn't see me. He was also at the restaurant. I didn't think of it at the time, but as I was falling asleep last night, I wondered . . ." I shake my head. "I don't know."

"But you recognized him? He was a patient?"

"He may have been. He seemed familiar."

"I thought there were several men following you?"

"Bowski thought three. He could've been one of them."

"You saw him with two others?"

I pause as I recall the times I'd seen him. "I didn't notice him with anyone else, but that doesn't mean he wasn't."

"That's true, I suppose," Katie agrees.

As Katie absorbs the details of my encounter, her expression shifts from curiosity to concern. The memory of being followed in a world already fraught with danger sends a shiver down my spine. We're used to being cautious, but this feels different, more personal somehow.

Katie's voice lowers to a hushed tone. "Do you think they were after you specifically, or was it just a coincidence?"

Considering her question, I chew on my lower lip and respond, "I'm not sure. It could be related to Bowski's dealings, or maybe they mistook us for someone else. But the way they were watching, it felt targeted."

A flicker of fear dances in Katie's eyes, mirroring my own apprehension. "What are you going to do? What's Bowski going to do?"

I take a moment to gather my thoughts, trying to push aside the rising panic. "I'll be cautious, as always. Thankfully, Mother Pearl left today for Opal's ranch. She'll be there until Tuesday. Maybe whatever is going on will be resolved before she returns."

"Do you think the people following you have something to do with the captain's house burning down?"

"Bowski thinks it might. He's going to use his contacts to see what he can discover."

Katie nods, the gravity of the situation sinking in. "I'll talk to Leo and tell him what Bowski suggested."

"Good idea," I agree. "Also, I wanted to tell you that Opal had Jason with her today when she arrived to pick up Pearl. At Opal's urging, he opened up to Pearl and me about his troubles."

"That's great," Katie says. "He didn't seem to want to talk with Leo or me. I'm glad he reached out to you."

"Well, I wouldn't go that far. He mostly seemed to gravitate toward Pearl. As gruff and difficult as she can be, she has a way of letting people know she'd do just about anything for them."

Katie snickers. "She scared me the first time I met her." Raising her chin slightly to meet my gaze, she adds, "And you intimidated me."

"What? Why?"

"You're so calm and put together and have an excellent grasp on the world. You knew just what you wanted. Even though you were grieving over the death of your husband, you were a rock. Plus, I admire how you stuck with Pearl. You left everyone and everything you knew to come here. To make sure Pearl was with her sister. Her people. She appreciates you."

"Sometimes she appreciates me," I say. "Other times, I make her crazy. I've never been the daughter-in-law she wanted."

"But you are the daughter-in-law who cares for her and makes sure she's safe."

"I hope you're right and we can shut down whatever weirdness is currently happening. Which reminds me . . . Bowski mentioned something mildly funny last night. Have you heard rumors about an angel of death in the care centers?"

"I haven't heard, but it doesn't surprise me. There's been a lot of deaths lately. Both at the care centers and in the hospital. When we had all the flu deaths, that was hard but understandable. This is . . . this is weird."

"And it has people spooked. Elaine Ebright practically begged Bowski to take her home. Marilyn visits the care center as often as she can and helps to keep her sister calm. Safe, too, since she's also buying the angel of death rumors." I glance down the hallway to ensure we're the only ones within earshot. "They've decided it's Alice Williams."

"What's Alice Williams?" Katie's eyes widen. "They think she's the angel of death?"

"Everyone's heard about her neighbors. Now they think she's on a spree of mercy killings."

"Of course, you know it's not Alice. If there really is someone going around killing people, it's not her."

"I know, of course I know. But rumors have a way of spreading like wildfire, especially in times like these. People are scared, grasping at anything to make sense of the madness."

"What do we do?"

The idea of an "angel of death" preying on the vulnerable residents of the care centers sends a chill down my spine. In a world already teetering on the brink of chaos, this new threat adds another layer of fear and uncertainty. We both know Alice Williams isn't responsible, and it's unlikely these deaths are anything but natural, but still . . . there's something about the increased number of dead that's concerning.

Katie opens her mouth to speak when the front doorbell chimes, indicating a patient, or at least a visitor. I crane my neck to look down the hallway, hoping the person I see is Bowski. While I can't get a view of his face, the size is all wrong to be the overly tall and stout Ritchie Kasubowski.

I temper my disappointment as Katie says, "I'll go see who it is."

As Katie heads for the front door, I make my way to exam room three to ensure it's set up to receive a patient. Our usual procedure dictates that we reserve the smallest examination room, room three, for ambulatory patients, reserving the larger ones for more urgent cases.

I swiftly check the supplies and make sure we have everything we might need for a routine examination or minor treatment. My mind races through the list of potential injuries or ailments that could bring someone to us at this hour. Absolutely anything is possible.

I straighten the sheets on the examination table and double-check the placement of the medical instruments. Despite the urgency that often accompanies late-night visits, maintaining a sense of order and readiness is crucial to providing swift and effective care.

Once satisfied that everything is in order, I take a deep breath and steel myself for the patient's arrival. Whoever it is, they can count on receiving the best care we can provide, even in the dead of night.

Katie pushes open the door of the exam room. "Merissa? He says he needs to talk to you. He's a friend."

Wrinkling my face, I shake my head. "My friend? You know all my friends."

"I don't know him. But that's what he said."

"He said he's my friend?"

"Not exactly. He said, 'Tell her it's a friend.' I can get rid of him if you want."

"Does he— "

"He seems normal. Mostly, anyway. Keeps looking around. That's about as normal as anyone these days." She flares her eyes and makes a face.

I can't help but laugh. "Come with me." I touch my hand to the small of my back, where my pistol is nestled in a belly band holster.

Noticing my gesture, Katie touches her own visible sidearm. In the apocalypse, doctors and nurses also carry weapons, even when on duty in the hospital. "I'm sure it's fine," she says with a quiver in her voice.

As Katie's words sink in, a mixture of curiosity and caution washes over me. The mention of a stranger claiming to be a friend sends a ripple of unease through my mind. Who could this person be, and what could they possibly want with me at this hour?

I glance at Katie, who waits expectantly for my response. Despite her attempt to appear nonchalant, I can sense the tension in her demeanor, a reflection of my own apprehension.

Taking a moment to gather my thoughts, I weigh the options before us. While the stranger may seem harmless, in our world, trust is a luxury we can't afford to give freely. But if he truly is a friend, as he claims, dismissing him could mean missing out on valuable information or assistance.

"Maybe I should get Kerry, too," Katie suggests.

"Kerry was going to take a nap in the break room. We won't bother her. Let's hear what he has to say." My voice is steady despite the flutter of uncertainty in my chest. "But stay close, just in case."

As we step into the dimly lit hallway, Katie nods in agreement. With a synchronized gesture, we make our way toward the front door, our footsteps resonating softly in the tranquil hospital corridor.

As we draw closer, I catch sight of the visitor standing in the waiting area; his back is turned to us. Despite my attempts to quell the rising unease in my chest, a sense of foreboding washes over me as we move nearer.

At the tap of our shoes on the tile floor, he turns to face us. He's in the shadows, and his face is unrecognizable.

"Merissa?" The man's voice is steady, but there's an urgency to his tone that sets me on edge. "I need to talk to you."

I step back slightly, allowing Katie to stand beside me, her presence offering a sense of reassurance in the face of the unknown. "Can I help you?" I ask, trying to keep my voice steady.

The man hesitates for a moment before responding. "We've spoken before. I've tried to get information to you. I was going to use the radio again, but I thought in person would be better, that you'd take me seriously. I tried last night— "

"Last night! It's you." I take a step back as I move my hand to the small of my back. This is the man who bumped into me before the concert and was also at the dessert speakeasy. "Why did you follow us?"

He raises his hands out to his side. "I wanted to talk to you. I was hoping to get you alone."

"To do what?"

"To tell you. I need your help so we can save as many people as we can."

Chapter 25

Merissa

The urgency in the stranger's voice sends a chill down my spine, and I exchange a quick glance with Katie, silently communicating our shared apprehension. The dim light casts shadows across the man's face, obscuring his features and adding to the air of mystery surrounding him.

"Who was with you?" I ask. "There were three people following us when we left the, uh, restaurant. The dessert place."

He shakes his head. "I didn't follow you. Not after that. I was hoping to get you alone, but when you left with Ritchie Kasubowski . . ." He lifts his shoulders.

"You said you were going to use the radio again? Did we—" Suddenly things become clear. "You're the prank caller, aren't you?"

He tilts his ear toward his shoulder. The movement puts more light on his face. It's definitely the man from last night that I saw not only at the concert but also at the dessert house.

"I guess you could call them prank calls," he admits in a self-conscious tone. "The first time I called on the radio, I was trying to, um . . . feel you out. See if you'd be able to help. *Willing* to help."

"I don't understand. Who do you want to save?"

He glances at Katie. "You're married to the guy with the busted-up arm, right?"

Katie lifts her chin defiantly. "I'm Sergeant Katie Burnett with the United Volunteers. I'm the nurse on duty tonight."

He appears to be confused by her response as he says, "Um, okay. But your husband does have a broken arm, right? And those bandages you're sporting were caused by a group of guys beating you up and leaving you for dead? How's your dog? Is he recovering well?"

A sinking feeling fills my stomach. This guy seems to know a lot about what's happened recently to Katie and Leo. Not that any of it has been a secret, but it's still concerning to hear him recount it as he is. I glance toward Katie. Her face is pale, and her lips are tight.

"I've done my homework," he says. "Figured it was best to see who I can trust. I considered approaching you, Sergeant Katie Burnett, but former Petty Officer Merissa Weaver carries a radio on her belt." He gestures toward the walkie-talkie. "And that seemed like a good way to make first contact."

"That's former Petty Officer *Second Class*," I correct him. "If you're going to throw rank around, do it properly."

His chuckle is louder than it needs to be. Several rapid blinks and a shudder that seems to start at his toes and end at the top of his head follow the friendly gesture. Does he have a tic? We see a considerable number of people with stress-related tics these days. The captain says it's to be expected with the way things are now.

"Enough of this cat-and-mouse game. What do you want?" I ask, my voice tinged with caution and irritation.

The man steps closer, his movements hesitant yet determined. "I can't talk about it here," he says, his voice barely above a whisper. "It's not safe. We need to go somewhere private. Whistleblowers end up dead."

My mind races with possibilities, each one more dire than the last. Who is this man, and what could he possibly need my help with? The gravity of the situation weighs heavily on me, and I can feel the weight of responsibility settling over my shoulders. "Whistleblowers?" I repeat. "Are you a whistleblower?"

"No. No way," Katie interjects, her voice steady despite the tension in the air. "Merissa isn't going anywhere with you. Say what you have to say—right here, right now. Like she said, enough of these games."

The man hesitates, his eyes darting nervously around the hospital lobby. "This place gets too crazy. I've tried to talk to you several times now. I've dropped by here two other times, faking sickness, so the front guards would let me in." He gives a fake cough before smiling. "See? I'm sick." He hesitates as he waits for our response.

With a shrug, he continues, "Anyway, the first time you were out with the patrollers, that was just a few days after I contacted you on the radio. Things went bad that night, and one of the patrollers got killed."

Nearly six weeks ago, I accompanied the team as a medic responding to a domestic dispute. The confrontation escalated, and a patroller got pinned down. The rest of the team moved in to assist, but somehow the suspect slipped past them and reached the truck where Patroller McKay and I were stationed. For reasons I can't explain or understand, the man opened fire, killing McKay and barely missing me.

"Then that flu swept through, and things went from bad to worse," he continues. "I thought maybe, with so many people dying so closely together, they'd stop. They'd have enough, and I wouldn't need to involve you—involve anyone. But I was mistaken. I dropped by again, but you all were a little busy that day being held hostage by that useless sheriff. I thought that when he was apprehended, maybe we'd once again caught a break, but then— "

The squeak of a door down the hallway captures our attention. I take a step to the side and see Dr. Murphy stepping out of the call room. "It's Dr. Murphy," I whisper.

The stranger gasps. "I-I've got to go. Don't tell him I was here. Don't tell anyone." He points toward Katie. "Not your husband." He points at me. "And not Bowski. They'd do something stupid and get themselves killed. You women are smart. You'll— "

The *tap-tap-tap* of footsteps grows louder on the tile, signaling Dr. Murphy's approach.

"Be safe," the man whispers. He slips out the front door, the bell announcing his departure.

Dr. Murphy steps near us and stretches his arms above his head, his hair disheveled from sleep. In a thick voice, he asks, "Did you have a patient?"

"Uh . . ." I hesitate. "No, Doctor. It was— "

"It was one of the guards," Katie interjects. "He was just telling us they saw a giant rat. There's getting to be more and more rats. It's a rat infestation."

"I've noticed the rats, too. Why— "

"He asked me if my dog can hunt rats. I told him I don't know. We're not really sure what breed he is."

Murphy cocks his head. "Wouldn't that be a rat terrier that goes after rats?"

"Maybe? Or maybe a wiener dog? My folks' dog liked to catch mice, and she was part dachshund. But Gerry's a bigger breed. Maybe rottweiler and German shepherd. We don't really know."

Playing along with Katie's story, I ask, "Are you going to take Gerry out rat hunting?"

"When he's feeling better. He's still moving kind of slowly. I think his ribs are still hurting him some."

"Probably a good idea to wait until he's a hundred percent," Dr. Murphy agrees. "He could get excited and reinjure himself. I'm going to get a cup of tea. Can I put water on for you two?"

Katie smiles. "Please. That would be very nice. We'll be right there."

He lifts his hand in acknowledgment as he walks away. When he's out of earshot, I turn to Katie, shaking my head. "What if he asks the guard about that?"

"It would be great if he did. I didn't make it up. Earlier, I had the exact conversation with the roving guard. I mean, hopefully Murphy won't mention the time he was supposedly here, but the conversation is real. And there really is a rat problem. They seem to get worse by the day. I heard they even got into some of the food storage."

"That's not too surprising. Speaking of food storage, have you noticed the rations have yet to increase? Bowski and I were talking about that last night."

"While you were having your dessert?"

Disregarding the teasing tone, I continue, "I asked him if he knew the reason behind the cuts and when they intend to raise them. I also asked how his friend ran the restaurant since food seems to be in short supply based on the decrease of rations."

"And he said?"

"He doesn't know why they cut them or when they plan to increase them. From what he knows, there should've been ample food to make it through winter, especially considering all the deaths from the flu."

"What do you think that guy meant? The whistleblower? He mentioned the flu deaths, too, and thinking things would be okay. What'd he say? That they'd stop? Do you think he's talking about the rations, too? Maybe he knows why they cut them, and he's coming to you to expose them."

"Why would he come to me for anything? I don't know him. I have nothing to do with anything in this town outside this hospital."

"You're Bowski's girlfriend."

I snort. "Hardly."

She holds up her hands. "You might not call yourself that, but it's obvious to everyone that he has feelings for you."

Considering what she's said, I hesitate before saying, "He could just go to Bowski if he has information. Bowski seems to know how to get things done, how to enact change while keeping himself out of trouble."

"But the guy said we can't tell Bowski or Leo because they'll do something stupid and get themselves killed."

Massaging the spot between my eyebrows, I say, "I think the guy might have some mental health issues. Did you notice how he kept rubbing his index finger against his thumb?"

Katie shrugs. "I didn't catch that but did catch the blinking and shivers. Maybe some sort of psychogenic tic?"

"A pseudo-tic. That makes sense. Coping skills are common. Some are minor, but others end up like Jason Wheeler. My guess is, there are dozens of Jasons in the Black Hills trying to relieve stress by cutting, burning, or hair pulling. Others choose things that are soothing instead of injurious, like this guy. What makes little sense is why he's here and why he calls himself a whistleblower."

"Maybe he's having a psychotic break? When I first talked with him—this guy, the whistleblower—he seemed fairly normal. Now I'm not sure what to think." Katie shakes her head.

"Let's go have a cup of tea. We'll talk more later."

"I'd like to say this seems weird, but I'm starting to think there's no such thing as weird anymore. Seems trouble flourishes in Rapid City."

Katie props open the break room door so we can hear the doorbell. The teakettle is already hot and steaming. Kerry, who had woken up a few minutes before Dr. Murphy entered the room, has already stoked the fire and moved the kettle to the hot spot.

With tea mugs in hand, Katie and I join the doctor and Kerry at the round table. Kerry looks better than the last time I saw her, but the grief of losing her husband is still clear on her face. I want to offer her condolences and tell her I know how she feels, but it's different for her than for me.

Rand Hendricks disappeared, and Kerry, who insists he'd never just leave, presumes he's dead. Whispers around town suggest that's exactly what he did, that he grew tired of his life and took off. There have even been rumors that people saw him on the interstate, walking toward Spearfish.

"How was the concert?" Kerry asks, as she pushes the honey in my direction.

As I dribble honey into my cup, I silently wonder how she knew I'd gone to the concert, but then I remember half the town was there, including Dr. Wolff. "It was great. The children were amazing and so adorable."

Tears fill her eyes. "Rand and I talked about adopting one of the orphans. We hadn't moved forward to the point of going and visiting or anything, but it was a common discussion." She wipes at her eyes before directing her attention toward Katie. "How are the children?"

"Great. They're doing great. Nico was pretty upset about the fire, but he seemed better when I left."

"It's good the Williamses have the guest house so you aren't all displaced. Are you moving back to your original home?"

Katie shrugs. "We don't know exactly what we're doing yet."

"I thought I heard someone was moving into your old place," Dr. Murphy says.

"Really?" Katie tilts her head. "I hadn't heard about that. We informed Shaw that we intended to stay with the Williamses for a while, but we hadn't requested to give it up. I guess we'll have to find out. I'm not even sure who handles that now. Captain Williams assigned us the house when we arrived, but now— "

"Right," Murphy agrees. "Now you'll need to go through Major Stone." He crinkles his brow. "In fact, I think that might be where I overheard it. The major was talking with someone about it . . . yes, that's right. One of the new nursing students. She lives in one of the dorm-style houses now, and he suggested she may want to get her own place because of all the studying."

"And he mentioned my house?"

"He said he had two med students not using their house after having moved in with friends. I simply assumed it was you. But you know what they say about assuming."

"It makes sense, though," Katie agrees. "We're the only med students not living in our assigned housing."

The casual conversation continues for the duration of our break. Even though Katie keeps up and seems to take part, it's obvious her mind is on other things. Is she thinking about her housing situation or our mysterious visitor?

Like her, I'm pretending to follow along with the chatter, but my thoughts keep circling back to the looming questions in the air. What did that stranger want? Why did he come to me to help him with whatever is going on? What exactly does he know?

Despite the jovial atmosphere around us, unease settles in the pit of my stomach, a feeling I can't shake no matter how hard I try. As the conversation fades into background noise, I glance at Katie and notice the distant look in her eyes. Kerry wears a similar expression, tinged with sadness. We may put on brave faces, but beneath the surface, we are grappling with thoughts that threaten to consume us.

Chapter 26

Katie

The city lies quiet around us as we trudge through the streets, our footsteps echoing in the early morning stillness. The faint glow of dawn filters through the early morning haze, casting long shadows that dance across the broken asphalt.

"Another night survived," Merissa says, her voice heavy with exhaustion.

"Yeah, barely," Kerry mutters as she rubs her eyes. "And we get to be back in, what? A little over seven hours?"

"Yep," I say, "Afternoon rounds at 1400 hours. At least we have only one more overnight shift and then get a couple of days off."

"If we actually have rounds," Kerry says. "As far as we know, Major Stone might pull the plug on the entire thing. No more med school and no nursing school."

"I think he's going to let us continue," I say, though I really don't know any more than Kerry or Merissa do. While he ordered the rounds to be canceled over the weekend, he led us to believe that we'd return to business as usual on Monday.

Kerry stops walking and turns to look at me. "Why do you think so, Katie? Did Williams talk to him? Did he tell you something?"

I splay my gloved fingers. "Nothing. As far as I know, the major doesn't share his plans with the captain. And if he does, the captain doesn't share them with me."

"What about Leo? He's the captain's aide— "

"Nope. He doesn't know anything either. We're out of the loop."

Kerry chuckles while shaking her head. "It's crazy how they send in someone who knows nothing about a hospital to run a hospital. I don't even understand who thought that was a good idea."

"The governor," Merissa answers. "Another person who doesn't know anything about running a hospital."

We share a laugh as we resume walking. Last night's shift brought emergency after emergency. It seems celebrating Valentine's Day during the apocalypse could be dangerous to one's health. While Leo and I did nothing to commemorate the once popular commercial holiday, others upheld the tradition—some with disastrous results.

The first patient last night was a woman around my age who'd surprised her husband by dressing up. She wore a beautiful red knee-length dress with a flared skirt, a black shawl over her shoulders, and black stilettos. Her husband carried her into the hospital, as mascara trails traveled down her cheeks.

This was the first time she'd worn high heels since the EMP. One missed step and she went down, fracturing her ankle. We saw two more wardrobe-malfunction-related injuries before the night was over, along with a couple of cases of food poisoning, a severe burn from a candle, and the successful birth of a baby.

Our hospital, which had been devoid of overnight patients when we arrived on shift, was filled to capacity when we signed out. After such a night, my feet ache and I want nothing more than to crawl into my bed. While I'm sure I'll get at least a few hours of sleep between now and when we need to be back for med school rounds, it won't be enough.

Even worse than missing out on sleep is missing out on time with the children. For what must be the millionth time since Nico and the babies came into our lives, I sincerely wonder how in the world I can continue with med school and keep the children. It was hard enough when we adopted our dog, Gerry. Then we had to rely on our neighbors to help.

If it wasn't for Alice, I'm not sure what we'd do. Alice, who always wanted a family, immerses herself in her role as honorary nana. She'd probably be more than willing to assume full guardianship, especially of baby Zach, who she has a particular fondness for. She certainly cares for Nico and Caleb also, but there's an undeniable bond between Alice and Zach. Not just from her end, but also from his.

I do sometimes feel a twinge of jealousy when I'm holding him and he reaches for her. But mostly, I'm just grateful she's so willing to help us.

With each passing day, I'm also keenly aware not keeping the children isn't an option. I love all three of them more than I'd ever thought possible.

As we reach Kerry Hendrick's house on the corner, I take in the frosted windows and front porch buried in snow. A single trail is pounded out, thanks to snow boots. It's been less than two weeks since her husband disappeared. Kerry spent most of that time as part of the search parties looking for him. When the official search was called off, she continued looking on her own.

Now that her bereavement leave has concluded, by orders of Major Stone, and she's back to work, I can't help but wonder if she'll continue to look for him during her off time—what little there is of that.

Where can she even look? Surely, if he were in the Rapid City area, he would've been found by now. I don't want to believe that he simply walked away, as the rumor mill suggests, but the only other alternative is Rand is dead.

Kerry covers her mouth to contain a yawn. "I don't even want to take time to light a fire, but it's too cold to go without."

"I thought the captain had someone helping you to keep the fire going when you were . . ." I hesitate to finish my sentence.

"He did. A few of the neighborhood folks have been great about helping me. Keeping the fire lit, bringing in wood, making sure I had food, water, and more. I told them I could handle it from here. Since I'm back at work, I hate to take advantage of their kindness."

"Seems to me, with working twelve-hour shifts, you still need the help," Merissa says. "It's not easy coming home to a cold house."

Kerry tilts her head at Merissa. "Isn't your mother-in-law gone and you're going home to a cold house, too?"

Merissa snickers. "That's true. But we have one of those rocket stove heaters. The fire might be out, but the rocks over the exhaust system warmed up while it was burning. They hold the heat. It'll still be warm in the living room, at least. When the fire's burning, the little house is almost too hot."

"We talked about converting our woodstove to something like that. A masonry heater is what Rand called it." The mention of his name causes Kerry's shoulders to drop. "I'll see you two later."

Merissa and I remain on the sidewalk, waiting until she's inside, before resuming our walk. "Are you talking to the major today about that house?"

"Hopefully. If we can catch him at the hospital. He seems to flit in and out."

"Flit? I guess that's a good word to use for the fact he's rarely there. Not that I mind. I think we'd all be better off if he'd spend as little time commanding from the hospital as possible and just let us do what we know best to do."

"Mm-hmm. Agreed." A faint glimmer of movement catches my attention up ahead, concealed within the tangled winter-bare foliage. Instinctively, I reach out and grasp Merissa's arm, halting her in her tracks. My fingers tighten around her arm as I lean in close, my voice barely more than a breathy whisper.

"Let's cross," I insist, the urgency clear in my tone.

I feel her body stiffen as she gives a nod, and we veer off the sidewalk and into the street. "Trouble?"

"There's something in the bushes up ahead."

"Something? Or someone?" Merissa's voice carries a hint of unease, her eyes darting nervously toward a neglected hedge edging the sidewalk.

I hesitate for a moment, my senses on high alert, before responding in a hushed tone, "It's hard to say. But I'm not interested in finding out."

Merissa's expression mirrors my own sense of urgency. Our footsteps quicken as we put distance between ourselves and the hedge.

As we reach the opposite sidewalk, a figure steps out from behind the brush, his sudden appearance causing us to pause. The recognition hits me almost immediately. It's him—the man who showed up the other night at the hospital, insisting there's some grand conspiracy happening in Rapid City and Merissa is the only one who can stop it.

"Merissa." I lift my chin in the man's direction. "It's your radio caller. The whistleblower."

She snorts. "Great. And I forgot my tinfoil hat at work."

He steps forward, his features partially obscured by the shadows cast by the barren branches. There's a slight tilt to his head, almost as if he's studying us, sizing us up. "Wait," he calls out, his voice low and urgent. "Don't go. I need to talk to you."

The hairs on the back of my neck prickle with apprehension, but before we can react, he raises a hand in a gesture of peace, his movements slow and deliberate.

"Please," he implores, taking a hesitant step closer. "Just give me a moment of your time. It's important."

"We're not going near those bushes," Merissa says, for my ears only. "We both agreed he's not right mentally, but what if— "

"What if it's more, and he's here to kidnap us?" While I don't actually believe this, with the trouble that seems to follow me around lately, it's certainly possible. "Let's talk to him. At the very least, maybe we can suggest he come to the hospital as a patient. Maybe he has something wrong that we can help fix."

"He needs a psychiatrist."

"We can talk in the middle of the street."

"Fine. But briefly. We encourage him to come in for a medical exam and then go. I'm tired, and I'm not up for his conspiracy nonsense."

I nod in agreement, though I really wonder if there might be some truth to whatever it is he thinks is happening. There's an awful lot of weird stuff we know about in Rapid, from the preacher and his followers to the former sheriff and his drug business.

"We'll talk to you," Merissa says, "But in the street."

He shakes his head. "Too open. Too dangerous. They might be watching."

"That's what we're comfortable with. Take it or leave it." She touches my arm. "Maybe he'll just go."

He hesitates and looks around, then finally steps fully out of the brush and moves toward the street. When we meet in the middle, he says, "You women are going to get us all killed."

Merissa and I share a look that includes an eye roll on her part. "About that," she says, "Katie and I were talking. We thought it might be a good idea for you to come into the hospital and let one of the doctors check— "

"Check what? Check to see if I'm crazy? I'm not. I know Chris Williams, and I'd like to believe he's not involved in this, especially considering the note Zadok left— "

"What'd you say?" I interrupt. My heart is suddenly pounding in my ears as I wonder if his concerns are valid.

He smiles. "I wondered if you knew about it. I'd heard Chris was going to be read in, but then with the complete debacle concerning his wife and him losing oversight of the hospital, I wasn't sure if it happened."

"Who are you talking about?" Merissa asks. "Zadok? Who's that?"

"The preacher," I whisper. "He used the name Justin Zadok."

"Huh," she mutters. "I thought he wanted to be called Preacher?"

"Yes, that's what most called him," the man agrees. "But at some point, he decided he needed a more formal name. Obviously, Norman Smith, his birth name that he used until he took up street preaching and leading a cult, doesn't have much . . . pizzazz."

"Obviously," Merissa mutters, her tone laced with sarcasm.

"Justin Zadok, which basically means Righteous Righteous, has a zing to it."

"What?"

He shrugs. "Justin means righteous or just, and Zadok means righteous or just. So, you could say his name is Righteous Righteous or Just Just." He chuckles. "The man had a sense of humor."

"The *man* killed thousands in his murderous rampage."

"And, in his mind, the killings were for a greater good or, in the case of the town of Black Canyon, were justified."

"In Black Canyon, he killed the innocent," Merissa argues. "The few who were behind the edict to eliminate all the pets— "

"The innocents were collateral damage. It's sad, but it happens sometimes. Ask Chris Williams about wartime and collateral damage."

I narrow my eyes. "Are you one of the preacher's followers?"

He shakes his head. "Nope. But I've met him. Interviewed him."

"Interviewed?"

"This whole mess is even bigger than the preacher—than Justin Zadok. That's why he's dead. Because he figured it out. Everyone who figures it out ends up dead."

Merissa motions toward him. "You keep saying that. Why is it you think everyone is going to get themselves killed?"

"Because everyone else is already dead or will be soon. They can't have this getting out. What do you think happened to your coworker? He didn't just disappear, you know."

My breathing becomes irregular. "Rand?" the question comes out in a gasp.

"Right, the hospital janitor. He— " The man's head vaporizes into a cloud of red mist, causing his next words to be lost.

"Move! We've got to move!" Merissa insists, grabbing my arm as the gunshot reverberates through the neighborhood.

Chapter 27

Katie

A second gunshot rings out as we dash to the sidewalk, taking cover behind the hedge where the man had been hiding. The bullet strikes a nearby tree, sending shards of bark flying—one of which grazes my cheek.

"Stay low," Merissa urges as we weave our way through a yard.

Heart pounding, I follow Merissa's lead, my senses heightened by the adrenaline coursing through my veins. I fumble with my holster, awkwardly drawing my pistol before holding it tight against my thigh. Merissa, too, has her sidearm at the ready. With each step, the weight of the situation presses down on me, the urgency of our escape driving us forward.

The echo of gunfire lingers in the air as we duck behind a house. Merissa's voice pierces the chaos. "We'll cut through there." Her grip is gentle yet firm on my arm as she points toward the alley behind the property.

As we emerge into the alley, Merissa's face is pale and strained, but there's a determination in her eyes that tells me she won't stop until we're safe. With her almost eight-month-pregnant belly, every step is a challenge, but she refuses to let it slow her down.

"Merissa, your home isn't far. Do you think we'll be safe there?"

The shooting has stopped, and while I'd like to think whoever it is has given up, it's possible they've only stopped shooting so they can come after us. I look behind me, searching for any signs of a pursuer.

"I'm wondering if we'll be safe anywhere," Merissa grumbles.

We move swiftly through the alley, our footsteps muffled by the soft crunch of snow beneath our feet. Merissa's hand never leaves my arm, a silent reassurance as we survey our surroundings, looking for danger.

As we move, my thoughts are all over the place. I'm scared. Will Merissa's house actually keep us safe? Or is it just wishful thinking? Everything feels so uncertain right now. One thing is crystal clear. The man who we thought was paranoid—who referred to himself as a whistleblower—is now dead. He said they were after him, and he was right. Now it seems they may be after us, too.

Merissa's breath comes in ragged gasps beside me, her strength wavering under the weight of both her heavy belly and the burden of our situation.

As we near the end of the alley, daylight filters through the houses and trees, casting a faint glow on the snow-covered pavement ahead. My heart skips a beat as I realize we're nearly at Merissa's house, the hope of finding safety growing stronger with each step.

As we step onto the deserted street, dread washes over me, gripping me tightly. Out in the open, we'll once again be prime targets. "Run," Merissa says, urging me forward.

Pumping my legs while holding onto Merissa's hand, I murmur a prayer for our safety. Will Merissa's home be the sanctuary we desperately need, or will it become yet another battleground in a conflict we never chose to be a part of?

As we reach the front porch of Merissa's house, the tension in the air is almost tangible, thick with the weight of uncertainty and fear. Merissa's grip on my arm tightens, and I scan her face, noting her clenched jaw and flared nostrils. "Are you okay?"

"Let's just get inside."

Merissa fumbles with the key, her hands trembling slightly from nerves and the physical exertion. With a click, the door opens, and relief floods through me. At least for now, we can get inside and figure out exactly what's happening and what to do next.

I'm relieved to find the house warmer than the chilly morning air outside. It feels good to be out of the cold and, at least for the moment, out of danger.

"Go check the back door," Merissa instructs, panting as she secures the front door and slides a brace under the doorknob. "Make sure it's locked."

After ensuring the door is secure, I go around the house and close all the curtains.

"Good thinking." Merissa collapses onto the couch. I move to the bench by the rocket stove heater; its rocks are still warm from yesterday's fire. The events of the past few minutes catch up to me in a rush of emotion, and my eyes fill with tears.

For a moment, we sit in silence; the only sound is the ragged rhythm of our breathing. But even as we catch our breath, the question still lingers in the air, unspoken yet ever-present: Who killed the whistleblower guy, and will they come after us? Will they raid Merissa's house or wait in the shadows until we step outside?

The adrenaline that had fueled our escape now ebbs, leaving behind exhaustion and apprehension. I glance at Merissa; her breaths are coming in labored gasps, and her hand is resting on her swollen belly.

"Are you okay?" I ask tentatively, my voice barely above a whisper.

Merissa offers me a weak smile, but I can see the pain flicker behind her eyes. "I'm fine," she replies, though her tone lacks conviction.

I scrutinize her features. A sheen of sweat shows on her forehead and upper lip—understandable, considering our recent run for our lives. Her face tightens, and she flinches, her hand moving to her back. I peek at my wristwatch and continue to watch her until she relaxes.

"Merissa? Are you having contractions?"

She takes in her upper lip as tears fill her eyes. "I pray I'm not, but . . ." She gives a slight nod before whispering, "I think so."

My heart sinks at Merissa's admission. Not only is it too soon, but we have the added problem of someone wanting to kill us. Is it even safe for us to travel to the hospital? Not to mention, walking could speed up Merissa's labor when what we really need is to stop it.

Before the EMP, a thirty-four-week baby would've likely gone to the neonatal intensive care unit and received extra care. In today's world, we don't have a NICU or all the gadgets needed to keep preemies alive. Panic threatens to overwhelm me, but I push it down and focus instead on Merissa and the baby growing inside her.

"Okay, let's get you to your bed," I say, my voice steady despite the turmoil churning inside me. "This could just be from the exertion and fright. We'll have you lie on your left side. I also want you to drink a big glass of water. Dehydration can lead to contractions."

"It's too early," she mutters as I help her from the couch and to her room. With her boots and blood-covered outerwear removed, along with the sidearms she had strapped to her back and ankle, she slips under the covers. As I'm smoothing the blankets, she says, "Here's another one."

Glancing at my watch, I note the time. Eight minutes since the last time I looked. I know that contractions closer than ten minutes can be a sign of preterm labor. I hold her hand until the contraction passes. "Okay. Let me get you a glass of water."

"There's some paper in the drawer by the kitchen sink. Pencils, too."

In the kitchen, I take time to wash my hands from the jug labeled "wash." Like Merissa, I caught some blood spray when the man was shot. After I've cleaned up, I fill two glasses with water from a second container marked "drinking."

After she drinks one full glass, I motion to the second one I placed on the nightstand. "I'm going to refill this one and get myself a glass."

On my way to the kitchen, I check all the windows, cautiously peeking out and searching for anything—anyone—out of place. As near as I can tell, no one's around who shouldn't be there.

It's after 0730; Leo must be wondering where I'm at. The captain went on shift at 0600 this morning. Leo's scheduled shift is at 0900. Originally, Poppy Gardner and her nursing school had him scheduled to work with them. Now, since Major Stone has put the nursing school on hold, I'm not exactly sure what he'll be doing. I know Poppy is hopeful, as are the rest of us, that classes will begin in the next day or so and the delay is just that, a delay and not a cancellation.

"What can we do to stop this?" Merissa asks, her voice now calm and sounding more like herself.

"Resting and rehydrating might be enough. Running like we did . . ." I shake my head. "Your baby probably wasn't a fan."

"I wasn't a fan either. Have you— " She motions toward the window, halting the movement partway as she scrunches her face.

I do my best to offer words of encouragement, to soothe her fears, as she rides out the contraction. But inside, I'm terrified. We're alone, with no one to turn to for help. What if something goes wrong? I still vividly recall the premature birth at the hospital when I lost not only the baby but also the mom. In the time since then, I've attended nearly a dozen births. While most have had a happy ending, not all have.

After the contraction ends, I record the time and duration before helping her drink more water. "I saw nothing concerning out the windows." From the kitchen window, I had a good view of the front yard, while the living room and laundry room provided views of the side yards. "I'll peek out this one, too, and if it's okay, I'll check Pearl's room."

"Yes, that's fine. Do what you need to do. I'm sorry I can't help."

"If you can relax, it'll help. I'm going to get a fire going. Maybe I should heat some water for a bath? Would that help?"

"I don't have enough water for that."

"Well . . . try not to worry. I know you're scared, but right now, everything is fine."

"Humph." She snorts and shakes her head.

After ensuring things look okay out each window, I make another round through the house. As I go, I worry about what will happen next. I know I told Merissa not to worry, but I can't seem to take my own advice.

If we can't get the labor stopped, how will I get Merissa to the hospital? At the hospital, we have not only a doctor who knows what he's doing much better than I do, but also a few different herbs that Stella Swensen has provided for preterm labor.

Merissa can't walk, so I'll need to leave her alone while I go get the pickup. I also need to let Leo know what's happening. On top of those needs is my concern that there's a killer waiting out there, just out of view, ready to shoot as soon as I step out the door.

I check my watch. It's been six minutes since the last contraction. I hustle back to the bedroom so I can be there if another contraction happens. I've counted three so far in less than half an hour, and my concern is increasing.

When the eight-minute mark comes and goes, I let out a breath of relief, thinking maybe we've stopped them. I'm just about to say something when Merissa grimaces. Looking at my watch, I again note the time. While I was hoping they were gone for good, if they get farther apart instead of closer together, that is also a good sign.

As the contraction subsides, I gently squeeze her hand. "You're doing great, Merissa. You're fine."

Her eyes squeezed shut against the residual pain. And in that moment, as we face the unknown together, I realize that no matter what happens, we'll overcome it. Because that's what friends do. They stand by each other through thick and thin, no matter what challenges come their way.

Chapter 28

Merissa

As the contraction gradually subsides, I release a long, slow exhale, feeling the tension melt away from my body.

"That one was nine minutes after the prior one." Katie's head bobs rhythmically. "I think that's a good sign, Merissa. An excellent sign. Maybe the running got things worked up, but we've got you settled in time and everything will be fine. Finish the water in your glass, and I'll refill it."

"I think emptying my bladder may help, too. If . . . if they don't stop . . ."

"Don't worry. I'll get us some help. I won't wait too long to go after the truck."

Katie helps me from the bed and asks if I want her to join me in the bathroom. "I've got this."

"All right. I'll get you some more water and check the windows again."

"We're sitting ducks. It wouldn't take much for them to get inside."

"How many shooters do you think there were?"

I pause as I try to remember the chaotic event. We were talking with the whistleblower, and the next second his head was gone and we were running for our lives. The shots were steady, but not excessive. "I think maybe only one? I don't know for certain, and I never saw anyone."

"Same. I never caught sight of the shooter, but I wasn't waiting to search him out either."

After using the bathroom and washing my hands, I make my way back to the bedroom. Katie used the time to get the fire in the rocket stove heater going. When she sees me, she asks, "Everything okay?"

I know what she's asking. Did I find any bleeding or other concerns? "As it should be. No contraction while I was in there, either."

"That's great. We're coming up on eight minutes, so . . ."

"Mm-hmm. I— " The pain starts in my back and travels around my stomach. Every breath I take feels like a battle against the chaos swirling around me. I put my hand against the wall as Katie rushes to my side and takes my other hand in hers, her grip offering a steady anchor in this sea of turmoil. We've been through so much together since I arrived in Rapid City, but this takes things to a new level of fear and danger.

I try to push aside the fear threatening to overwhelm me. Katie's presence beside me is a comfort; her friendship and calm demeanor help to keep me grounded. Oh, I know she's scared, as am I, but she's doing her best to not show it and be the professional she needs to be.

But as this contraction grows stronger, I can't help but feel a rising tide of panic clawing at my insides. Each wave of pain serves as a stark reminder of our precarious situation, a reminder that in this unforgiving world, even the miracle of childbirth is fraught with danger.

It's too soon for my baby to be born.

What may have been fine before, when the hospitals were fully functioning, could be a death sentence now. When Dr. Wolff examined me last week, she said my baby was probably around five pounds in weight, maybe a little less since I've had trouble putting on weight.

Nothing is easy in the apocalypse. Low weight gain combined with chronic stress can also be a contributing factor to preterm labor. Even though both of those are issues, I've been surprisingly healthy and without complications. I guess getting shot at was a little much for my baby and my body.

As the contraction finally begins to ease, leaving me drained and shaky, Katie squeezes my hand gently, her concern etched in the lines of her face. "Merissa, we need to stay calm and focused. We can handle this." Her voice is steady despite the circumstances.

"How long was that? Between contractions, I mean?"

She pulls her lips into a tight line as she stares at her watch. "Just under seven minutes. But . . . it may be okay. The last couple were irregular. It may still be stopping. Let's get you back to bed and on your left side. I've already freshened your water, and as soon as the fire gets going a little better, I'll put a kettle on for tea."

"If nothing else, I'll be well hydrated," I joke. "I'll have so much liquid in me, I can float to the hospital."

"That would be a help," she laughs while her eyes communicate her concern.

As we reach my bed, a knock sounds at the front door. Katie and I make eye contact, and my heart rate instantly increases.

"It's probably someone you know," she whispers. "The killers didn't strike me as the knocking type."

"Let's go find out."

"You should get back in the bed. Let me— "

"If it's not a friend, we're better off together. Let's just hope it doesn't take more than eight minutes."

"Six and a half now," she mutters as she hands me my 9-millimeter from the nightstand.

We walk quietly, me in my stockinged feet and Katie in her insulated boots, both of us with our guns at the ready. As we approach the door, I motion to the window near the side. "I'll take a look. Stay back from the door and be ready."

I consider the best way for me to peek out the window without catching a bullet, should that be the visitor's intention. I finally settle on moving to a window in the dining area that will still have a view of the front porch but from farther away. When I motion my intentions to Katie, she responds with a nod and positions herself at the edge of the hallway, where she'll have some cover should bullets start flying.

Reaching the window, I view the porch through the still-closed curtains. The light fabric is too heavy for me to see through clearly, but opaque enough for me to make out a shape on the porch. It looks like one person, probably a male. I have a fleeting hope it may be Bowski, but I don't think the figure's tall enough or stout enough.

I reach out to touch the curtain as a second knock sounds. "Merissa?" the voice calls out. "Merissa? It's Leo. Is Katie with you?"

"Leo," I say with a sigh as I part the curtain to assure myself it really is Leo.

"Is it him?" Katie whispers.

"It's him."

"I'll let him in," she says, already moving toward the door. "He can get the pickup so we can take you to the hospital. I guess . . . I guess no one is shooting at him, so that's a good thing." She releases a nervous laugh.

As soon as Katie has the door open, she pulls him inside and melts into his arms, rapidly describing the shooting and my contractions. I watch for a moment as the tightening in my back begins. I reach out to grab the countertop, balancing myself as the wave of pain envelops me.

Katie realizes what's happening and rushes to my side, wrapping an arm around my waist to help balance me. I know she's being kind, but right now, even her touch feels overwhelming in this moment of intense discomfort.

Once the pain subsides, Katie says, "I missed the beginning, so I'm not entirely sure of the timing, but I don't think it was any closer than the last. I'll write an estimated time so we can continue to keep track. Let's get you back to bed and send Leo for the pickup."

"How did you know we were here?" I ask Leo as we start toward the bedroom.

"Someone heard the shooting and saw the body. When it was over, he ran to the patroller's depot and reported it. Oscar Harrington was one of the responding patrollers. He asked the neighbors and one of them said they didn't see what happened but looked out the window and saw two women running away.

"Since you were near Kerry Hendrick's place, the investigators also interviewed her. She heard the shooting but saw nothing. Too far away. When he mentioned two women running away, she instantly mentioned you two. He came to the house to check on Katie, and here I am. Oscar and a couple of other patrollers positioned themselves around the house in case there was something hinky happening."

"Are they on foot?" Katie asks. "We need to take Merissa to the hospital."

"We're all on foot, but I'll go tell them and have one of them go after the pickup truck."

As he moves to leave, a sudden realization grips me like a vise. "Wait. The shooters . . . are they still out there?"

Leo's jaw tightens at the reminder of the danger lurking beyond our doorstep, but his gaze remains steady. "Not that we've seen."

I manage a weak smile, though the fear still gnaws at the edges of my mind. "Okay. If it won't be long until the truck arrives, maybe I don't need to go back to bed."

Leo shakes his head while Katie says, "The less pressure on the baby, the better. Leo will bring a stretcher and— "

"Argh, I don't— "

"Merissa." Her tone stops me from arguing. "Let's get you in the bed. Leo, please get the truck on its way. Make sure they know we need a stretcher and tell them to inform the captain of what's happening. Let yourself back in. Merissa, where are your house keys?"

Understanding Katie is right and is doing what's best for me and my unborn baby, I point to the drawer holding a spare set of keys before allowing Katie to lead me to the bedroom and into bed. "Would you mind packing a bag for me? My nightgown, robe, and slippers, at least."

"Sure. Yes. How about . . ." She pauses and swallows. "Do you want me to pack some things for the baby?"

I shake my head. "It's too soon for her to be born."

"I'm sure the captain will know what to do. He'll use some of Stella's potions or something. Maybe even alcohol intravenously."

"Yeah, that'd be great. Get me and the baby drunk."

"Alcohol was one of the earliest forms of tocolytics."

"I know alcohol was used to stop preterm labor, but remember that report from one of the captain's medical journals? They compared ethanol with a sugar water placebo, and others compared ethanol with other drugs that slowed or stopped uterine contractions. The alcohol didn't do any better than the sugar water."

"Really, Merissa, let's just try to get you to relax. Move to your side, and I'll pack a bag for you."

As she speaks, a new wave of pain washes over me, stealing my breath and leaving me trembling in its wake. I clutch the sheets, willing myself to endure as the seconds tick by agonizingly slow. Katie comforts me with her words, urging me to breathe and go with the pain.

By the time the pain dwindles to nothing, I notice Leo is standing in the bedroom doorway. "One of Oscar's guys went after the truck. They've got more patrollers out there, making sure there's nothing awry. Deputy Shaw is on his way, too."

Finally, the sound of the pickup's engine rumbles outside. "I'll go get the stretcher," Leo says in a clipped tone.

I ride out another contraction before Leo returns. Jesse Talbot, back from bereavement leave after losing his brother, is with him. "Hey, Weaver," he says. "Captain Williams is getting the presidential suite put together for you. You can expect celebrity treatment at *Hospital del Distrito de Guardia.*"

"Is Spanish supposed to make our crummy Guard District hospital sound more appealing?" I ask with a shake of my head. "Because it doesn't. I'd much rather stay at *mi casa.*"

"Yeah, well, let's get you fixed up, then you can be back here in a jiffy."

As he brings in the board stretcher, I gently ease myself into a sitting position. "I can walk, you know."

"Sure, but when else am I going to have a chance to carry you around? Allow me my fun."

"Great, Jesse. Why do I get the feeling you are going to remind me of this every opportunity you get?"

"Because I will."

I convince them to at least let me get to my feet instead of trying to transfer from the bed to the stretcher being held by Jesse and one of the patrollers. Leo offers to hold the other end, but Katie tells him no because he's not cleared to use his surgically repaired arm yet.

As we make our way outside, I cast a fleeting glance back at the home I share with Mother Pearl. If Captain Williams can't get my labor stopped, someone will need to go to the ranch and bring her to the hospital. I reach for Katie's hand.

"I'm here, Merissa," she says.

"Will you pray with me?"

"Absolutely."

I close my eyes as she increases the pressure on my hand. "Father God, please be with Merissa during this time. Help Captain Williams know what to do to allow the baby to stay where she needs to be for now. You, Lord, are the Mighty Healer, the One in which all things are possible. We pray these things in the Precious Name of Your Son, Jesus. Amen."

Chapter 29

Merissa

The journey to the hospital feels like an eternity, each bump in the road sending waves of discomfort rippling through my body. Katie's prayer seals any lingering questions or doubts that I may have had. Now, I realize that the path I've been on since marrying Braedon, with his insistence on a loving God, is reaching its culmination tonight.

When we first met, Braedon was a believer, albeit not fervently. He occasionally accompanied his parents to church, but his commitment was lacking. After we married, his attendance waned further until his father passed away. It was then that a shift occurred within him; he prioritized his faith and expressed a desire for children—neither of which aligned with my own plans.

While the idea of God held some appeal, it wasn't a necessity for me. As for children, they simply weren't part of my agenda. Braedon and I were content with our careers and our shared passions for horses and hobbies. It seemed inconceivable to me how children could fit into our carefully constructed plans, so we went our separate ways.

Despite the separation, our love persisted. As the attacks on our country unfolded, Braedon still ensured my well-being, checking in to see if I was all right and providing whatever support I needed.

When the cyberattack disrupted the electricity and water supply at our former condo, Braedon brought water to me. During what was supposed to be a tranquil breakfast of pancakes cooked on the balcony grill, our phones blared with alerts, forewarning of an imminent missile strike. In mere moments, we abandoned our meal and hurried to Pearl's home, where Braedon had been staying since our separation, seeking refuge in the basement.

Livingston, Montana, which we called home, didn't sustain any direct hits, but the nuclear weapons set off high in the sky changed our world forever. I stayed with Braedon and Pearl in their gated community. Braedon's brother, Tomas, and his brother's wife,

Courtney, lived in the same community, allowing all of us to work together to survive.

I attended weekly church services in the public house alongside the family. It was there I started feeling that maybe I wanted to learn more about God and His ways, but it was all still very confusing. Sometimes, the preacher's words seemed almost contradictory. After the attack on our community resulted in the deaths of Braedon and Tomas, Pearl and I came east to South Dakota. Attending services at Opal's place, the feeling grew stronger.

Shawn Maher's preaching and being around the Maher family, plus becoming friends with Katie, has shown me a truly loving God. Sometimes, I still question how God could allow so many terrible things to happen. The attacks on the country, the nuclear bombs that destroyed both the East and West Coasts of the United States of America, the EMP that destroyed the remaining forty-eight contiguous states, and the death of my husband.

Then I remember the same God has given me a child, a part of my husband to hold and have and remember him by. *In everything, give thanks . . .*

The Bible verse is one that's easy to remember but sometimes so hard to follow. There's been so much tragedy, how does one really give thanks?

Mother Pearl comes to my mind again. God has given me Pearl, who is not merely my mother-in-law but genuine family. Closer than family. Pearl and I have encountered many challenges in our relationship, moments when I was convinced she would've preferred anyone else for her son.

Nowadays, we occasionally share a laugh about those troubles as we reminisce about Braedon and Tomas while pondering how Courtney is faring. She chose to head west to be with her relatives. Has she found happiness? Is she safe?

The tightening in my back returns me to the present. "Mmm . . ." I hum.

Katie glances at her watch and jots down the time before turning her attention to me. "We're almost there. I know this isn't great, bouncing around in the truck bed. Breathe, Merissa, breathe."

As the pain subsides, I feel the truck slowing for a corner. "See?" Katie says. "We're here now. Just passing the guard station." There's a pause as Katie peers out the windows of the recently replaced camper shell. The attack that killed Josiah Talbot also destroyed the previous shell.

She turns back to me, a wide smile covering her face. "The captain is waiting in the driveway. He has a gurney. Stella's here, too. I'm sure she has something in mind to help you."

"Good." I let the breath out through my nose. Master herbalist Stella Swensen is a wealth of knowledge. Having started med school with me and the others, she now acts as our pharmacist, deciding that was a better fit for her.

She loves the medicine part of doctoring; it's the people part that is a challenge for her. This is something to which I can relate. My bedside manner is less than desirable. Interacting with patients is something I have to focus on, and it's still awkward.

Before the EMP, I worked for the Forest Service, fighting wildland fires. Prior to that, I was in the Coast Guard. Neither of those things required me to be a people person. Captain Williams originally hired me to work as an orderly, or what they call a medic, because of my training in the Coast Guard and with the Forest Service in emergency medicine.

When the captain suggested I join the med school, I wasn't sure it'd be right for me. Some days, I still wonder. Especially now. If the captain and Stella can get my labor stopped, I'm well aware the goal will be to keep it stopped for at least three more weeks.

Delivering at thirty-seven weeks is an entirely new ballgame for the baby compared to thirty-four weeks. At thirty-seven weeks, she'll be full term. I can't imagine they will allow me to do much of anything between now and then.

If they can't stop the labor . . . I squeeze my eyes tight to stop the thoughts.

"Are you having another contraction?" Katie asks, her tone laced with fear. "Already?"

"No, no. I was just thinking."

"Whew. I was worried." The truck comes to a stop. "Here we are. Let's get you inside."

At Katie's suggestion, Leo had ridden in the front seat with Jesse. He pops the gate of the truck open and lifts the door of the shell.

"Well, Ms. Weaver," the captain says, "you've had quite a morning."

"Yes, sir. A morning I could've done without."

"Indeed." He agrees before turning to Katie. "Sergeant Burnett, please give me the report."

Katie shares the contraction history with the captain while Jesse Talbot and Austin Chambers remove me from the bed of the truck, positioning the board stretcher on top of the gurney. "We'll get you inside, Weaver," Jesse says. "You'll be fine in a jiffy."

Inside the hospital, they move me to exam room two. Jesse and Chambers help me transfer from the gurney to a slightly softer bed. Slightly, but not by much. Hospital exam tables don't have a reputation for comfort.

Nurse Jacquie takes my vitals while tsking over the fact that I'm here. "I knew you were pushing yourself too hard, Merissa. A woman in your condition needs to take things easy."

"Jacquie," Katie says with a bite to her tone. "Let's save that talk for another time."

She huffs. "I'm just saying— "

Katie raises her hand. "Stop. Just stop." Katie turns from the older woman toward me. "The captain will be in shortly."

"Thanks, Katie." The tightening begins again. "Here we go."

Checking her watch, then scribbling on her paper, Katie tells Jacquie to give me a minute. As I'm riding the pain wave, Jacquie transforms into a caring and comforting nurse as opposed to the meddlesome busybody she can sometimes be.

When it's over, Katie sends me a smile. "Good news. That one was shorter than some of the others, and you went almost ten minutes between contractions."

Tears of relief fill my eyes. "That's wonderful. Maybe . . ." I bob my head several times. "Maybe it's stopping."

The next bit is a whirlwind as Captain Williams and Stella enter the room. Katie stays with me while Jacquie goes to check on a patient who's ringing the bell for help.

The exam is brief and external only, as the captain says he doesn't want to disturb anything that doesn't need disturbing. He asks Katie to start an IV to make sure I'm well hydrated, and then he confers with Stella about the medications.

Since the EMP and the cessation of pharmaceutical production, herbal remedies have become commonplace. The captain isn't as knowledgeable about these remedies as he was about commercial medicine, so he's taken to calling Stella for difficult cases. She's also created a book for hospital use with extensive information.

As she shares her plan, I nod my agreement. The herbs are in line with what I thought she might use. An alcohol IV was discussed but discarded for now.

"No sense having you on this uncomfortable table." The captain motions at the examination bed. "You're going to be with us a day or two. We'll put you in the presidential suite."

I give a courtesy laugh. "That's exactly what Jesse said you'd do. I appreciate it, Captain."

In a more somber tone, he says, "I heard your mother-in-law is out of town, visiting her sister at the ranch. Would you like me to send for her?"

I take in a deep breath and consider the best choice. Mother Pearl wants this baby as much as I do. She's loved him or her since the moment I told her about the pregnancy.

I'd waited, probably longer than I should have, to share the news out of fear of not keeping the pregnancy. The stress of losing Braedon, combined with traveling from Montana to South Dakota, as well as my poor diet, didn't make for the best home for a growing baby. When I finally told her, I was already showing but hiding my expanding midsection underneath winter clothes.

I'm fairly certain Opal knew I was pregnant, but it was still a surprise to Pearl. A surprise that has brought us closer than I ever believed possible. Now I can honestly say I have a deep and abiding love for my mother-in-law that was never there before. I don't know if it's because of the baby entirely or because of our shared losses, but it's there.

"She's supposed to be home on Tuesday. She looks forward to her time at the ranch with Opal. I hate to take that from her."

With an understanding gesture, the captain adds, "Tuesday is tomorrow. We could give it a few hours and see how you do, then reevaluate sending for her. You wouldn't be cutting her getaway too short."

"I know she'd want to know, especially if . . ." I release a sigh as my words drift off. Before the apocalypse, a baby at thirty-four or thirty-five weeks gestation would likely do fine. They'd give me shots to strengthen the baby's lungs, and maybe she'd need to stay in the NICU for a few days or be under the lights to help with jaundice caused by a buildup of a substance in the blood called bilirubin and common among newborns, especially those who are preterm.

While jaundice cases are typically mild, severe cases require light therapy to prevent brain damage. Unfortunately, the EMP destroyed most of the special phototherapy lights, and as far as I know, the Rapid City area doesn't have a light therapy option.

Fortunately, so far, we haven't encountered any babies with severe jaundice. However, our hospital hasn't seen any live births at a gestation as early as mine. We've experienced stillbirths and other losses, including mothers. Despite our knowledge of birthing practices, without the advanced machinery that doctors once relied on, we've regressed hundreds of years in terms of infant and maternal mortality rates.

I am determined not to contribute to those statistics.

Chapter 30

Katie

"Thanks, Katie," Merissa says, her voice barely above a whisper. We've done what we can to make her comfortable in the bed, adding extra pillows to position her on her left side.

With the IV drip running and the first dose of Stella's herbal concoction administered, it's now just a waiting game to see how her body responds. So far, we're optimistic, as the contractions are at irregular intervals and shorter durations.

I sit by Merissa's bedside, my heart heavy with concern yet buoyed by the improvement in her condition. The light from the lantern casts long shadows in the small room, amplifying the sense of urgency. Despite the makeshift arrangements and the limitations we face without modern medical equipment, we're determined to do everything in our power to help Merissa through this.

"Is there anything new about the shooter?" Merissa asks.

"Not that I know of."

She nods before gesturing toward the clock on the nightstand, positioned there so whoever is sitting with her can time her contractions. "It's getting late. Are you going to go home? Get some sleep before rounds?"

"I'll grab a nap in the call room."

"What about the children?"

"The captain sent a message to Alice about the situation. She'll take care of them. The wet nurse is there this morning, too. It'll be fine."

"Would you mind asking the captain for an update on the shooter? Maybe see if they were able to identify the whistleblower? I'd love to know who he was. Maybe then we could figure out exactly what he was talking about."

"I guess he wasn't having a mental break."

"Yeah . . ." Merissa shakes her head. "He was just so twitchy and out there. I feel terrible— " Her words halt as her face contorts with another pain.

"Hang in there, Merissa," I encourage, my voice steady despite the concern within me. Glancing at my watch, I note it's been almost sixteen minutes since the last contraction. Within about thirty seconds, she visibly relaxes. "Better?" I confirm.

"Better. They're easing off." Her smile shows relief. "I guess, though, that even if we get them stopped completely, I'd better get used to this bed. I can't imagine Captain Williams is going to let me return to work or even school. It'll probably be bed rest until the baby is born."

I dip my chin in acknowledgment.

She rushes on with, "I know it's the best choice. Every day she stays in utero is going to help her. I'm not really complaining, just . . ."

"Just wondering how you'll keep up with med school?"

"I am. Does that make me selfish?"

"Not at all. I— " I clear my throat and lower my voice. "I completely understand. Since the boys started living with us, I've wondered if I'm doing the right thing by continuing with the school, especially considering I only became an official student about the same time as Mindy died and Kemeera took off.

"Part of me thinks I should've immediately told the captain I was out. Leo could stay in the training, but I'd just be a nurse and a mom. Of course, Leo and I keep insisting that we haven't finalized any decisions about our plans, but neither of us intends to relinquish the boys. The truth is, if it wasn't for Alice, we couldn't do it. Losing the house is going to make things more difficult."

"Will you talk with Major Stone today?"

"We planned to, but he hasn't arrived yet, at least not as far as I know."

"With the way things are concerning the major and his disdain for our med school and the nursing school, it may be a moot point for both of us. He could easily decide to pull the plug on the schools, and we'll both go back to being only hospital employees. Of course, in my case, he may also decide to fire me from that, too. He said he doesn't care if I have a doctor's excuse; he'll still expect me to perform the duties of my position."

"I'm pretty sure this situation is going to qualify as not able to fulfill your full duties."

We both release a small, nervous laugh. I sober quickly and say, "Seriously, though, if by some miracle he doesn't cancel med school, I'll do what I can to help you keep caught up. Even if restricted to your bed, you can still read and study."

"Thanks, Katie. Would you mind popping out and seeing what you can find out about the murder this morning? Also, um, maybe if there's not much info, we could check with Bowski, ask him what he knows."

A smile creeps over my face as I realize Merissa is asking me to let Bowski know about this situation. "I'm sure he'll want to visit you."

She blushes as she averts her gaze. "I'd like it if he would."

"I'll take care of it. I won't be gone long, but if another contraction happens, try to note the time, okay?"

"Oh sure, if I'm not too busy being in pain." She laughs, then waves her hand. "I'll be fine."

I slip out of the room in search of either Leo or the captain and any information I can find about the shooting this morning. Even though Merissa says she'll be fine, I don't want to be gone for more than a minute or two.

Austin Chambers is at the nurse's station and informs me both Leo and the captain are in the break room with Deputy Shaw. "How's Weaver?" he asks.

"Better. Listen for her bell for me? Is Stella still here?"

"She's in the medicine room. Said she wanted to update the pharmacy book. Do you need her?"

"No, just wondering." I make my way to the break room, which Captain Williams now uses as his office after being displaced by Major Stone. I give a solid knock on the door and wait for an invitation to enter.

"Perfect timing," Leo says. "Deputy Shaw is ready to interview you."

"Okay," I agree while making eye contact with the deputy. "I don't want to leave Merissa for too long. She asked me if I'd see what I could find out about the dead man. Also, if you found the shooter."

"We didn't find the shooter. Why don't you have a seat and tell me what happened this morning."

"I'll go stay with Merissa," Leo offers.

I send him a grateful smile. "She's asking for Bowski. Do you think he's monitoring Hugo's radio and we can reach him?"

Leo defers to Deputy Shaw, who says, "Let's try."

He uses his radio and tries Hugo's frequency. Bowski is out on a pickup. Shaw is very discreet, preserving Merissa's privacy when he asks if Bowski can be sent by the hospital when he's available. Hugo agrees to send him.

With those plans in place, Leo excuses himself to sit with Merissa. He'll let her know about Bowski. The captain also steps out with Leo, leaving me alone for my interview with Shaw.

"Were you injured?" he stares at my cheek as he flips his notebook open.

My hand goes to my face, the opposite side of the wound I'm still sporting from the attack a few weeks ago. "Just a scratch."

"And Merissa?"

"She didn't sustain any injuries when we were being fired upon." Even though I could tell him she's in preterm labor, likely caused by the exertion of running for our lives, combined with the stress of being shot at, I choose to keep her medical conditions to myself. No doubt, he already knows some of what's happening. I'm sure the captain gave a general overview. "Do you know who the dead man was?"

"I was going to ask you the same question."

I nibble the inside of my cheek as I consider my response. I know I need to tell him about meeting the man the other night, but I'm not really sure where to begin. "I don't know his name. I was hoping you might recognize him."

His expression shifts into one of solemnity, his eyes locking onto mine. "Facial recognition wasn't an option due to the wounds he sustained from the large caliber weapon."

Making a face, I shake my head. "We both had blood spatter on our jackets, and Merissa said he was dead. But I was too busy moving to check his condition." I don't want to admit to Shaw the guilt I'm feeling. Maybe if we had met the man in the bushes like he asked, he'd still be alive.

"Can you give me a rundown of what happened?"

Licking my dry lips, I consider pulling out my tiny jar of tallow lip balm. I know, though, the action, while comforting, would really just be another way to buy time and not tell Shaw what I know. "We were walking home when he called to us from the hedge edging the yard nearby where he was killed. We, uh . . . we told him to step out to the middle of the road and we'd talk to him."

Shaw crinkles his brow. "Did you know him?"

"Not, uh . . . not by name. He was here before."

"A patient?"

"Not exactly. We thought he was at first, but he was here to see Merissa." I pause and then quickly add, "She didn't know him either. Had never met him before that night . . . not really, anyway."

With his pencil paused above his notebook, Shaw gives me a serious look. "What's going on here, Katie?"

"It's going to sound crazy," I warn him. "At the time, we thought he was having a mental breakdown of some sort. We didn't know . . . I promise we had no idea what happened was going to happen. It's like something out of a spy novel or . . . or some kind of movie."

He stares at me. With a nod, he urges me to continue.

I clear my throat and pull my lip balm from my pocket. I don't care if it is a way to delay telling him. Once I've finished, he still hasn't spoken. I start with what I know. "You know about the prank calls the hospital has received over the walkie-talkie?"

"I took the report the last time it happened. Someone claiming to be a doctor from Deadwood said there was a biohazard event. People were dying. That was . . ." He sighs and shakes his head.

"Josiah Talbot died that day. It took me a few days to follow up with the Deadwood hospital, but they said they didn't have a Dr. Wainwright there and weren't having any issues. The first time the call came in, Shroeder—that louse—was on duty and took the report. He followed up with Garcia from the Main Street District, who said he hadn't made the call. We chalked it up to a kid with a radio and too much time on his hands."

"But after the first prank call, you changed the radio frequencies, right?"

"True."

"The dead man was the guy on the radio. At least, he claimed to be."

Shaw is silent as he contemplates what I've told him. I fight the urge to ramble on. Instead, I wait with my hands folded in my lap, my index finger rubbing along the edge of my thumb, similar to the nervous habit the whistleblower had.

"Did he say why he made the radio calls?"

"He said he needed help, and he was assessing Merissa to see if he could trust her. He also said he tried to meet her in person before the other night, but with the flu and all the other trouble we've been having, things didn't work out. Then he said he thought the flu epidemic would stop them and things would be okay."

"The flu epidemic would stop who?"

I lift my shoulders toward my ears as I shake my head. "No idea. As I said, we honestly thought he was having a mental break. He wasn't making much sense. He insisted we couldn't tell anyone—not Leo and not Bowski—or they'd try to track down whoever was doing whatever he was concerned about, and they'd end up dead.

"When Dr. Murphy came out of the call room, the guy left, warning us not to tell anyone and to be smart. Merissa and I discussed the man's visit and chalked it up to . . . well, as I said, mental health issues. It wasn't until the shooting started that we figured there might be something to it."

"To what?"

I raise my hands. "That's the thing. We don't really know. He mentioned Melvin Cabal, expressing his belief that after authorities took him into custody, maybe they would stop. But he didn't specify what needed to be stopped. Just that he wanted Merissa's help.

"I guess he wanted mine, too. He seemed to know a lot about both of us. Too much, really. Said he contacted Merissa because she wears a radio, and it was an easy way to feel her out." I realize I'm repeating info I've already told him as he bends his head and scribbles in his notebook.

Without looking up, he asks, "And he never told you his name or how he chose you two?"

"He didn't. But as I said, he seemed to know an awful lot about things. This morning, before the shooting started, he mentioned knowing the captain and some . . . some private information." I shrug as I consider what the dead man said. He knew the name the preacher used in the suicide note, which, as far as I know, nobody has publicly disclosed. At least, I'd never heard the name Justin Zadok until reading the note myself.

Shaw must see a change in my demeanor. "What is it? Did you remember something?"

"Maybe. He mentioned he interviewed the preacher." I lean forward in my chair and lower my voice. "He knew the name the preacher was using."

Leaning back in his chair, Shaw says, "He told you he knew the preacher's real name and that he interviewed him?"

I shake my head. "Not his real name. Not Norman Smith. The, uh . . . the other name."

Shaw narrows his eyes. "Is he in law enforcement or the military?"

"I didn't get the impression it was that kind of interview. I could be wrong."

"What kind of interview did you think it was?"

"I don't know. I was going to ask him, but then the shooting started. But he said the preacher knew about whatever was happening. He said that's why the preacher and his people ended up dead. At first, we thought it was more of the delusions, but now he's dead, too, and . . ." I end with a shrug.

"What name did he use for the preacher?"

I hesitate. If I give him the name the dead man used, which matches the name from the copy of the suicide note Lieutenant Paul shared with us, things could go badly for Paul and the captain. "I'm not comfortable sharing that," I mutter as I lean back in my chair and cross my arms.

Chapter 31

Katie

Deputy Shaw mimics my actions, placing his pencil on the table next to his notepad and leaning back in his chair, even crossing his arms.

"Now, Katie, you were saying the dead man mentioned the preacher by name? That he somehow knew him. *Interviewed him.* You didn't get the impression he was military or law enforcement. Do you know about the newspaper that's put out each month? Any chance he worked with the woman running it?"

Relieved Shaw isn't pressuring me about the preacher's name, I relax. "He didn't say he worked with her. And I didn't think it at the time, but now . . ." I bob my head. "Maybe? Do you know her? Can you ask her?"

"And you said he mentioned Captain Williams by name?"

"He did. Only he didn't call him Captain Williams. He said Chris Williams. I remember because I found it odd. No one calls him by his first name except Alice . . . um, I mean, Mrs. Williams. She said before everything fell apart, he only went by his rank on his drill weekends or annual training. He was Dr. Williams in his office and at the hospital, and Chris when not working."

"So, you're thinking maybe the man knew the captain from before?"

"Maybe? He said something about thinking Chris Williams is a good guy and not involved." I take a deep breath. "That's when he mentioned knowing the preacher."

"Anything else?" Deputy Shaw's chair creaks as he leans forward.

"Um, no. Sorry. I wish I had done more. I feel awful that we didn't believe him. Maybe . . ." I shake my head. "I should've believed him the first night. Told Leo and the captain. They would've brought you in. The man might still be alive."

"Not necessarily. I suppose you know that we're going to need to put you back in protective custody."

"Are you sure that's necessary? Maybe the shooter doesn't know— "

"Maybe he doesn't know who you are? Who Merissa is? We didn't find him. We don't know if he followed you to Merissa's home. My understanding, from Captain Williams, is she'll be here for several days at least. Possibly until the baby is born. We think we can protect her here. You, however . . ." His words fade away as he shakes his head.

"How exactly do you think that's going to work? We already moved in with the Williamses out of fear that Julius MacAllister and his group would come after me again." My right hand instinctively travels to hold my left, the pinky finger still bandaged from the frostbite I sustained the night the men attacked me and left me for dead.

It was a case of mistaken identity, as they were apparently after my neighbor Oscar Harrington. Out of an abundance of caution, Leo and I, along with the Harringtons, moved out of our homes. After the whole Melvin Cabal debacle, when Geoff Landers informed us that Cabal had eliminated Julius MacAllister, Oscar and his family moved back home. The babies came into our lives at the same time, so we remained with the Williamses.

A thought occurs to me. "We were looking at a new house, one on the same street as the Williamses house, bigger than the little guest house. We were going to ask Major Stone if we could get approval to move there. I heard he was moving one of the nursing students into our old home. Do you know anything about this?"

"Yes, he is. I saw the paperwork come through. Moving you all to the new house may solve the issue for a day or two, but it wouldn't take much to follow you from the hospital. You'd be a target going back and forth and easy to follow to your new house."

Crossing my arms, I release a sigh. "What do you have in mind? You want to put me in the bed next to Merissa?"

A slow smile spreads across his face. "I considered that."

Shaking my head, I put up my hands. "My children . . . I mean, the boys. I wouldn't— "

"Relax. I said I considered it and quickly realized you'd put up a fight. The house next door to mine is vacant. One of my patrollers lived there, but he and his wife moved to Monument District where her folks are. It isn't huge, but it's large enough for all of you."

"I don't know how that would work. It's the other direction from Alice Williams. She helps with the children."

"The captain said he and his wife would move in with you. It's a four bedroom, not nearly as large as their destroyed home but larger than the guest house. It's still within the range of distance deemed suitable for those working at the hospital. And if Weaver stabilizes to the point the captain is able to release her, he suggested she could take one of the bedrooms."

"How would that be safer than living where we do? We'd still have the same issue of being followed."

"Except the bulk of my crew lives on the same street. We can coordinate escorts and guards easier."

"You already spoke with Leo? He was in favor of this?"

As much as I agree it may make sense, I already had my heart set on the blue house. I've been to Deputy Shaw's place several times, even staying there for a few days when necessary. I hadn't paid attention to the house next door, but certainly liked the neighborhood and the many green spaces and parkland. It's closer to the creek than where we were living before, and much closer than the captain's place. This proximity to waterways, however, holds a sobering reminder.

In 1972, heavy rains and a dam failure caused a disastrous flood that claimed the lives of over two hundred people. In the flood's aftermath, a designated flood plain was established to prevent a reoccurrence of this tragedy. Where flooding was probable, authorities prohibited construction. Instead, they implemented parks and greenways and built houses outside the areas likely to flood.

Even with these changes, I'd heard plenty of people concerned about the possibility of one of the dams upriver being destroyed, resulting in another catastrophic flood. The National Guard still posts people at Pactola Dam, and other dams, to prevent anyone from messing with things.

"He understands the need for it and agrees it may help keep you safe. The captain also seemed to think it was smart. Williams suggested his wife would find it to be a preferable arrangement compared to living in separate homes."

"She loves the children. It's been truly life changing for all of us to have them in our lives. And to be quite honest, I'm not sure how Leo and I would handle all of this without her."

"Leo said the same thing."

I offer the deputy a small nod. "I should go check on Merissa. Then I need to take a nap before it's time to start rounds. I'm on again tonight, so I guess you'll at least get your wish for today."

As the words leave my lips, a sudden surge of apprehension floods my senses. "Do you suppose Alice and the children are safe today?" I can feel the weight of unease settling in, a nagging worry that claws at the edges of my mind, causing my words to tumble out. "Could the shooter know— "

"I've got a team at the house with them."

"And everything is fine?"

"Last I heard. One more thing. If you had to guess, what do you think the man was concerned about? You mentioned he thought the flu epidemic would stop whatever was happening?"

"The flu epidemic and the situation with the sheriff . . . former sheriff."

"In what way?"

"That I don't know. He spoke in a jumbled manner, making it difficult for us to follow his line of thinking, causing us to suspect he might be having a psychotic episode."

"I'll let you check on Merissa, then I'll be in to chat with her in a few minutes. Please don't discuss what you've told me. I'd like to get her statement directly from her."

"Of course."

"When I'm finished getting Merissa's statement, can I take a few more minutes of your time and you can describe the dead man to Captain Williams? Maybe he'll be able to give him a name."

After leaving the break room, I notice Leo and Captain Williams at the nurse's station. Hearing the click of the door, Leo lifts his gaze from whatever he's looking at. He says something to the captain before quickly moving in my direction.

"Are you okay?" he asks, brushing his finger against my cheek, below where the woodchip caught me.

"I'm fine. Is it bleeding again?"

"No. Just a little red and puffy. It may scar."

"Humph. I'm sure. I'm a roadmap of scars since the EMP. How's Merissa?"

"The contractions have backed off. She's only had one since you left her."

"Timing?"

"Close to twenty minutes between them. Stella's in with her. She thinks you caught it in time."

I lift my shoulders. "Perhaps. I'm going to pop my head in. Shaw's catching up on his notes before he sees her. Think she's up to it?"

"I think the captain will allow it as long as it doesn't take too long. Did Shaw mention the housing situation?"

"Do you think it's the right choice?"

"I think it's the only choice. As soon as we tell him we're in, his people will move Alice and the children. After the fire, there's not much to move."

"That's for sure." I take a step closer to my husband and lower my voice. "Do you think Stone will be here today? I guess we don't need to ask him about the blue house, but . . ."

"He's not coming in today. But David Paul stopped by. He said the major will allow both the med school and nursing school to continue. The captain is relieved."

"So am I," I agree. "Shaw's probably going to ask the captain some questions about the shooting. Well, not about the shooting, but about the dead man. He mentioned knowing him."

"Knowing him? The dead man knows the captain?"

"Yes, only he called him Chris Williams and not Captain Williams."

"You spoke with the dead man?"

I scrunch my face as I nod. I thought I'd mentioned that to Leo, but maybe I didn't. Everything has been so crazy since the shooting and running for my life with Merissa.

"I think we need to have a long talk about this whole thing, and you can catch me up on how you happened to be there."

"Sorry, honey. Let me check on Merissa and get a nap in. Maybe we can talk after rounds. And yes, let's get Alice and the children moved to the new house where they will be safe. I have to admit, I'm beginning to wonder why these troubles keep happening. It seems like it's been one thing after another since we arrived in the Black Hills. I'd love to have just a few peaceful days."

"And a hot bath?"

I snicker out a laugh that ends in a snort. "I'd love a hot bath."

He puts his hand to my face, and I turn to kiss his palm. Even that light touch is probably more PDA than we should be showing while on duty and in our United Volunteers uniforms. Not that there's much to the uniforms, considering the Volunteers didn't exist until the apocalypse, and clothing isn't being manufactured in bulk. But we're both wearing our stripes, so that counts.

Merissa looks much better than she did when I left her for my interview with Shaw. Stella excuses herself and says she'll give us a few moments of privacy. "Then you need to get some rest." She points at me. "With the fire, then two overnight shifts, and now this, you must be dead on your feet."

"Pretty close," I agree. "One more overnight and then I have three days off."

"But you'll have school."

"You heard?"

"I heard. It is wonderful news. Med school—being a doctor—isn't for me, but it's certainly needed in this crazy world we're living in."

"Your skills are very much needed, too," Merissa says. "Between the herbs you put me on and Katie's quick thinking, I'm feeling fairly confident my baby will stay put for now."

Merissa gives me a smile that lights up her entire face. Stella again admonishes me to get some sleep, then she slips out of the room.

Once we're alone, I ask Merissa if she's up to giving her statement to Shaw.

"Is there any news about the shooter?"

"No. Nothing new. He's confident you'll be safe here, so that's good."

"And you?"

"I'm going to nap in the call room, then do regular rounds and my shift tonight. We're moving—again. Next door to Shaw. The captain and Alice will go with us."

"Good. That's good. He thinks he can keep you safe there?"

"He does." I hesitate to mention that Shaw had suggested Merissa could also move in with us. While her mother-in-law is currently at the Maher ranch, she'll be back tomorrow, and I'm certain Merissa won't leave her at the house alone.

Will Pearl Weaver be willing to move in with us, too? Is the house suitable for three families? The realization of just how dangerous things have been since we arrived in the Black Hills sweeps over me again.

I wish I was home in Wyoming.

Chapter 32

Merissa

From the expression on Katie's face, I can tell she has more to say but is holding back. I wait a few moments, giving her time to collect her thoughts.

She finally speaks up, "You look so much better, Merissa. Relaxed and— " she gestures toward the half-empty bag of intravenous fluids " —well hydrated."

"A little too well. I had Stella help me to the toilet. She's right about you getting some sleep." I gesture toward the clock. "It's almost 1100 hours."

"I know. Shaw's going to talk with you—chat, he said." She quirks her eyebrows at me. "Then he wants to interview me again, this time with Captain Williams, so I can tell the captain what the man looked like."

"Why the capt—Oh . . . I forgot he said he knew him. How'd he put it? 'I know Chris Williams, and I'd like to believe he's not involved in this, especially considering the note . . .' Goodness, Katie. I just remembered how the man knew more about the preacher than I'd heard before." Pausing, I fix her with a piercing look. "And so do you."

Katie shrugs and avoids looking at me.

"What'd he call him? I remember the name was a play on words. Justice Justice."

"Or Righteous Righteous," she adds.

"What I didn't understand, Katie, is how you knew the name. You seemed completely shocked he'd heard it. As far as I know, no one ever called him anything except Preacher. They didn't even use his given name any longer, and certainly not the new name . . ."

I pause until she whispers, "Justin Zadok."

"How do you know it?"

Katie scrunches her nose. "I can't tell you."

I reposition myself slightly and pull my arm up over my head to achieve a mild stretch. "I already know lying on my left side is going to get old fast."

"Can I get you another pillow?"

"I have enough. Thankfully, this is just a regular twin-sized bed, not a hospital one, so I suppose I should be grateful. I can only imagine how uncomfortable that would be. The blocks under the legs make it challenging to get in and out, but once I'm settled in, it's bearable."

I take a deep breath before leveling my gaze. "Maybe if we had fewer secrets around this place, we'd have fewer people dying." My words come out much snippier than I intended, betraying my frustration simmering beneath the surface—frustration over this entire situation.

"Perhaps," Katie agrees. "But this isn't my secret to tell. Believe me, I wish I could. I wish I could talk to you about it."

I notice Katie's face change. Her eyebrows scrunch as if she's contemplating something, and her lips press together tightly. It seems like her mind is somewhere else, lost in whatever she's thinking about. But behind that faraway look, I can tell she's feeling something strong, like she wants to say more but won't. Or can't. It's like her face is begging for me to understand without her having to say a word.

As I'm observing Katie, the all-to-familiar tightening begins in my back and rapidly encircles my midsection.

"Another contraction?" Katie checks her watch.

"Mmm. Yeah. Mild, though, and already subsiding."

"Good. Good." She marks on the paper. "It's been almost half an hour since the last one. Is it gone?"

"It's gone. Maybe that'll be the last one? Can I hope?"

"Maybe it will be."

"You were in deep thought."

Katie releases a weighty sigh. "I think . . . I think maybe it's all related—the preacher, the hospital, and the whistleblower. I need to go talk with Leo and the captain. Let me see if Stella can sit with you again."

"Shouldn't Shaw be showing up to take my statement?"

"I'll find out what's keeping him," she says as she rises to her feet.

"Take care of what you need to do, then get that nap in," I encourage. "You look like death warmed over."

"That good?" she snickers. "I feel like I'm in a fog. I'll see you later, probably when we do our rounds."

It's only about two minutes after Katie leaves before Stella and Deputy Shaw come in.

"Katie says you only had the one contraction while she was with you." Stella smiles, the lines on her face smoothing.

"Just the one." I glance between Stella and Shaw. "I'm ready to get my statement over with and try to get some sleep."

"Would you like me to stay?" She asks as she checks my pulse.

"Not necessary. I'll let you get my vitals and then the deputy and I can get started."

"Thanks, Weaver," Shaw says. "I'll be quick. I need to talk with Burnett again before she gets her nap in."

After Stella finishes taking my vitals, she tells me to ring the bell if another contraction starts. After she's gone, Shaw asks if he can take the chair next to the bed.

"That's best. Otherwise, I won't be able to see you. I'm stuck in this position for now."

He slides the chair back before sitting and stretching out his long legs. He has his notebook at the ready and his pencil poised. "Why don't you take me through your morning, beginning with when you left the hospital? You were with Katie Burnett and Kerry Hendricks? Just the three of you?"

"Yes, just the three of us."

"You didn't have one of the guards escort you? Isn't that standard procedure?"

"There's usually someone walking with us when it's dark, but the days are getting longer, and by the time we got out of here, it was light enough to walk. We figured with the three of us, it was fine."

"Kerry had already gone inside her home?"

"Correct. Plus, we'd gone about half a block when Katie said she thought she saw movement in the bushes. We crossed to the other side of the street. Then the man called out to us. I'm sure Katie already told you he'd been to the hospital the night before?"

"Tell me about that."

I spend many minutes detailing how the guy not only showed up at the hospital but also how he admitted to being the prank caller. I also stress that Katie and I thought he needed psychiatric help.

"Honestly, it seemed like a conspiracy theory brought on by a mental break. He was twitchy and out of sorts."

"Out of sorts? Had you met him before and had a baseline of how he should act?"

"No. That's not what I mean. We see many people here. I'm sure you're aware. Sometimes, we see people having issues with reality. The apocalypse isn't easy, and we have people who may— "

"Lose their marbles?" he offers.

"Not the phrase we prefer, but something like that. This is what the whistleblower seemed like."

"The whistleblower?"

I lift my hand. "Sorry. That's how Katie and I referred to him. *At first.* We said it in jest, and probably not as professionally as we should have. Then, when someone killed him in front of us, well, we thought maybe he wasn't, as you said, losing his marbles. Especially when the shooter started gunning for us."

"So, you referred to him as the whistleblower, but you thought he was some conspiracy theorist?"

Nodding, I say, "Now I don't really know what to think. He probably had some mental health issues, but obviously, he was in real danger. I can't say whether it was something major like he suggested or just someone chasing after him."

"Burnett mentioned that the man claimed to know Captain Williams. Why did he approach you, someone you claim not to know, instead of going directly to Williams?"

"He said something like he didn't want to think the captain was involved, but he couldn't be certain." An overwhelming feeling of exhaustion hits me. I don't bother to try to hide my yawn.

Taking the hint, the deputy shuts his notebook. "I'll let you get some sleep. It's possible that I'll have some follow-up questions. In addition, I want to bring you, Katie, and the captain together for a description. But we'll wait on that until you've both had a nap."

Waking up sometime later, the first thing I see when I open my eyes are knees clad in brown-patched, heavy-duty twill pants. The smile on my face is instantaneous. "Bowski?"

He slips off his chair and kneels next to my bed, his face in line with mine as his eyes sparkle. "Hey. I was trying to be quiet so as not to wake you."

"I don't think you did. How long have you been here?"

"Not long. Stella was sitting with you before. She said you're doing better, but that when you woke up, I was to call her in."

"Wait a minute before you do." I reach my hand toward him, and he grasps my fingers. "They told you about the contractions? The dead man?"

"I heard," he confirms. "Stella asked me to watch your face and, if I noticed you grimacing, to write the time down. She said you could still contract in your sleep, but they may be light enough not to wake you up."

"Did I?"

"Not while I've been here, but she said it happened once while she was sitting with you. She also said if they were light enough for you to sleep through, you were probably not in active labor."

I have a floaty memory of something in my dream that may have been a contraction, but nothing severe enough to pull me out of it. "Did you retrieve the body of the dead man?"

He shakes his head. "Hugo handled it. I was on a pickup from one of the care centers then . . ." He glances toward the door before whispering, "I moved Elaine out of the care center. She and Marilyn were both certain that if she stayed in there, she'd end up dead."

"Did the captain say she was well enough?"

"I didn't clear it with the captain or anyone. I think . . . the sisters' concerns may be accurate."

"Their concerns that Alice Williams is the angel of death? That's absurd. I'm sure you know— "

"Not Alice. I agree with you, that's just a nasty rumor, but I think there's some validity to the concern. More people are dying than there should be. I found someone to stay with the sisters, to watch over Elaine and make sure she's healing okay. She'll still have her physical therapy and everything to regain her strength."

"And she'll be home where she feels safe. I guess that'll be fine. But you really should discuss it with the captain. What about her medicine?"

"That's sorted out, too."

"Of course it is," I snicker. "You and your contacts, Bowski. I guess I should've figured you'd have it all planned out. I'm sure Elaine is happy to be home."

He shoots me a glance that suggests he's on the brink of contradicting my words, his mouth forming a taut line, his lips vanishing beneath his mustache. I narrow my eyes. "What?"

"It's not important. Now, other than the contractions starting, were you injured?"

"Scared beyond belief but not physically injured. The running and fear are probably what started the issues with the baby."

"I'm sure. Shaw asked me to see if I can find out who the dead man is—discreetly, of course. He said you and Katie both spoke to him, and he's the man who's been doing the prank radio calls. What'd he look like?"

There's a bite to Bowski's voice when he says prank radio calls. "I need to visit the toilet. Let me take care of that, then I'll give you a description."

"Should I get Stella to help you?"

"No, I'm fine. Just help me get the IV stand moving." This intravenous pole was homemade; it was modeled after the metal ones that used to be common but was instead made from some scraps of PVC pipe. Our hospital has a few of the commercial ones, but not enough.

When setting up the various district hospitals and clinics, Monument Hospital and other places shared what supplies they could, but there simply wasn't enough of anything to distribute.

Same thing with the beds. We received a few hospital beds and examination tables, but for the rest, we brought in standard twin-sized beds, adding risers underneath to help the hospital staff not have to bend over so far. Since our building was a dental office, we kept one of the dentists' chairs to use in an exam room and passed the others on to whoever could use them. Learning how to improvise is an important skill during the apocalypse.

Bowski waits outside the closed door, telling me he'll get me help if I need it, just to let him know. Once I've done my business. I stare in the mirror as I wash my hands. Stella must have freshened up the water container when she was here, as the water is warm and soothing.

Despite the fatigue weighing heavy on my shoulders, a flicker of determination ignites within me. I need to stay focused and handle whatever comes my way. For the sake of the baby, for the sake of Mother Pearl, and for the sake of all those who depend on me. With a steadying breath, I square my shoulders and return to the room, ready to face whatever challenges lie ahead.

Chapter 33

Merissa

With damp hands, I finger-comb my hair. It's resting against my shoulders, the natural waves now frizzy and wild. There are dark circles under my eyes, and my face is puffy. I glance down at my ankles. They're swollen, but not terribly so. I'll mention it to Stella or whichever doctor comes in next. I doubt it's anything too concerning.

The swelling could be an indicator of preeclampsia, but my blood pressure was fine the last time Stella checked it. I know they also checked my urine using one of our precious dipsticks to show if there was any protein. That, too, was fine. I'm sure the mild fluid retention is from the IV and extra hydration.

After I return to the bed, Bowski fusses over me more than necessary, even tucking in the covers. My heart flutters with a mixture of gratitude, affection, and vulnerability as I silently acknowledge his tenderness, despite my verbal attempts to downplay his fussing.

Once I'm settled, he tells me that Stella popped her head in while I was in the bathroom and said she'd be in soon to take my vitals. He fixes me with a steady look. "Can you describe the whistleblower?"

I not only give him a description, but I share all the information I know, plus attempt to recall everything the man said, including how he said he knew Captain Williams and how he interviewed the preacher. I even mention the name he used for the preacher and how Katie seemed to know that name, too, but won't say how she does.

From the look on Bowski's face, I can tell he also knows the name Justin Zadok as well as Norman Smith, the name the preacher used before he became a self-appointed prophet.

When I'm finished, Bowski shakes his head. "From the description, nothing jumps out."

"He didn't seem familiar to me, and as I mentioned, he was just an average-looking guy. Other than the twitching, nothing stood out about him. Average height and looks, regular clothes . . . just normal. Oh! I forgot to tell you. I saw him at the concert the other night. He bumped my elbow when we were going inside, and then I saw him again when we left the auditorium. He was also at the dessert house."

Bowski's bushy brows shoot up. "Really? That's quite a coincidence. Was he— "

"He said he wasn't following us. Not after we left the restaurant, anyway."

"Do you believe him?"

"I think so, yes. Did you see the body? I know the bullet left him unrecognizable, but maybe he has a tattoo or something like that?"

"Maybe. I'll check with Hugo. Did the captain say when you'll be able to return home?"

I shake my head. "Not yet. And I'm not sure Shaw is going to allow it. He thinks Katie and I may still be in danger. They're moving Katie and her family . . ." I hesitate a moment as I realize even Bowski probably shouldn't be told where they're going. "Somewhere safe with protection."

"It's a good idea. Until we figure out who the guy is and what the situation is, you and Katie need to be kept safe."

"You knew the names the preacher used?"

"Norman Smith?"

"Not that one. I heard that name, too. Katie told me about learning that name when RJ Kittleson and Bryson Young held her hostage."

Bowski nods. "I was part of the team that went looking for the preacher after the tip Young gave Katie. I didn't know the man, but I knew of him. After his death, I heard he'd written a suicide note and signed it Justin Zadok. But to my knowledge, none of his followers called him that. You were helping to care for the two women, Mindy and Kemeera. Did they ever refer to him by name?"

Suicide note? I wonder if that's where Katie heard the name. If so, how was she privy to the note? "I never heard them refer to him as anything except Preacher. We always called him the preacher, but they dropped the '*the.*' I thought it was more of a term of endearment, you know? And I've heard nothing about a suicide note."

He leans closer before whispering, "A few people are questioning the validity of the suicide note based on the discrepancy with the name."

I can't help but laugh.

He gives me an odd look.

I wave him away and say, "I was telling Katie this morning about all the secrets around this place and how maybe there'd be less killing if there were fewer secrets. Doesn't it seem strange to you? I truly thought Pearl and I would move here and at least have some sort of stable life. In all honesty, I didn't expect it to be entirely safe. I'm well aware of the kind of world we live in.

"But this is all just nuts. From the preacher—or whatever people want to call him—and his murderous cult to the former sheriff and his drug ring. Not to mention whoever blew up the holding cell at Camp Rapid on Christmas Day. And now this . . . whatever this is. The whistleblower made it sound like it was a much bigger deal than anything the preacher or Melvin Cabal had been up to. With this craziness, I'm beginning to think coming here was a mistake."

I rest my hand on my stomach as tears fill my eyes. I know my emotions are running wild, thanks not only to my pregnancy hormones but also to the lack of sleep and the massive dump of adrenaline from earlier when Katie and I were running for our lives.

I close my eyes and allow the tears to flow freely while Bowski tenderly strokes my forearm. His comforting touch soothes the ache in my chest, and for a moment, the weight of my worries feels a little lighter.

In the quiet of the room, with Bowski's presence as my anchor, I gradually feel the tension ebb away. I take a deep breath, allowing his kindness to envelop me like a warm embrace, and I find solace in the simple yet profound comfort of his companionship.

Of his love.

My breath catches and my eyes pop open. That four-letter word. Neither of us has said it, but that's what this is. With a soft exhale, I realize the truth in that simple word. Love. It hangs in the air between us, unspoken yet undeniable. In Bowski's gentle touch, in the way he stays by my side through each storm, I feel his warmth, his constancy.

My heart swells with a bittersweet joy, knowing that in this moment of vulnerability, we're bound not just by affection, but by something deeper, something enduring.

As this realization washes over me, a memory suddenly surfaces, vivid and bittersweet. I'm transported back to a night not long after Braedon and I first met. We were lying on a blanket in a meadow, stargazing. The air was crisp, and Braedon had wrapped his arm around me, pulling me close.

"You know," Braedon had said, his voice soft and playful, "I think the stars aligned just for us to meet."

I remember snorting and elbowing him gently. "That's the cheesiest thing I've ever heard."

He had laughed, the sound rich and warm. "Maybe. But I mean it, Merissa. I've never felt this way about anyone before. It's like . . . I don't know. Like I've found a piece of myself I didn't even know was missing. And I know it wasn't the stars. It was God. God chose you for me."

I had turned to look at him then, seeing the sincerity in his eyes, feeling the same indescribable connection. It was the moment I knew, without a doubt, that I loved him.

The memory fades, leaving me with a familiar ache, but also a newfound clarity. The love I had with Braedon was real and precious. And now, with Bowski, I'm experiencing something equally genuine but different.

Another familiar sensation swiftly follows this revelation: guilt. My husband's been dead only five months, and here I am lying in this bed trying to keep Braedon's child from being born too soon while realizing my love for another man.

As the guilt settles within me, I feel torn between Bowski's warmth and the memory of Braedon. His absence looms large, a constant reminder of the life and future we once shared. The ache of loss mingles with the tenderness of Bowski's presence, generating a storm of conflicting feelings.

Bowski's expression softens as he meets my gaze, his eyes reflecting the same mix of emotions swirling within me. "I know it feels like everything's spiraling out of control," he murmurs, his voice a soothing balm. "But I'm here with you. We'll figure it out together."

Hope surges through me. With a shaky breath, I nod, silently grateful for his unwavering strength and knowing that if anyone can get answers, it's Ritchie Kasubowski.

For a moment, we simply exist in the quiet space between us, bound by an unspoken understanding that transcends words. And in that moment, I realize that perhaps moving to the Black Hills of South Dakota wasn't a mistake after all. Despite the dangers lurking in the shadows, I've found something worth fighting for—a love that's as unyielding as it is unexpected.

As I look at Bowski, I see not a replacement for Braedon, but a new chapter. A chance at love that honors my past while embracing my future. And in this realization, I find a measure of peace.

Chapter 34

Merissa

As the weight of guilt begins to lift, replaced by a newfound sense of determination, I reach out and intertwine my fingers with Bowski's.

"I've been thinking about so many things today. Not just today, but in the last few days . . . weeks, even. You belong to the men's prayer group that Leo goes to?"

He nods. "I meet with them as often as I can."

"Remember our conversation the other night at the dessert speakeasy? I asked you about your belief in heaven. You said, 'The Bible says it, so it is so.'"

He tilts his head. "I think what I said was, 'What the Bible says is so.'"

Scrunching my forehead, I ask, "Is that different from what I said?"

"Maybe not, maybe so. I guess my position is, many people can pervert the true meaning of the Bible. Take the preacher, for example. He took something good in the Bible and transformed it into an excuse to murder people. Even now that he's dead, there are people learning of the things he did and calling him a hero."

"What? Who's doing that?"

"Many. There's a new group that calls themselves the Disciples of Zadok, after the leaked suicide note. It's not a huge group yet, but it is gaining traction. They're embracing his message of agrarianism and being against the redevelopment of our country. Which reminds me . . . did you hear there was a radio talk from both the president and our governor this morning?"

"What? No . . ."

"I didn't listen to the originals, but I caught the replays. The president had little new info. Spoke about the demarcation lines of the Wastelands and said that the United Volunteers have helped move people out of the Wastelands and into the safe zones. He mentioned they were putting plans into place to fill the seats of the elected officials who were lost in the mass assassination, along with any deaths that have occurred since then."

"It's about time," I say. In the early days of the attacks, after the cyberwar but before the EMP and nuclear bombs that turned the East and West Coasts of the United States into what's now referred to as the Wastelands, more than half of our US Senators and Representatives were killed.

When the bombs arrived a few days later, people became too busy with survival to give much thought to who may be leading us. We didn't even hear from the president for some time. I was living in Montana then, and we never heard from our governor or people at the state level. The truth is, I don't even know who all was killed in the assassination or in the time since. If they weren't people I knew or loved, I gave them little attention.

Here in South Dakota, the governor has made radio addresses and even the occasional public appearance throughout the emergency. When I first arrived here, there was a lot of public support for the office, but I've heard rumblings lately, especially during the time the preacher was in his killing heyday, that the governor needed to do more.

Now the preacher is dead, but the rumblings continue, mostly focused on the bombing at Camp Rapid, which was not attributed to the preacher, and also the decrease in rations.

Like Bowski, many people believe it's time to return to some semblance of normalcy and embrace capitalism again.

"What'd the governor have to say?" I ask.

"That there will be some changes happening in the near future to rebuild the economy and put South Dakota in a better position."

"A better position?"

"That's the phrase verbatim. I listened to the broadcast twice so I could make sure I got it right."

"What does that mean, exactly?"

"That I don't know. There wasn't anything additional said to elaborate on how we're going to get into a better position or what exactly the end plan is. There's talk— "

"Of course there is," I scoff.

He chuckles. "There always is. The talk is that maybe we're going to step away from what's left of the United States and form our own country. I didn't hear any of the transmissions, but someone said several governors came out with nearly identical statements. So . . . I guess we'll see. But anyway, let's go back to your question about the Bible. I believe the Bible is the Word of God and all scripture is God-breathed and is useful for teaching, rebuking, correcting, and training in righteousness."

"But how do you know this?"

"Research. Unlike other old writings, the Bible has a lot of evidence to back it up. Old history books, letters from Roman soldiers, and writings from early church leaders all talk about and confirm what's written in the New Testament. This shows that the Bible is accurate. When I was younger and questioning things, I saw videos and read many different accounts that proved the legitimacy of the Bible." He pauses as he lets out a breath.

"In those days, when I was doing my research, even though I called myself a Christian, I hadn't truly given my life to Christ. I did little to stop my sinful ways. Take my marriage, for example. We've discussed how it fell apart. But it wasn't entirely my wife's fault. The Bible says I should've loved my wife the way Christ loved the church. I should've treated her better than I treated anyone or anything. I didn't do that. While I'd like to lay the blame on her fully for our marriage failing, I know I can't. As much as I try to, I can't blame Austin either. We used to be friends; you know."

I mentally register his words, surprise flooding through me before I manage to respond, "I didn't know."

"Forgiving him and forgiving her is something I should do. I want to, but so far . . . it seems beyond my capabilities. Every time I see the man, the betrayal comes back front and center."

"And now that he works here, you see him every time you come by the hospital."

He shrugs. "Nothing new. We've worked together on various crews since the EMP and the rebuilding. I may say things about him, but the truth is, he's a hard worker and cares about what's happening here and in the Black Hills.

"Like I said, I know I need to forgive him. He didn't really do anything wrong. My wife and I were separated. Sometimes I pretend we were trying to work it out. But we weren't. Not really. I wanted to be a family for my daughter's sake, but the marriage was over, and

I knew it. That is until she started dating Austin Chambers, then I made it my mission to steal her away from him." He gives a sad chuckle.

"It didn't work. Instead, she got a job offer in California and begged me to allow her to take it. It really was something she couldn't pass up, and we made a visitation schedule for our daughter that was very generous. She was supposed to spend the months of July and August with me. But with the attacks and then the EMP and bombs, and now California being declared uninhabitable . . ." He shakes his head. "I don't even know how they are."

"But at least they weren't where there was a bomb, right?"

Just then, a loud crash echoes from the hallway, followed by raised voices. Bowski and I exchange startled glances. A moment later, Nurse Jacquie bursts into the room, her face flushed.

"I'm so sorry to interrupt," she says, not sounding sorry in the least. "But we need some help. A patient fell trying to get out of bed, and we're short-staffed . . . as usual. Bowski, could you lend a hand?"

Bowski squeezes my hand. "Of course."

As they hurry out, I consider the things Bowski told me. People actually think the preacher was doing something good? They call themselves the Disciples of Zadok? There's no way that nut having new followers, even in death, can end well. After a few minutes, Bowski returns, looking slightly disheveled but relieved.

"Everything's under control now," he says, settling back into his chair. "Where were we?"

I take a deep breath, gathering my thoughts. "You were telling me about your family in California."

"They were in Northern California. As far as I know, there weren't any direct hits there, but who knows about the radiation? Hopefully, they were able to get out of the Wastelands and are in one of the aid stations or camps. I've got ham radio people working to help me locate them, and I keep praying."

"I've started praying about things. Privately, and with Katie a few times. When Landers was having his allergic reaction, we prayed. But I think . . . I'm not sure if I should be. I'm not sure that God hears my prayers if I'm not an actual Christian." I drop my gaze from his.

He crinkles his brow. "We haven't really discussed this before. I knew you went to church services, and . . . I guess I thought you'd already given your life to Christ."

Shaking my head, I say, "You know Shawn Maher? Opal's son, who does the preaching out at the ranch? He did an entire sermon about this one time. I'm pretty sure he was talking directly to me when he said something about God not listening to sinners, only those who openly worship him."

"Okay . . . so, what's stopping you?"

"Stopping me? Oh, from worshipping Him?" I blink my eyes a few times as I consider the question. "I don't know." There's a long silence interrupted only by the overly loud ticking of the clock on the nightstand before I add, "What if I'm not good enough?"

"Good enough for God?"

"I used to tell Braedon that church wasn't for me, but the truth is, I thought it shouldn't be for him either. In my mind, church was only for weak people who couldn't handle life on their own. They used God as a crutch and Jesus as a scapegoat. Then all this happened— " I motion about the dark room to indicate the apocalypse.

"And I wonder how in the world this supposedly loving God could allow this. How many millions of people did God allow to die? Braedon tried to explain to me that during this tragedy, he wasn't using God as a crutch. Jesus's death on the cross gave him the hope he needed. When Braedon died, I knew without a doubt that as miserable as I was over his loss, as much as I grieved him, he was celebrating with God. With Jesus."

I glance at Bowski as he nods and urges me to continue.

Taking a breath, I press on, "I started wondering then if I was wrong. Spending time with Pearl and knowing that, even after losing both her sons, she continued to trust in God . . . I think that's why I came with her to South Dakota. She was so . . . I don't know. We'd never been close, not until the EMP. And even then, things were sometimes strained. But after Braedon and Tomas died, Courtney— Tomas's wife—went to be with her family, and I couldn't leave Pearl on her own."

"Your people will be my people and your God my God." Bowski dips his chin.

I crinkle my forehead in question.

"It's from the book of Ruth. You should read it. I think you'll find it interesting."

"Okay. Anyway, I came here and started listening to Shawn's sermons and got to know Katie, who has faced her own challenges but still tries to live like Christ. And then, when Josiah passed away and Katie mentioned how Josiah said he would soon be dancing for Jesus, now I realize that's what I want for myself, too."

Tears fill Bowski's eyes. "You can have that, Merissa." His voice is husky and low. "The Bible tells us that if you confess with your mouth the Lord Jesus and believe in your heart that God raised him from the dead, you shall be saved."

"I know. I'm just . . . I'm not sure I'm ready."

His smile falters slightly. "I understand. When you are, let me know—or Katie or your mother-in-law. I know any of us will be ready to rejoice with you."

Chapter 35

Katie

Waking from my all-too-brief sleep, I'm instantly confronted with the memory of the whistleblower's death, just feet away from where I stood. These past months have brought an onslaught of tragedies—some through violent acts like shootings, others, like my mother, due to my inability to save them despite my medical training.

Each loss weighs heavily on me, even with my attempts to keep them separate. In these vulnerable moments of waking, memories flood back, a relentless montage of recent deaths, Josiah Talbot's among them.

Josiah knew he was going to die. He accepted it and said he was ready to dance with Jesus. Likewise, my mom knew she would die. She wasn't very coherent in the last few days of her life, but at the very end, she was smiling. She, too, understood she'd soon be rejoicing in heaven.

Their acceptance, their peace, it's something I both envy and admire. I know for a fact that heaven exists, that they're in a place of eternal joy and serenity. But even with that certainty, I can't help but wrestle with the grief and questions that come with each loss.

Did the whistleblower know Jesus? The short conversations I had with him didn't include discussions of heaven and hell, just his concerns that something terrible was happening in Rapid City—maybe the entire Black Hills—and how it needed to be stopped. If Merissa and I had believed him from the beginning instead of labeling him as batty, he may still be alive.

Stretching my arms above my head, I lengthen my body as I curl and uncurl my fists and toes. Rounds will start soon, but all I really want is to keep sleeping. Even better, I'd love to be home cuddling the babies and Nico.

I wonder where they are. Before I slipped into the call room, unable to keep my eyes open a minute longer, Shaw said he'd take care of Alice and the children, then he'd be back later to put both

Merissa and me together with Captain Williams to see if we could describe the whistleblower to him.

I release a sigh and shake my head. "Lord, please help us get through this. Whatever is happening here, please protect the children—*my* children—and Alice. Please be with Leo and me, too. And, of course, be with Merissa and all the others we love and care for. I don't know what's happening here, but I trust that You will bring us through this." As I quietly whisper the words, I'm again reminded of the dangers we've faced since arriving in Rapid City.

When we got here, I was so proud to be with the Volunteer Unit. Leo and I both thought we were doing something important to help our country get back on its feet. When Captain Williams gave us the opportunity to work directly under him at the hospital, with me as a nurse and Leo as a medic, I believed I was fulfilling God's purpose.

I joined the Volunteers partly to help ease the grief of losing my mom. Being at home in Wyoming, everything reminded me of her. The trip across Wyoming, traveling on foot, helped some, but I felt I'd have a fresh start in South Dakota. At the time, I didn't realize I had packed that grief in my backpack along with everything else.

The governor unceremoniously ousted the United Volunteers from the state, making our first few days here rocky. Leo led the campaign for us and a handful of others, those who wished to do so, to stay behind and become part of the South Dakota National Guard. The crusade succeeded, and the Guard quickly swore in the others while Leo and I waited for his recovery from falling off the horse and breaking both his arms.

Now those who used to be Volunteers with us have either died or disappeared. Leo has tried to find the ones he lost contact with, but so far, he's been unsuccessful. He's even asked Lieutenant David Paul if he could check on the men for him, but we haven't heard where they may be.

Is it possible that the remaining Volunteers were the source of the concerns the whistleblower had? I shake my head. No, that makes little sense. If that was the case, then why was he mentioning the preacher— or, as he wished to be called, Prophet Justin Zadok? Whatever happened with our fellow Volunteers is probably not what the whistleblower was concerned about.

Most likely, there's nothing suspicious there. We know that Tigger and Barnsey died in the Christmas Day blast at Camp Rapid, along with dozens of others. They might have moved the remaining Volunteers to Custer or other parts of South Dakota where there was a need for them. Maybe we'll find out more, but with the way the world is, there's a chance we won't.

I suppose we can say the same about discovering what concerned the whistleblower. Now that he's dead, maybe, just maybe, the danger died with him. Maybe, but unlikely. Somehow, I think if that was the case, then the shooting would've stopped when the man went down. Shaw is doing the right thing by moving us somewhere safe . . . safer, at least. Is anywhere actually safe in this world?

Home.

The desire to go home to Wyoming is almost overwhelming. While we had our own dangers there, including an attempted coup d'état that killed several of my friends and my sister's mother-in-law, plus an attack on our community when we were living at the ski lodge that killed several, it was a much smaller, close-knit, geographically contained community, especially during the winter months when we moved up to a nearby ski lodge.

I don't think I would've left Bakerville had I not been grieving for my mom. I knew Leo wanted to help with the rebuilding efforts, thinking he could go right back into the Marines, but with the computers out and his documentation in a bank in Manhattan along with his college degree, he could only get into the United Volunteers, who were taking anybody and everybody.

They sent most of the Volunteers from Wyoming to the Western Wasteland Demarcation Line to assist with the resettlement efforts. I'm still puzzled about how they sent us to the Black Hills, but it truly felt like a blessing back then. Not so much now. Not with everything that's happened since we arrived. If I didn't know better, I would suspect someone had cursed us.

A light knock at the door interrupts my thoughts, followed by Leo's voice. "Katie? Are you awake?"

I swing my legs off the bed. "I'm up. I'll be out in a minute."

My body protests as I drag myself out of bed and plod to the bathroom. When this was a dental office, the call room was a windowless storage room with a smaller locked closet that housed precious supplies. They converted the locked room into a bathroom with a compost toilet and sink.

The hospital staff hauls in water and keeps it in containers, just like all the water in the building. They added foot pedals in the surgery and exam rooms for hands-free dispensing. In this bathroom, along with the patient and guest baths, we keep water in large coolers. It's awkward to dispense the water with one hand while rinsing the other, so we set the plug and add water there. Is it the best setup? Not even close. But it's what we have for now.

There's talk of strengthening the solar system, which currently is only large enough to provide lights to the surgery room and two of the exam rooms. The goal is to not only light the entire building but also provide us with running water. We have enough solar panels and batteries to do the job, as the EMP didn't affect them.

Finding a controller or controllers is the problem. The system we're using was still in a box and was unaffected, but it's only large enough to do what it is doing, even with the addition of more panels and batteries.

Cleaned up and in some semblance of put-togetherness, I join the rest of the med students in the break room. With Merissa now on bed rest, there are only five of us. The other three—Matt, Jeff, and Kerry—have been official students since the inception of Captain Williams's med school back in November.

Leo and I started as honorary faculty, with Leo and me helping lead some of the classes. I worry that missing those first three months will be a problem, but Leo reminded me that both of us kept up on the reading assignments so we'd know what the others were learning. Now, with the children . . . I force the concerning thoughts from my mind.

Today's trouble is enough for today. I need to find that verse and study it. Back in the day, I could grab my phone and instantly find information with a quick Google search. I think it's in the New Testament. Matthew, maybe?

The captain starts by informing everyone about Merissa being on bed rest until her baby is born. "I'd like everyone to help keep her in the loop on her studies so she can stay up to date as much as possible. We may try to come up with a safe way for her to join us, assuming I get approval for cadaver use. I'm not sure how yet. Maybe we can put a cot nearby so she can have plenty of lie-down time. We'll have to see."

I'm mildly surprised the captain doesn't detail why Merissa went into preterm labor, but since he said nothing, I don't either. Kerry, who knows about the shooting since the patrollers interviewed her, raises her eyebrows at me. I respond with a slight lift of my shoulders.

After a quick briefing during our last rounds together, where the captain outlined today's expectations, it's time to begin.

Merissa alone occupies one room, while two additional rooms accommodate five other patients. In one, three men share the space; one with a broken ankle, another believed to have experienced a mild heart attack, and the third complaining of stomach pain with an undetermined cause.

The doctors also admitted a woman with a broken collarbone. She claims it was due to an accidental fall down the stairs. We've had this woman visit us before with other "accidents," her husband always fawning over her while chiding her for being so clumsy. Many of us have let her know we can help her, but she insists she really is simply accident prone. None of us believe her.

The second lady is recovering from what we believe to be a bout of food poisoning following her Valentine's Day meal. She's on the mend, and the doctor thinks we'll be discharging her today. All the people we'll be seeing were admitted over the weekend when I was on duty, so I'm familiar with each case.

After we've finished with our hospital rounds and are writing up the discharge orders for both the woman with the suspected food poisoning, who's now holding down food, and the man with the broken ankle, who will continue to recover at home, Deputy Shaw returns. Spotting him, the captain gestures for him to take a seat as we conclude our discussion.

When the hospital duties are done and we're ready to continue on with rounds at the various care centers in the district, along with our weekly visit to the orphanage, the captain asks Leo and the others to go on ahead. "I'll meet you at Poppy's place," he says. "Katie and I need to speak with the deputy for a few minutes."

As the rest of the students don their outdoor wear, the captain, Shaw, and I head toward Merissa's room. During rounds, I marveled at the noticeable improvement in her appearance. The best part is she hasn't had any contractions for hours. The captain wants to keep her until tomorrow but may then discharge her to continue her bed rest at home. I truly wonder if Shaw will allow that or if he'll move her into protective custody, as he suggested earlier.

After we pull chairs around the bed to allow Merissa to engage with us, the captain says, "I've been racking my brain trying to think who the man might be. You said he called me Chris, which leads me to think he must know me outside of the military."

"That's what we thought, too, sir," Merissa confirms.

"Let's see if we can come up with a description," Shaw says. "I tried to find someone who had some sketch artist training. They're amazing at getting the info we need, but the only person we still have around isn't able to get here until Wednesday. She gave me some pointers that I'll try to use. I won't be sketching, but maybe it'll help."

"Why don't you have Katie do the sketch?" Merissa points in my direction.

"Can you draw?"

"She majored in art in school," Merissa adds.

With a nod, I indicate my agreement. "I can try. Drawing has taken a backseat lately due to how busy things are, but Merissa's correct. I did study art in college, and . . . well, I'll give it a shot."

"Will copy paper be acceptable to use?" the captain asks. At my nod, he adds, "Go get what you need." He glances at his watch. "My guess is that the sketch may take some time. I'm going to continue rounds at the care centers. Don't worry, Burnett, you can review the notes and be there for our recap. We'll stop back by here before we go to the orphanage."

I take a few minutes to get some paper, a pencil, and a clipboard. My hand shakes as I put the pencil to paper. I'll admit, I'd considered offering to draw the whistleblower when Shaw was asking for his description, but I'm rusty with my skills, and most of the portrait drawings I've done have been with a photograph or digital picture to copy.

Shaw guides us as I do my best to recreate the image of the whistleblower from what Merissa and I remember. After what feels like forever, I show Merissa what I've come up with. She wrinkles her brow as she says, "That's pretty good. Not exact, but pretty good."

"What would you change?" Shaw asks.

"His nose. Was it wider at the top?"

Tilting my head, I try to picture him as I make the change she suggested. After many more minutes of fiddling, I show her the sketch again.

"Better," she agrees.

"May I see it?" Shaw requests.

I flip it in his direction. He stares at it for many minutes before saying, "There is something familiar about him."

"He said he'd been to the hospital a few times, faking illnesses so he could see Merissa," I say. "Do you think it'd be worth taking it to the guards to see if they recognize him?"

"I wish we would've gone ahead with writing names down at the guard stations," Shaw says. "We discussed it, but we were worried a medical emergency would happen in the process and our red tape would be at fault."

"It's doubtful he would've given a real name, anyway," Merissa says. "And it's not like people carry identification with them these days."

The lack of identification is frequently discussed. Some in charge of the area's reorganization want IDs to be required in order to receive our ration chips, but with the way things are, that isn't realistic. The proponents of the ID requirement insist that requiring IDs can cut down on the black-market issues, but others say that's unlikely.

Some people, including Bowski, suggest the time for ration chips has run its course and we need an actual trade system put into place. Then, and only then, will the black market become nonexistent.

"Think it'd be okay for me to use your break room to make a cup of tea?" Shaw asks while sliding his chair back. At my nod, he offers to get us both a cup. We agree tea would be great, and I tell him I'll join him in the break room shortly to help with the preparation and carrying the mugs.

Chapter 36

Katie

"Let me check your vitals before I go," I say to Merissa. "Any contractions?"

"Not for hours."

"Back pain or any weird twinges?"

"Nothing. I feel good. Except I need to use the toilet again."

"Can you wait a few and I'll get your BP and everything before you get up?"

"You bet."

I check Merissa's vitals, which are all within normal limits, and wait while she goes into the bathroom. I get her settled back into bed and excuse myself to help Shaw gather the mugs of tea.

By the time I reach the break room, the kettle is already whistling. Jacquie Haley is there with Shaw, animatedly recounting a story. Shaw gives a polite chuckle and says, "That's something, for sure."

"Isn't it?" she says with a bright smile. In her forties and unmarried, Jacquie often tries to charm certain men, though it doesn't always have the desired effect. Deputy Shaw is one of her favorites, but her attempts at flirtation, like batting her eyes and sharing what she believes are amusing stories, often fall flat.

I've seen her do the same with Bowski, though it's less frequent now that he's seeing Merissa. Interestingly, she doesn't behave this way around the male hospital staff. I'll admit, I find her quirk somewhat amusing. However, Deputy Shaw clearly doesn't share my amusement.

"Katie. Great," Shaw says, looking relieved to see me. "I've got the mugs ready. We can let them steep in Merissa's room."

"Sure. I'll bring a tray with honey and milk." As hospital staff, we bring our own food, but the kitchen workers provide us with milk, honey, and a few other treats when they deliver meals for the patients. It's not much, but we certainly appreciate it.

"Do you need me to come in and check Merissa's vitals?" Jacquie asks while swirling the tea in her mug.

"I just did. Everything's good."

"M-kay. I'll take my break now, then." She moves to the recliner and picks up one of the old magazines she's likely read a dozen times.

We've finished our tea and made a few additional changes to the sketch by the time Captain Williams, Leo, and the med students return from rounds at the care centers.

While the students take a break, the captain joins Shaw and me in Merissa's room to review the sketch.

The recognition is instantaneous. "Are you sure this is the man?"

Merissa and I make eye contact before simultaneously responding in the affirmative.

"I know him. His name is Hank Timbs, and he used to work as a reporter." He turns to Deputy Shaw. "I bet you know him. He was the one who always covered the crime stuff. He used to be at all the trials and stopped at the police stations for reports. I met him when I testified— "

"Oh, yes. I remember him," Shaw says, his voice dripping with disdain. "We called him Hack Hank. That guy had a nasty habit of writing biased articles against law enforcement. Can I see the sketch again?" Shaw looks it over with a frown. "Didn't he wear glasses?"

"Some funky sunglasses with yellow lenses," Williams agrees. "He had problems with the fluorescent lights bringing on migraines."

"Guess the EMP solved that issue for him." Shaw motions to the dead ceiling lights in the room.

"That makes sense," Merissa adds. "He said he interviewed the preacher— " She gives me a pointed look. "Or whatever his name is."

Williams points at the sketch again. "Wasn't Timbs working with the gal who's trying to get the newspaper up and running?"

"More like in competition with her. He was trying to take it over. Either way, I hadn't heard of anyone outside of military and law enforcement, plus a few people from the Office of the Governor, who were allowed to see the preacher and his followers. Not sure who would've authorized letting Hack Hank in. He didn't have many fans among LEOs. I think I'll do some poking around, see if I can find out how he got in there."

"You think it's related to his death?" I ask.

Shaw raises his shoulders. "I have no idea. You and Merissa both said he mentioned the preacher, so it seems a logical place to start."

"He also mentioned Melvin Cabal," Merissa adds.

Shaw sighs. "He's off-limits. Even if I wanted to interview him, and part of me does, no one is getting in there. Not after what happened with the preacher and his followers. Something Katie mentioned . . ." He flips the pages of his notebook.

The rest of us are quiet for several moments while he searches for what he's looking for. "Here it is. She mentioned Timbs said he thought it may have been over when the flu epidemic happened. Katie, you said he said, 'Maybe they'd stop.' Merissa, do you remember him saying that?"

Merissa closes her eyes as her face tightens. Opening her eyes and releasing a breath, she says, "Maybe? It was something similar. Like how he thought it was over when so many people died from the flu."

"Not over . . ." I shake my head. "I think he said he thought they'd back off."

"You're right." Merissa bobs her head. "He said they'd back off. Then he added, 'They didn't,' and he thought maybe with Cabal out of the way, things would change. Out of the way . . . that's what he said, right?"

I lift my shoulders as I try to recall what Hank Timbs said. "Seems so, yes."

"So . . . this is related to Cabal." Captain Williams splays his hands. "You need to interview him. See what he knows."

"I can ask. But it won't help. Besides . . ." Shaw glances toward the door before leaning forward and lowering his voice. "They're moving him to Pierre. The governor will oversee the whole circus as they put both him and his nephew on trial."

"We all know how it'll end for them. Sometimes, I think we should've just finished it here." Captain Williams gets to his feet. "Burnett, would you like to join us to visit the orphanage?"

"Yes, sir, I would." I pop to my feet.

"Me too," Merissa says with a chuckle.

"You're doing the most important thing you can do right now, Weaver. I know it's frustrating and you're worried you're going to fall behind, but I promise you, we'll do all we can to keep you caught up in your studies. It's a relief knowing our program may continue and the nursing program will begin tomorrow. And as long as things stay calm with you, I'll allow you to go home tomorrow to continue your bed rest."

Shaw clears his throat.

"Oh, yes. I almost forgot. Not your home, but to the safe house." He gestures toward the deputy.

"Even though it may be crowded, I believe it's best for you and your mother-in-law to stay with the captain and the Burnetts, at least until we can get a handle on what's happening."

"Have you sent someone to the Maher ranch to let them know? Pearl will come home tomorrow. She'll go to our house."

"I'm going to go out there personally tomorrow morning. I've got a man watching your place in case anyone should go there today."

"Anyone? Do you mean my mother-in-law, or the shooter?"

Shaw raises his hands, palms up. "I mean anyone. I intend to get to the bottom of this. There're too many things happening in our district—in all of Rapid City—for my comfort."

As Shaw exits through the front door, we opt for the back, a more convenient route for visiting the orphanage. Established during Leo's recovery from his horse accident, the orphanage is a recent addition to our district's programs. Dr. Wolff recommended its inclusion in our hospital rounds, having volunteered there since shortly before Christmas. During the flu epidemic, the orphanage went into lockdown to protect the vulnerable children, allowing only resident workers to care for them.

During this period, the staff and children prepared for the recent performance they put on. As a newly appointed med student, I've only visited the orphanage once, just last week, shortly after Nico and the babies came to live with Leo and me.

While I believe the children's home is fulfilling a crucial role, my visit reinforced my decision to keep the boys. Not that I seriously considered otherwise, but seeing the orphanage gave me a strong nudge. There are already too many orphans, and it's distressing to know that not all the children there are true orphans; some were abandoned like Caleb.

When we arrive at the locked door of the orphanage, Jeff rings the bell, and we wait to be let inside. A few minutes later, one of the residents unlocks the door and ushers us in. "I'm glad you're here. We were wondering if you'd show up today."

"Sorry. We're running behind." The captain offers an apologetic smile.

She steps back and ushers us inside. "We had a new child brought in early this morning. I'm not entirely sure what's wrong with her, but she isn't well."

As we enter the orphanage, a sense of unease settles over me. A solemn quiet has replaced the usual lively atmosphere, and the caregiver who welcomed us appears tired, her eyes reflecting the challenges of caring for the children here. She leads us to a room near the entrance where we see the new arrival—a small, fragile figure lying on a cot, her shallow breaths filling the room.

"When did she arrive?" The captain asks as he moves to the side of the cot.

"A few hours ago. I can check to find the exact time, but it was probably around eleven. We hadn't started setting up for lunch yet."

Captain Williams does a quick exam while asking questions about the girl's condition; she's skinny and underweight, as many are these days.

"We put her in a diaper," the caregiver says, "but it already needs to be changed."

The smell is overpowering, a mix of sweat and sickness that hangs heavy in the air. The girl, about the same age as Nico, lies on the cot, her small frame shrouded in blankets.

Her skin appears ashen and dull, lacking the healthy glow of youth. Dark circles mar the flesh beneath her eyes, and her cheeks are gaunt, evidence of her illness. Her eyelids flutter, briefly revealing dark brown eyes before closing again. Despite her youth, her face carries the weight of suffering, her features drawn and weary.

"She's been vomiting, too," the caregiver motions to the bucket next to the bed with about an inch of liquid in it. "She has a fever and is mainly sleeping. Barely acknowledges us."

"Who brought her in?"

"We don't know. The doorbell sounded, and when we got there, she was sitting on the stoop, propped against the wall. A thin sheet was wrapped around her. We've given her water and broth, but she isn't keeping anything in."

"Why didn't you bring her to the hospital?"

She widens her eyes. "Because it's your day to come to us. Had it not been, then we would have."

"Let's get her cleaned up. Jeff? You go back for the truck. We'll have her ready when you return." He looks at the caregiver. "Did you know we're starting our nursing school? I hadn't considered it before, but perhaps it'd be smart to have a few of you attend some of the classes."

"Perhaps." She takes a step closer and lowers her voice. "I live on site along with three others, but mostly, this is just a crew assignment. A way to collect ration chips. You probably wouldn't find much interest in advanced learning."

"Are you interested?"

She glances at the sick girl. "If it'll help keep these children alive, I am, but I already put in eighteen-hour days. I don't see how . . ." She shakes her head. "I'm exhausted as it is."

"Understood. I'll talk to the director and make sure he understands the importance of the staff seeking medical care when it's necessary. Now, if you would please find clean clothing and a diaper for this sick child, I'd sincerely appreciate it."

Chapter 37

Merissa

In the dimly lit hospital room, I groggily blink my eyes open, feeling as though I've barely slept. Despite Katie and the team's best efforts, the night was a restless blur. Hospitals, I've realized, are designed for everything except sleep.

As if tuned into some sixth sense, Katie gingerly eases open the door, hoping to stifle the inevitable creak. Predictably, it fails. How did I never register the deafening noise of that door during my time working here? It's impossible to ignore as a patient. "I'm awake," I assure her. "That door needs some oil on it. It's terrible."

"Good morning, Merissa," Katie says, sounding as tired as I feel. "I'll take your vitals one last time before my shift ends."

"Are you finally going home?"

"I wish. We're doing morning rounds beginning at 0800 hours. I'm going to rest in the call room until then."

"Is Jacquie on again today?"

"Jacquie and Dr. Murphy, along with Chambers and a new woman they brought in as a janitor."

"Think they'll let me go home today?"

"There's a good chance. Captain Williams said if you didn't have any contractions, he'd discharge you, but . . ."

"Shaw isn't letting me go home."

Katie flashes me a sheepish grin. "We'll be roomies."

"Have you seen the house? Is it nice?"

"I haven't been there yet. They moved Alice and the children yesterday. Leo and Captain Williams went straight there last night, but I've been here since . . . oh, forever." She snickers. "I'll get the details when they show up for morning rounds. I'm sure it'll be fine, and hopefully, we'll only be there for a few days. Maybe Shaw can get to the bottom of whatever's happening."

"Maybe. Or maybe nothing really is happening."

"Meaning?"

"I was thinking last night, what if Hank Timbs wasn't on to some big conspiracy thing but rather had someone after him on a more personal level and that's what got him killed?"

"If it was personal, why'd they keep shooting at us after he was down?"

"Witnesses? We both agree it was only the one shooter, right?"

"I don't know, not for certain. It was so crazy, and— " Katie lets out a long breath. "Like you, I just wanted to get out of there. It sounded like only one gun, but I can't be certain. Can you?"

"No. You're right, I can't. Perhaps I'm just wishing there's a simple explanation and not some big rigamarole that's going to change our lives. I get Shaw wanting to keep us safe, and I agree. I'm just thinking about what Mother Pearl's going to say about it. She will not like it, and I can almost guarantee she won't be a very good roommate."

"I don't know about that. Alice is looking forward to having Pearl around. She's heard how Pearl is a great help at the daycare in our neighborhood . . . former neighborhood."

"How's the little girl? Did she improve overnight?" I received an update on the child from the orphanage's condition when the med students reviewed yesterday's rounds in my room, allowing me to take part.

Her symptoms are worrying, and her condition is grave. The captain expressed gratitude that they kept her isolated at the orphanage in case she was contagious. Many precautions are being taken while caring for her in the hospital, too.

Katie's face falls at my mention of the child. "It'll take a miracle for her to recover. She's not any better, and . . ." Her words trail off as tears fill her eyes.

Clearing her throat, she speaks again, her tone only slightly stronger. "I think the captain has a good idea about sending all the orphanage workers through at least some of the nursing classes. He's going to talk with Poppy about how they could make that work. Kerry suggested the daycare workers should go through the classes, too. Most of them have infant and child CPR, as do a few at the orphanage, but it's not enough. There are too many things that could happen. Of course, Stone might not agree to it, and then . . ." She raises her hands.

"Hear anything about Major Stone? Will he be at the hospital today?"

"He sent word late yesterday afternoon that he'll be out all week. Whatever he was working on yesterday required him to go to Pierre. I don't think anyone is upset about that." Katie wiggles her eyebrows at me.

"Pierre? Didn't Shaw say Cabal and Landers are being moved to Pierre? Do you think he's part of that?"

Katie shrugs. "Anything's possible. I'm beat and can barely keep my eyes open. Let's get your vitals done so I can give Jacquie the report and be in that bed one minute after my shift ends."

"Ha. You wish. You know Jacquie will bend your ear as long as possible."

"Not today, she won't. Not today."

After Katie leaves, I drift off into another fitful sleep. When I wake up, Pearl is by my side. "Hey," I say, adjusting myself to sit up.

"I heard you're supposed to keep yourself in bed."

I sink back into the mattress. "How long have you been here?"

"A few minutes. That nice Deputy Shaw showed up at Opal's place right after sunrise. Told me about what happened." She leans forward and narrows her eyes. "He said someone got shot right in front of you, and you and that little Katie had to run for your lives."

I smile at her reference to Katie. Even though Katie is several inches shorter than me, she's taller than Pearl, which makes the description funny. "What else did Shaw tell you?"

"You mean about how he wants to put you in witness protection or some such thing? I know all about it. He took me to our house before bringing me here so I could pack us a few things." She scoots even closer to the edge of her chair. "Are you truly okay? The nurse said they stopped the labor— "

"I'm okay. I haven't had any contractions since yesterday. They even stopped the IV drip last night, and things continued to be fine. Have you seen the house we'll be staying in? Did Shaw tell you— "

"He told me we'll be roommates with Katie and her husband, along with the captain and his wife."

"The children, too. You're okay with that?"

"Seems to me it's the smartest thing. At least until they catch whoever was shooting at you two." With that, Pearl slides back in her chair and crosses her arms. "Really, though, I'm wondering why these things keep happening."

"Me too," I agree. "Me too."

When making their rounds, the captain declares me his star patient and says I'm almost ready to be discharged. "I'd like you to stay until after lunch. I'll be back from the rest of the rounds by then and pop in for a last check." He turns to Pearl. "We'll make sure you have a tray as well."

She gives him a nod as the group leaves. Before the door closes, Katie turns back and offers me a thumbs-up. Letting out a sigh of relief, I settle back into the bed. "It'll be good to get out of here, even if I'll still be stuck in a bed most of the day."

"While listening to him speak of your condition, I realized it'll be a blessing we'll be staying at the captain's place. Not only will he be around, but so will the Burnetts. How many babies has Katie delivered?"

"You're right. It probably will be a good thing."

"Plus, the captain said you'd be able to rest on the couch, not just in the bed. But no picking up the children."

"I heard."

"Three little boys. My, they must have their hands full. And how old are the babies? Only a few months? It must be like having twins."

"More difficult, maybe. Zach is a few months older than Caleb and is doing more. Nico is a help. He really tries to be the big brother."

"But he's not related, right? Are any of the children related?"

I shrug. "Not as far as we know. When Zach's mom Mindy was dying, she admitted that the father of the baby was the preacher— "

"That awful man. How many thousands of people did he kill?"

"Too many," I agree. "Anyway, Mindy admitted that he's Zach's father. Kemeera always said she had a boyfriend who died in the early days of her pregnancy, but we aren't certain if she was truthful. She lied about so many things; we've wondered if the preacher might be Caleb's dad as well as Zach's. There are a few similarities in the babies."

"Yet babies often tend to look alike."

"True. I suspect as they age, we'll know more. Without DNA, though, they'll probably never be certain."

After a few minutes of chitchat, Pearl says, "I think I'll walk around a bit. Stretch my legs." As she rises from her chair, there's a knock at the door before it opens a few inches.

"Merissa?"

"Bowski. Hi." My heart does a crazy little flip as he opens the door the rest of the way. With the light shining from behind him, it almost looks as if he's wearing a halo. My heart beats harder.

"Well, hello, there," Pearl says as she glances from Bowski toward me. I feel my cheeks heat.

Bowski steps into the room, followed by a shorter, heavier man. Heavy by today's standards, anyway.

"Do you know Hugo?" Bowski asks, motioning toward the man.

"Of course." Despite not being formally introduced, I've seen him around the hospital when he's picked up remains. Hugo is our district's coroner, mortician, and coffin maker, all wrapped in one.

During the winter months, there are no burials because of the frozen ground. His primary task is collecting and storing the bodies. When spring arrives, the burying will begin, but according to what I've been told, there will be multi-person funerals and shared graves. In some cases, this makes sense. The flu took out entire families, as did the explosions.

Bowski introduces Pearl to Hugo. As soon as the introductions are done, Hugo turns in my direction. "I heard you were with the man who was killed."

"Um . . . not exactly with him." I shake my head.

"But you were there when it happened? Did you see the shooter?"

Bowski glances at his coworker before I shake my head again. "I'm not really sure I'm supposed to discuss this. Deputy Shaw . . ."

"Of course. Of course." Hugo bobs his head, which sends his jowls rippling like a gentle wave on a still pond. "I was just concerned about how you may have been in danger. I'd hate to see Bowski's girl get caught up in any trouble."

My breath catches as I glance toward Pearl. Any hope that she might have missed Hugo's statement evaporates as a knowing smile spreads across her weathered face. She raises an eyebrow and shoots me a pointed look, silently conveying her awareness.

I quickly change the subject. "Are you here for a pickup?" As soon as the words leave my mouth, I regret them.

Bowski pulls his mouth into a tight line, his lips disappearing into his facial hair.

Hugo sighs. "A little girl."

"Oh, that's terrible," Pearl mutters.

I drop my shoulders as I release a quiet breath. I know Katie said they weren't expecting her to make it, but it's still sad. Now the hope is whatever her illness is, it isn't something contagious like Typhoid—one of the concerns—and others don't come down with it.

Would bringing her to the hospital a few hours earlier when she was first found on their doorstep have made a difference? This is certainly an excellent case for extra training. Hopefully, Major Stone won't make a fuss about it.

"Did you know the dead man from yesterday?" Hugo asks.

"Um . . ." I hesitate as I consider my response. Surely, Deputy Shaw would've shared the man's name with Hugo. "Have you spoken with Shaw?"

"Haven't seen him. Does he know who the man is?"

"I-I'm not sure." It'd be easy for me to give the name Captain Williams used for the man, but something about Shaw not yet telling Hugo raises a red flag for me. It's probably nothing. Most likely, Shaw has just been busy and hasn't had the time to share the info with Hugo. He said he was going to find out who allowed Timbs into the main jail to interview the preacher. Maybe he went to do that instead of sharing the man's name with Hugo.

"Hmm," Hugo hums as he stares at me. "I guess I'll just have to find Shaw and see what he knows. Too bad it'll delay notifying the family even longer. I'd really like to get that job done. Are you sure you don't know the man's name?"

I shake my head in response. Hugo sighs and taps his fingers impatiently against his leg. He glances around the room, his frustration evident on his face.

"Welp, Bowski. Ready to go?"

Bowski seems to hesitate in his response before giving a nod. "I'm ready." His smile sends my heart fluttering again.

I don't dare look in Pearl's direction for fear of her knowing exactly what I'm thinking and feeling. Will she be upset with me? When she met Bowski before, she seemed to almost encourage me to become better acquainted with him. She's told me more than once in recent months she wants nothing but happiness for me.

Still, I don't want to flaunt my relationship with Bowski in front of her and cause her pain. Losing Braedon was as difficult for her as it was for me. Probably even more so. And I still have some serious guilt over the quickness of my new relationship. My brain tells me I should still be in mourning. It's my heart that refuses to listen.

Chapter 38

Katie

My eyes and nose still sting when I think of the little girl we lost. No one even knew her name, not for sure. The worker at the orphanage said she had tried to respond when they asked her, but she was so out of it they thought she said Thindy. But they weren't certain.

Stella, who was still at the hospital performing an inventory of the various herbs and medicines, suggested maybe she had a lisp and her name was Cindy. The little girl never came around enough to be asked and passed this morning while the rest of us were out on rounds. Stella, who never had children of her own but acts as an aunt or grandma to many, stayed by the little girl's side the entire time.

Now, with our rounds completed and all the reports finished, buttoning my jacket takes just about every bit of energy I have left. I've only slept a few hours in the past forty-eight. I know this is a common thing for medical residents, often working long hours.

Even though we're referred to as medical students, our training is a combination of school, first-year internship, and residency all wrapped up into one. As Doctors of the Apocalypse, we're expected to be practicing medicine and performing surgeries on our own in only two to three years, as compared to the ten to thirteen it would take when our world was whole.

The nursing school, which began with basic classes today, will have an even more abbreviated schedule. Many of the students will finish in under a year. Their training will be much like the training I had with Belinda Bosco and Kelley Hudson back in Bakerville. Undoubtedly, the crash course in medicine was among the key reasons Major Stone contemplated shutting down the programs.

As Leo and I step out the front door of the hospital, I turn my face toward the sun, basking in the warmth it's providing. The day has warmed up to the point where there are puddles of water on the concrete driveway giving a glimpse of the pavement beneath.

"This slush might make it slick in places," Leo cautions.

"Do you think the guard is waiting for us?"

"Should be. I called Shaw on the radio about half an hour ago to let him know we'd be leaving soon."

"I completely understand why Shaw thinks an escort is needed, but how long will it continue?"

"Unknown. Shaw's still working on finding out exactly what happened. So far, he hasn't been able to make any headway on . . . well, anything."

"He said he was going to keep working on it, right?" Shaw believes I not only need an escort, but he himself served as an escort for Leo and the captain earlier today, accompanying them from our new house to the hospital for rounds. Shaw granted Alice emergency leave and authorized her to stay in the safety of the house and care for the children, as she typically works at the hospital and fills in for various work crews.

Once Merissa leaves the hospital, she and Pearl will move to the house, where Merissa will continue her bed rest. Pearl, like others her age, contributes by purifying water, mending, and working at the daycare. While the work is encouraged, it's not required to receive ration chips.

Leo touches my arm as the guard station comes into view. I immediately start scanning for our escort. Leaning against the shack is a man chatting with the station guard. I can't recall his name but recognize him from previous times he's walked me home after late shifts. Straightening up, he acknowledges us with a nod before turning back to say something to his coworker.

Our escort speaks into his radio, "M–Ten in motion."

"Copy that," a voice replies.

"Ready to go?" our escort asks, his voice tense, as he adjusts the three-point sling holding his rifle and brings his weapon into the ready position. Like Leo and me, he's also wearing a sidearm on his hip. I glance at his ankle, briefly wondering if he, too, has a second pistol concealed somewhere, as Leo and I do.

"Ready," Leo replies. "Have you heard from Shaw? Any updates?"

"Shaw's at Weaver's house. The man watching the place saw someone in the neighborhood who seemed suspicious, but by the time backup arrived, the suspect was gone. Could have just been someone walking through, or . . ." He lifts his hands as if in a question.

"D-did he know him?" I ask, my voice trembling as fear tightens its grip on me.

"Never got a good enough look. He was wearing his winter gear, more than necessary for today, which was part of why he was suspicious, and he kept his face down with a cap pulled low."

"Were you part of the backup team, Miller?" Leo asks. Miller, that's right. Gabe Miller.

"Not me, nope. They assigned me to your neighborhood."

"Our neighborhood?" I ask, alarm rising in me. "Who's watching there now?"

"Don't worry," Miller assures us. "Your family is safe."

We've gone about a block when a sudden noise erupts—a sharp crack, like a firework. Our guard reacts instantly, ordering us to get down behind a car stalled alongside the road. The ping of metal against metal leaves no doubt about the nearness of the second bullet.

Grabbing his radio, he says, "M–Ten is under fire. Repeat, M–Ten and party of two are under fire." He then rattles off the street and nearest crossroad before adding, "Send backup." Turning toward Leo and me, he shouts, "Stay down!" He leans out from the front of the car and raises his carbine.

Huddled behind the rear tire, Leo pulls me closer and shields me with his body. "We need to move," he whispers urgently. Even though Merissa and I felt certain there was only one shooter the other morning when the whistleblower died, the current rapid gunfire sounds like an entire squadron is firing.

As Miller pauses to add a fresh magazine, Leo fires a couple of shots in the direction of the shooters. "We've got to move," he says again, this time loud enough for Miller to hear.

"Yep," Miller agrees. "I'll cover you. Get to the next car, then you cover me. Wish you had something more than a pistol." He motions to Leo's pistol.

"You and me both," Leo agrees. He touches my arm. "Ready to go?"

I nod in response, my voice too shaky to use.

"Go!" Miller fires his rifle as Leo and I dart out.

We scramble toward the next car, my heart racing faster with every second. Once we're behind cover, it's our turn to shoot while Miller runs. "Are you ready?" Leo asks.

"Ready." I scan for the shooters. Movement catches my eye near a dilapidated house across the street. Pausing, I wait to confirm it's one of the assailants. Seeing his rifle, I steady my pistol and fire a shot in that direction. Leo joins in with his .45 booming. At this distance, our accuracy may be in question, but if nothing else, we'll make them think twice about shooting.

Miller takes the opportunity of our cover and sprints toward us. As he reaches the midpoint between the cars, a sharp cry escapes his lips. He stumbles. Clutching his side, he collapses about ten feet from the car. Blood seeps through his fingers as he grits his teeth against the pain and gets to his knees.

"Leo, he's hit!" I cry out, panic rising in my voice.

Leo's face hardens. "Keep firing, Katie," he orders, moving from behind the safety of the car and putting himself between Miller and the shooters, his pistol firing.

Miller struggles to his feet while Leo maintains his position in front of the injured man.

"C'mon!" I call, urging Miller to come to safety.

He staggers the few remaining feet, just as my slide locks back. I quickly eject my spent magazine and insert a fresh one.

"Katie, check his wound," Leo instructs, as he puts in a new magazine of his own.

Taking out a field dressing from my pack, I move to Miller's side. The return shots are fewer now, more sporadic, but still dangerous. I work quickly, applying pressure to Miller's wound.

"You're going to be fine. Just fine," I say, forcing calm into my voice.

Miller's face is pale. "Hurts," he mutters through gritted teeth.

Just as I finish bandaging Miller's wound, the gunfire seems to pick up. "We're pinned down," Leo declares. "Is he stable? I need you shooting again, Katie."

I meet Miller's gaze, and he gives me a nod. "Take my pistol, too."

A moment later, the crackle of Miller's radio cuts through the tension.

"Hold your positions! Reinforcements are on the way!"

Relief floods through me as I recognize the voice. It's our former neighbor, and part of the Citizen Patrol, Oscar Harrington. Within moments, the street erupts in a flurry of activity. Armed figures move swiftly, taking up defensive positions and returning fire with precision.

Oscar and a team of officers pour in, their weapons at the ready. "We've got you covered!" Oscar shouts.

"Miller's wounded!" I cry.

"Let's get you all out of here!"

Two patrollers move to Miller's side and expertly lift him in a two-person carry. Leo and I exchange a look, exhaustion and relief mixing on our faces.

Additional officers have formed a protective perimeter. The shooters have been driven back, and the street is now secured.

"We need to get Miller to the hospital," I say.

"We've got transport waiting," Oscar says. "Let's get you all to safety."

The pickup truck arrives with a roar and a screech of the tire. They place Miller in the bed of the truck. While Leo is giving Oscar a quick report of the incident, I take a moment to check his vitals.

"What do you think, Doc?" Miller asks.

"I think I'm glad you had a radio and got us help so quickly."

"Always good to have the cavalry on speed dial."

"Indeed."

Leo climbs into the bed of the truck. "Vitals?"

"Strong."

He squeezes my shoulder. "We're going to be okay," he whispers.

"They were waiting for us. They knew— "

"We're fine, Katie. And Oscar assured me the children are fine, too."

"He did? When?"

"Just now. Right before I climbed in with you. They've got people with eyes on the house and someone inside. They're fine. I hate to tell you this, but your nap is going to be delayed."

"I'm not even tired now."

"You will be. The adrenaline crash will happen sooner than you'd like. We'll make sure Miller's all set. Oscar's man will wait to take us to the house. No more risking you walking out in the open."

Captain Williams and Dr. Murphy take our report before dismissing us, ordering me to go home and get some rest. "I don't want to see you back here until afternoon rounds tomorrow."

"Okay," I agree. Miller's wound is just above his left hip, but it didn't appear to strike anything vital, and I'm hopeful he'll make a full recovery. Of course, the gunshot isn't the only concern. Secondary infection is always a possibility.

The patroller who drove us to the hospital is waiting for us when we come out. He gives us a nod and tells us we can both sit up front with him. "Harrington requested we stop by the location of the incident before getting you home."

"Really?" I ask. "Why's that?"

"He didn't say, ma'am. Sorry."

Ma'am? I give him a look. I'm not that old. Of course, he's young. Really young. Maybe eighteen . . . maybe younger. He must be at least sixteen, the minimum age to join the Citizen Patrol, though they have a cadet program with youth as young as twelve.

When we reach the location of the shootout, Oscar motions to where he wants the truck parked. "Sorry to call you back," he says as Leo and I get out of the cab. Our driver remains behind the wheel.

"It's fine," Leo declares. "What's up?"

Oscar beckons us to follow him to where a body rests by a bush. "Do you recognize this man?"

He's a bloody mess, but it's obvious someone has wiped his face to make him recognizable. I squint my eyes and scrunch my nose. There's something familiar about him, but I can't honestly say I know him.

"I don't know him," Leo says before turning toward me. "Katie?"

"I'm not sure. I don't think so, but . . . maybe? We see a lot of people."

In a low voice, Oscar says, "This is Julius MacAllister."

"Julius— " Leo starts.

"The man who attacked Gerry and me?" I interrupt. "Are you sure? Geoff Landers said he was dead."

"I'm sure." Oscar nods. "I guess it's another instance of Landers telling stories."

"Either that or he shared what his uncle had told him," Leo adds.

"But why?" I ask. "Why tell us Julius MacAllister is dead if he wasn't?"

"Well . . ." Leo hesitates. "Landers didn't outright say MacAllister was dead. He said he couldn't hurt you. That his uncle made sure of it. He also pointed out that MacAllister wasn't after you but was after Oscar."

"That's what we believed," Oscar agrees. "But I'd say he's definitely not going to hurt either of us now. No one else either."

Chapter 39

Merissa

"I know that boy Jason is struggling to get through his difficulties." Mother Pearl's fork, laden with mashed turnips, pauses halfway between her plate and her mouth. "Even so, he's a nice boy. Hard worker, too. I don't know why he thinks it's okay to harm himself."

As I finally swallow the tough elk meat, I nod several times and reach for my water glass. Taking a long sip to help wash it down, I manage a grin. "This meat is quite the workout."

"Mercy! I'll say. Roast isn't usually so dry and flavorless either. 'Course, I hate to complain. We haven't been getting meat in our rations since . . . I don't remember when. It was nice of Captain Williams to arrange a plate for me."

"I'm sure Jason doesn't actually think it's okay to hurt himself. From the talk we had with him at the house the other day, it seemed obvious he felt guilty after doing it."

"Then why does he do it? He admitted it hurts—causes physical pain."

"He also admitted the pain helps him feel better. Feel something different."

"But he has cuts and burn scars. If he doesn't want to do it, I don't understand why he doesn't just stop."

I lift my shoulders and shake my head, then murmur my agreement before adding, "I'm sure he'd like to, but he isn't able to do so on his own. Captain Williams has reached out to his contacts at the main hospital. We're going to have someone with better skills for this examine Jason, and then we'll . . ." I lift my shoulders. "It'll take time and work on Jason's part."

"Well, I certainly— " A noise from the hallway interrupts Pearl's words. Her eyes go wide. "Someone's in a hurry."

"Sounds like an emergency." As I strain my ears to hear what's happening, part of me feels guilty that I can't offer my assistance. The other part of me knows I'm doing exactly what I need to do for the sake of my unborn child.

About an hour after Pearl and I finish our lunch, there's a soft knock at the door. Captain Williams and Stella enter. "Well, Merissa," Williams says, "I've heard a rumor that you're ready to get out of here."

"More than," I agree. "Is, uh . . . is everything okay?"

He glances toward Stella before again offering me a less-than-convincing nod. "Ms. Swensen is going to go over the medication plan with you."

Stella has an assortment of bottles and jars, each with handwritten labels attached, along with a separate sheet of paper, detailing times and doses. She makes sure not only do I understand the medication plan, but that Pearl does, too.

"Now, when you get home, remember you're still to take it easy. Bed rest, mainly. Lots of fluids." She points to one of the small jars filled with powder. "Add this to the first glass of water you drink in the morning. Most people wake up dehydrated. This will help rehydrate you. Add it to a second glass in the midafternoon. Any questions?"

I glance toward Pearl, who shakes her head. Even though she and I know we'll soon be staying at the safe house, Stella remains unaware of this information. None of the medical students or staff have been told we've all moved.

Deputy Shaw has even tried to limit those under his authority from knowing the full details of our protection, though I doubt that's helped much. It's likely that everyone heard about the shooting and connected the dots to figure out who moved into the empty house next to Shaw and why. Still, I think the fewer people who know, the better.

With the medicines all sorted, Captain Williams turns to Stella. "Thanks for going over it all. If you would update the chart notes at the nurse's station, I'd appreciate it."

Stella understands she's dismissed, so she says her goodbyes and assures me she'll see me soon. "Remember, herbs can be very strong. They are medicine. The dosages I gave you are safe as long as you follow them. Anything else . . ." She shakes her head.

When it's just Pearl, the captain, and me remaining in the room, he clears his throat. "I suspect you heard the commotion earlier?"

"What happened?"

"While walking home to the new house, someone ambushed Katie and Leo."

Pearl gasps as I ask, "Are they okay?"

"The Burnetts are fine, but a bullet struck the patroller who was with them."

"You used the word ambushed," Pearl says. "Does this mean the . . . the assailants were waiting for them?"

"Seems so."

"They know where the new house is?" I ask, fear settling over me.

"We're not sure if they know exactly where it is, but it seems they know the general direction."

"Who is this *they*?" Pearl asks, annoyance dripping from her tone. "Do you even know who is responsible?"

"Shaw still isn't sure exactly who's behind it, and there was no one to question. The patroller was able to call for help on the radio. Oscar Harrington and his team got there and stopped the attack. The patrollers killed several of the assailants, but at least two got away. One was injured pretty severely based on the blood trail, at least that's what I was told. Oscar and his people recognize most of the dead. It's the usual people who cause trouble in the district, including . . ."

Captain Williams pauses, a tightness in his jaw betraying the effort to rein in his anger. "Including Julius MacAllister, the man believed to have attacked Katie Burnett and left her for dead."

My thoughts swirl as I consider this information. "I thought he was dead? Landers said— "

"Landers was wrong, apparently. This time, though, there's a body and confirmation."

I crinkle my forehead as I consider this latest info. "Could this be unrelated to the shooting of Hank Timbs? If it was MacAllister, maybe he was actually after Katie and decided to finish what he started."

"Shaw suggested the same thing, but it's believed that attack was a mistake. They thought they were at Oscar Harrington's place. MacAllister had a beef with Harrington for something law-enforcement-related. If the attack on Katie was a mistake, then why go after her now?"

"What does this mean for Merissa?" Pearl asks. "For her safety?"

"At the moment, nothing changes. Shaw will be here in about an hour to drive you to the house. There are people stationed around the neighborhood and even in the home, providing around-the-clock protection."

"But if you and the Burnetts continue to work, isn't there a chance someone will see you walking back and forth? Won't that put Merissa in danger?" Pearl reaches for my hand. "Doesn't it make sense that may be how the ambush was arranged?"

"Yes, Mrs. Weaver. It certainly does. And because of that, Katie, Leo, and I will stay elsewhere. Shaw allowed the Burnetts to go to the house and gather a few things, plus visit with the children and their dog briefly. They've relocated. I'll join them after I've wrapped things up here. We're hoping you're willing to help Alice with the children."

"Of course, I will." Pearl's tone leaves little doubt about her dedication to help where she can. "I'll also be making sure Merissa is doing what she needs to do. Will it be safe for her to even leave the house to come for checkups?"

"We'll have to find a way to work that out. My guess is it'll be fine, but we'll wait and see what happens over the next few days."

After the captain leaves, Pearl says, "Well, that's a fine kettle of fish. Poor Katie, being targeted like that. What do you think, Merissa? Is it because of the shooting a few days ago or the incident from before?"

"I don't know. Given that it has been weeks since the other incident and only days since the shooting, it seems it must be connected to the shooting of Hank Timbs. That said, maybe MacAllister was holding some kind of grudge and decided he needed to finish what he started."

"But if it really was a case of mistaken identity, seems to me he'd not bother going after Katie but his intended target instead, that Oscar fella."

We discuss the situation for several more minutes, reaching no additional conclusions but agreeing the plan of us staying in the house together while the others have a secondary location makes sense.

The less chance there is of whoever it is following someone to the house, the better, whether related to the original attack on Katie or the shooting of Hank Timbs. Keeping the babies and Pearl safe, along with my own unborn child, is certainly a priority. No doubt Katie and

Leo will miss the children and Gerry, but I'm sure they, too, understand it's for the best.

After Jacquie comes in and removes the IV port and instructs that I can get dressed and ready to go, Pearl bustles around, helping me as best she can. I'm ready to leave when there's a knock at the door.

"Come in," I say, expecting it to be Jacquie with my official discharge papers. But to my surprise and delight, Bowski enters the room. "Hey." I smile as my cheeks warm.

He glances toward the hallway as he softly shuts the door. "Merissa, I— " He hesitates as he looks from me to Pearl. In a lower voice, he says, "I've been doing some digging. Trying to figure out what the whistleblower may have been on to. I found out his name. Hank Timbs."

I answer with a nod. "I would've told you when you were here before, but Hugo— "

"You were right to keep quiet. I think he's in on it."

"Hugo? In on what, exactly?"

"Something big. Too big. That's why Timbs is dead. He figured out what's going on. Why he came to you . . ." Bowski's giant fists clench at his sides. He speaks again in a measured tone. "Why he came to you, why he dragged you into this mess, I have no idea. Truthfully, though, you were probably already part of it. All of you were. So was I."

"Bowski." I shake my head. "You're not making much sense."

"Remember how the Ebright sisters and others from the care centers were worried about the angel of death?"

"Of course. But you took Elaine home, right? Is she still concerned?"

"I didn't take her home. I took them somewhere else. A place that's safe. Marilyn believed Elaine would be in just as much danger at home as in the care center. She may have been right. I think there really is something going on. I know there is, and it's put you and everyone else working at this hospital and in the care centers at risk."

As Bowski's words settle in, a chill sweeps through the air, sending shivers down my spine. "What do you mean? How are we at risk?" I whisper, my voice barely audible over the pounding of my own pulse.

Bowski's eyes narrow, his gaze piercing through the shadows that linger in the corners of the room. "It goes deeper than we ever imagined," he says, urgency lacing his voice. "The whistleblower, Timbs, stumbled onto something sinister, something that reaches far beyond the confines of these walls."

My mind races as I try to connect the dots of the cryptic puzzle before me. "But what is it? What could possibly put us all at risk?"

Bowski's jaw tightens briefly before he continues, his words measured and deliberate. "It's a network—a web of corruption that spans across the entire healthcare system."

"What exactly is it?" Pearl asks, her words tinged with exasperation. "Just tell us."

He takes a step closer to Pearl and me, his voice a whisper. "It's the dead. The remains. They're using them for . . ." His nostrils flare as he releases a breath. "The fat on the bodies, what little there is of it, is being harvested and melted down. They're using it to make biodiesel."

In horror, I instinctively bring my hands to my mouth as I try to process what I've just heard.

"What?" Pearl's voice trembles with disbelief.

"I don't think Timbs is the first to die while they've tried to keep this secret. Your coworker, Rand Hendricks, I believe he may have been a victim, too. Several others as well."

"What are we going to do?"

"You're going to follow whatever instructions Captain Williams gives for your baby's needs while ensuring your safety. For now, go to the house Shaw has set up for you. I'm going to see if I can find you someplace else. Someplace away from here."

"How? With the baby— "

Bowski reaches for my hand. "We'll figure it out. For now, let's get you home. I've brought Shaw in on what I know—or what I think I know—and he asked me to take you to the house." Bowski glances around the room. "Are you ready to go?"

His words sink in, and a glimmer of hope sparks within me. I squeeze his hand and nod in acknowledgment. I trust that Ritchie Kasubowski will do everything in his power to ensure the safety of not only me but also Mother Pearl and the others at the house while putting an end to the despicable crimes against our dead.

The adventure continues in Unleashing Mayhem, the sixth and final book in the Dakota Destruction series.

In a dangerous post-apocalyptic world, how much would you sacrifice to help your community?

In the final showdown of the Dakota Destruction series, chaos reigns as Katie and Leo confront the dark forces threatening their fragile survival in the Black Hills. With danger lurking at every turn, trust becomes a luxury they can't afford.

As Merissa and Bowski join the fight, can they unveil the truth before the next strike destroys Rapid City?

The stakes have never been higher—will they unleash mayhem or rise from the ashes?

Learn more at MillieCopper.com/Unleashing.

Thank you for spending your time on our new South Dakota adventure.

If you have five minutes, you'd make this writer very happy if you could write a short review on Amazon, Goodreads, Bookbub, or your favorite review site.

I appreciate you!

Join my reader's club!
As part of my reader's club, you'll be the first to know about new releases and specials. I also share info on books I'm reading, preparedness tips, and more.

Please sign up on my website:
MillieCopper.com

Also by Millie Copper

The Havoc in Wyoming Series

When a series of coordinated attacks devastate the United States, the people of Bakerville, Wyoming, must come together to survive. Unfortunately, not everyone has the town's best interest at heart. Some are striving for personal gain during the apocalypse.

The Montana Mayhem Series

A group from Bakerville, Wyoming strikes out on their own while searching for the desires of their heart. Unfortunately, the road will not be easy, and sometimes the heart is hardened and deceitful.

The Dakota Destruction Series

After a series of coordinated attacks devastate the United States, Katie and Leo sacrifice everything to help their country. But some things aren't as they seem. Is it time to go home and start fresh, or can something good come out of this terrible situation?

Wyoming Fall Series (In The October Fall World)

In the blink of an eye, an EMP changed everything for Lauren and her family. Now they are in a fight for survival, trying to keep their loved ones alive as society collapses around them.

Nonfiction Books

Millie has penned seven nonfiction, traditional food focused books, sharing how, with a little creativity, anyone can transition to a real foods diet without overwhelming their food budget. Many of her books also include preparedness and food storage tips.

Find these titles at: MillieCopper.com

Acknowledgments

Thanks to:

Ameryn Tucker, my editor, beta reader, and daughter wrapped in one. I had a story I wanted to tell, and Ameryn encouraged me and helped me bring it to life.

Dee from Dauntless Cover Design.

My husband, who gave me the time and space I needed to complete this dream and was very patient as I'd tell him the same plot ideas over and over and over.

Three more adult daughters and a young son, who willingly listen to me drone on and on about storylines and ideas while encouraging me to "keep going."

My amazing Beta Readers! Thanks to Barbara, Christine, Glen, Linda, Melonie, Tammy, and Tracy for your help in creating the final story. Your insights and abilities to see the things I miss are very much appreciated!

A special thank you to Kristy who gave me a peek inside the world of the Coast Guard and Forest Service. And also a special thank you to Tim, a specialist in all things that go boom, for always answering my questions and pointing out things I wouldn't even think about.

And to you, my readers, for spending your time on our new South Dakota adventure. If you have five minutes, you'd make this writer very happy if you could leave a review. I appreciate you!

About the Author

Millie Copper, writer of Cozy Apocalyptic Fiction and preparedness mentor, was born in Nebraska but never lived there. Her parents fully embraced wanderlust and moved regularly, giving her an advantage of being from nowhere and everywhere.

Millie Copper lives in the wilds of Wyoming with her husband and young son, tending chickens and attempting a food forest on their small homestead. After living off the grid for several years, they've recently gone back on the grid. Four adult daughters, three sons-in-law, and five grandchildren round out the family.

Since 2009, Millie has authored articles on traditional foods, alternative health, homesteading, and preparedness-many times all within the same piece. Millie has penned seven nonfiction, traditional food focused books, sharing how, with a little creativity, anyone can transition to a real foods diet without overwhelming their food budget.

The twelve-installment *Havoc in Wyoming* and six-installment *Montana Mayhem* Christian Post-Apocalyptic fiction series use her homesteading, off-the-grid, and preparedness lifestyle as a guide. The adventures continue with the *Dakota Destruction* series.

Find Millie at www.MillieCopper.com
Facebook: www.facebook.com/MillieCopperAuthor/
Amazon: www.amazon.com/author/milliecopper
BookBub: https://www.bookbub.com/authors/millie-copper